LOOK OUT FOR
HYDROPHOBIA

LOOK OUT FOR HYDROPHOBIA

Stories

Betsy Wing

A BIRCH LANE PRESS BOOK
Published by Carol Publishing Group

FOR NAT
More Beyond

A Birch Lane Press Book. Published by Carol Publishing Group.
Editorial Offices, 600 Madison Avenue, New York, NY 10022.
Sales & Distribution Offices, 120 Enterprise Avenue, Secaucus, NJ
07094. In Canada: Musson Book Company, a division of General
Publishing Co. Limited, Don Mills, Ontario. All rights reserved.
No part of this book may be reproduced in any form, except by a
newspaper or magazine reviewer who wishes to quote brief
passages in a review.

"Cotillon" first appeared in *The Southern Review.*
"Possum Triptych" first appeared in *The Southern Review.*

Queries regarding rights and permissions
should be addressed to: Carol Publishing Group,
600 Madison Avenue, New York, NY 10022

Manufactured in the United States of America

10 9 8 7 6 5 4 3 2 1

Library of Congress Cataloging-in-Publication Data

Wing, Betsy.
    Look out for hydrophobia : novella and stories / by Betsy Wing.
      p. cm.
    "A Birch Lane Press book."
    ISBN 1-55972-050-6 : $17.95
    I. Title.
PS3573.I5314L6 1990
813'.54—dc20   90-41898
                                        CIP

Carol Publishing Group books are available at special discounts
for bulk purchases, for sales promotions, fund raising, or
educational purposes. Special editions can also be created to
specifications. For details contact: Special Sales Department,
Carol Publishing Group, 120 Enterprise Ave., Secaucus, NJ 07094

CONTENTS

WARM SPRINGS

Charles Vetuste stood half-naked in his office admiring the autographed slicks on the wall opposite his window. There was no more room for glorious memories: every square inch was taken. "Vetuste, Vetuste," he whispered to one of them. He sucked in his gut and felt as if it all tucked in again like in the photo—under the striped jersey he wore then to swim (two pieces with pants nearly to the knee). He thumped his sternum twice, testing the resonance, the power of his lungs but, though he shifted his eyes to the adjacent photo, he gave no Tarzan yell. He was still startled to be introduced to prospective clients as the man who trained Tarzan to swim. And what about the gold? he wanted to ask. But his charming old-world manners made him bow his head, blush, and give them two or three lessons before he showed his young, dripping charges his glorious moments, medal on chest and the later gold on the chest of pre-Tarzan Bob.

There were no regrets displayed and few hidden. But there was one: he had never trained an Olympic girl. Never even a channel swimmer. Each one had left him at a crucial moment for dresses and tennis. Then later they would pop in, all golden fluff, and give him their children to teach—but survival skills were all they had in mind: for the brats to learn to survive, not underfoot, while their mothers played more tennis or, in the worst case, cards. He thumped his chest again

1

and had to bring the gut back into position. Where it used to stay of its own accord.

"Mr. Vetuste. Mr. Vetuste." He heard someone calling.

"I need a girl," he thought. "Just one before," thinking: "I die" and quickly revising to: "I retire." He turned around and looked through the window toward the blue water and the voice and there she was, stepping into the quavering, green light of the pool building. Her slim but stolid frame, her square shoulders were backlit by the brilliant July day framed in the doorway. He stared. There she is. Praise God, he thought. What a good life this is.

The other three were almost to his office before he stepped out to greet them. "This is the Mr. Vetuste I told you about," said Dorothy Manning. "He taught Tarzan to swim! Mr. Vetuste, this is Mrs. Frazer..."

"Oh, I'm so admiring of you," said Mrs. Frazer. "How exciting that must have been! How proud you must be!"

Charles bowed his head and blushed and waited to be given his girl. From the corner of his eye he could see her as she slowly rimmed the length of the pool, centering her steps in the square tiles with a precision and control that told all.

"This is my son John," said Mrs. Frazer. "I would like him to have swimming lessons while we are here."

Charles looked down and there was, indeed, a curly-headed boy of about five, with the same solid build, the same square shoulders, holding up a hand to be shaken. Charles took it and said, "Well well, a fine young man. And what about your sister?"

"He doesn't like his water wings anymore and I'm afraid he'll take them off and drown," said his mother.

"Of course, I understand. We'll fix that. And what about you, young lady?" he said to the girl, who had arrived at the group and placed both feet carefully inside a tile next to her brother.

"I can swim," she said.

"She spends the afternoons with her grandmother," said Mrs. Frazer.

"I do give morning lessons occasionally, in exceptional cases," Mr. Vetuste offered.

"That would interfere with our excursions I'm afraid. We like to walk or ride before the heat of the day. No. The lessons are for my son. Would three o'clock suit?"

"Mrs. Frazer," said Mr. Vetuste. "It is a little early to tell about your son, but your daughter has the makings of a champion. Look at those shoulders, that chest capacity. Turn around dear."

Kathleen Frazer stared straight ahead at the lower half of her admirer and then carefully turned inside her tile without once transgressing its limits.

"Behave yourself, Kathleen. This is not the moment for games."

"You can see already," said Vetuste. "She has a strong strong back and it will be long besides."

"Yes, yes, I see. Run along, Kathleen. Run along, John. I'll be right there."

John took off for the door followed closely by his sister, who hollered after him, "Step on a crack. Break your mother's back!" Even running fast, she kept her feet inside the lines.

Blue-green water, high glass windows prolonged the shout in echo as she raced away.

"She's a natural athlete, Mrs. Frazer."

"John! Stop that!" He was spinning out of control trying to make his sister miss her step. "You'll fall in and drown!"

"Dumb dumb game," John hooted, stomping deliberately on all the lines.

"The problem is the boy, Mr. Vetuste. I'll bring him tomorrow at three."

Charles Vetuste sighed and went back to his office to write down John's appointment.

Outside the poolhouse, Mrs. Manning left them to return to

her post behind the hotel desk. "Why did he wear a baby bathing-suit?" asked Kathleen as the three Frazers wandered across the first tee toward the white verandah.

"Baby?" said Mrs. Frazer.

"Like John has. Too little and showing all his lumps."

"Mine is *not* a baby suit," said John.

"That kind makes them go faster, Kathleen. You have to learn not to stare."

Next day at lesson time for John and Grandma time for Kathleen, Mrs. Frazer put on her white clothes for tennis. "I don't want to play cards with Grandma any more," said Kathleen.

"Oh, she would be so sad to hear that, Kathy dear. You mustn't hurt her feelings."

"She always wins."

"And I happen to know she has a surprise for you today."

"But I don't like those special cough drops she gives me. That's not a surprise."

"It's not that. But I'm not going to say what it is."

"All right. I'll go," said Kathleen. "But it had better not be cough drops."

Kathleen found her Grandma pinning the rolls of her hair up into an old lady's heap. "Did you have as nice a nap as I did, Kathleen? I dreamt all my cares away. Did you?"

"I just read. I can't ever sleep."

"You'll find," said her Grandma, "that a little afternoon nap is a wonderful treat for your body. . . And guess what!"

"What?" said Kathleen. This was to be the surprise. Body treats sounded like more cough drops to her.

"We're going to the springs today. You and me."

"We are! Oh Grandma!"

Indian braves bathed in the springs. They ran until they dropped and there the springs were to bring them back to life, to give them back their power. The springs, hidden inside two round wooden buildings with oblong windows and barnswallows under their eaves, were the whole magic of the place. Mens' springs and ladies': they were Warm Springs. That was their name.

"I'll get my bathing suit," said Kathleen.

"No. There's a lady there with suits everyone has to wear." The lady with suits was a huge one in black with blue rubber swimming shoes. She had whiskers and a whole room of dark red wool suits in piles. She tried to find a pile of Kathleen's size. "Children are discouraged," she said to Kathleen's grandmother. Kathleen felt particularly discouraged, in the tiny white closet with a bench, putting on her suit. It didn't cover her chest, it dangled below her knees, and it itched. She bungled it up in a big stomach lump and held it there when she came out. There was something to be said for baby suits like Mr. Vetuste's.

"Don't worry," said her Grandma. "They all fit like that. There's nobody to see you."

On the contrary. There were a lot of women floating around the pool edge like hippos at the Washington Zoo with nothing to do but stare. Kathleen's Grandma sat down on the edge and put her legs with their lavender veins in. The water was clear and from the round stones on the bottom came strings of bubbles. "That's the spring isn't it, Grandma?"

"There are several. See, more over there. Wherever it bubbles up that's a spring."

Kathleen picked a long stream of silver air beads for her target and did a cannonball. Most of her suit came off and she came up struggling with its armholes and spouting whalewater. "Phew! Phew!" she said. "This water doesn't feel like you're anywhere! There's no difference between you and it!"

The floating ladies around the edge were glaring now as Kathleen's tsunami washed over their spluttering lips.

"No splashing, young lady," said the big one who guarded the pool. "Or it's out you go."

Kathleen's Grandma did a few sinking sidestrokes to an empty floating spot. "Come over here and float with me,

Kathy. That's how you take in the minerals."

The whole center of the pool was empty.

"Can I just swim around in there, Grandma? I won't bother anybody if I stay in the middle."

"I think so, dear. But you should float. It's not good to exert yourself in warm water. Do a little sidestroke maybe."

But Kathleen's was not a sinking sidestroke. Her unruly feet broke the surface and the wake from her circling began to build and crest at the floaters' face level. They shook their jowls at her.

"Out you go," said the guardian with whiskers and blue rubber feet. "That's enough. Children should not just be discouraged they should be forbidden."

Where were the Indian braves?

Kathleen climbed out and let the water spill out of the baggy wool crotch, then she hiked her droops. "Grandma," she said. "I can't swim that slow. Can we go back now?"

"Let me soak up my minerals, Kathleen dear. Try to calm down. Just go sit in the sun a bit."

Kathleen looked for the little closet where she had left her clothes. The door was shut and there were fat white feet showing underneath. She looked at all the doors and they all had fat white feet. She went out to sit on the bright steps and wait.

That must not have been the magic spring. There was another in a shady part of the grounds. It had its own round house, just smaller, a version for children perhaps. It probably had a half-size moustache lady with blue shoes. Kathleen's suit was very heavy. It had gotten longer with the weight but she arranged it again by twisting the middle in a knot when she stood. More water ran out, cool now on her sunny legs. She meandered toward the little spring house. No one was guarding it. It was a drinking spring with two tin cups chained on either side of a running faucet. It stank. Apparently, all magic had some drawback. There were no warnings though, no "Drink me" or "Eat me" to make her feel like a nervous Alice who might suddenly dwarf a whisker lady or find herself treading water in a pool of tears. No. The light came slanting through a crack and touched the right hand cup. She took that one and held it under the faucet. She didn't take much—just enough to get back her strength. She could hardly put the rotten smell to her mouth but bravely took a big gulp. "Waah!" she shouted, "Waaagh!" she gagged. "EEEaah!" She began to run top speed, anywhere, away. Toward the first tee. — EEeeaah—She was running in the rough where the dry, coarse grass chewed her legs. She churned them as hard as she could, because past the foursome tossing for first shot, behind the gangly caddies with golf bags on their backs she could see the tall windows of the real pool building. The one with real water where you could swim as fast as you wanted.

It was very very close now. She was running for her life. The magic water was working its powerful spell.

Charles Vetuste looked up. His hand was under John's belly and he was trying to persuade the boy's knees not to bend. Something wild was flying at the bright door. It gave a whoop and suddenly moulting burst out of the dark thing on its body and then he could see clearly just as it took off in the golden light, naked and pure, it was his girl yelling like Tarzan, diving into the deep end.

TRADERS

Chris and Izzy basked in their love. They lay naked in the sun watching each other grow so warm they had to touch. They pulled back the shower curtains in the old clawfoot tub to watch the soap suds run down each other's body. They would watch, rinse, get wet, mop up. When Izzy was pregnant, Chris took pictures of her luminous belly in front of the bright leafy window behind the tub. She was standing up to rinse and the light seemed to come from inside and to glow out through the water. Neville was born soon after that and the kind of brightness and warmth they were feeling just spread to include him.

At the time, they lived on nothing, or practically nothing, in a small house in Maine Chris had inherited from his grandmother. It came with beautiful things in it: a sewing basket woven of sweetgrass still smelling of summer, years and years after it had been picked; mismatch old china, with handpainted flowers on one sugar bowl; wool blankets in soft colors that Izzy promptly shrunk because she thought that when you changed your bed, you threw, not just sheets and pillowcases, but blankets too, into the machine. They were the color of strawberries and cream with a new reassuring density to them—a sense they would never wear out or fade. All that had already happened and now they fit the bunks that would be the children's, when the others after Neville came.

Chris limped a little because he fell and broke his left leg when he was twelve and afterward it didn't grow quite as fast as his right. It had seemed terribly unlucky then, but now it kept him from Vietnam. He found a job in Maine with a potter who gave him space for a darkroom as part of his pay, solving what seemed to be Chris and Izzy's only problem—it was almost impossible to shut off any dark space with running water in their house. Light snuck in the cracks. Chris wanted to be a photographer and worked hard at it. Sometimes it seemed almost all their money went for film and chemicals, but his parents wanted him to be a photographer too and occasionally sent them a check to help out—nothing regular, but often surprisingly big, and Chris and Izzy could make it last. After Neville came, Izzy ran an ad in the town paper, saying she would sew for people. She had a few jobs that way. Before the baby, she had done some waitressing and picked up a cleaning job here or there if she felt like it. The house was the only possession they really wanted, and they had that, free and clear. They didn't need much else. In 1968, earning for the future didn't seem to make sense. The world was about to change radically for the better, though some of its best dreamers were dead and buried. They knew now that this change could only come painfully; times were likely to be worse. Already there were riots, fires, looting. Chris and Izzy wanted wealth to change hands, rearrange itself more fairly perhaps. But they hoped that somehow they would still have their house with its hundreds of pictures of Izzy and Neville tacked around the windows.

Chris decided to go back to school. He had never had any formal training in photography and he felt there were some technical things he needed to know. First try, he got a good scholarship, and there was cheap, furnished student housing, so they packed up and went to the city for the winter. They didn't take anything from the house because it all belonged where it was.

The university was in an old industrial city whose rough

bustling edges were filmed over with dinginess and grit. Chris spent more time in studios and darkrooms than outside, so he didn't mind much. He exploited the heavy, smoky light and his pictures—even of his bright-cheeked baby and smooth-limbed wife—took on a grainy quality. Izzy hated grit but was excited by exposure to city sights and sounds. Surprisingly happy, she walked Neville in his stroller up and down the city streets. Unlike Chris, who snapped pictures everywhere, she liked just looking at the details around her, trying to sense where she was in relation to them all. Another sort of horizon stretched out of the long streets almost sucking at her eyes. There was an edge of terror for her in the way she saw, but she had a firm anchor in the things she knew best. She was in the city on a time swing, as if riding a tide or wind shift (predictably reversible), a swing away from the granite ledge looking out to sea, from the yellow pine walls of the house smelling of balsam and the sweetgrass basket.

By spring, however, both could hardly wait to get back to Maine. In June, they finally were there—breaking in through their own front door because each thought the other had the key. (A month or so later, they found it in the ashtray in the front seat of their third-hand Volvo—carefully put there in September, so they would be sure to have it when they returned.)

They burst in and breathed deeply. The first smell was intoxicating: sunbaked dust and firewood and pine needles and whatever animals had spent the winter inside, usually squirrels or mice—an edgy, acid touch in the air. And there was probably a little mildew, their own leftover dirt, the soap they used. All unmistakably the warm breath of the cottage taking them in, greeting them. They went around and opened curtains and windows to the breeze. Everything was in place and they dropped their bags and car clutter to be attended to in the morning, so glad just to be where they really belonged.

By noon the next day, they were lying in the sun on their ledge, looking out to sea. "Who do you suppose we've got for neighbors this year?" asked Izzy. Their house was on the crest of the hill and, depending on where you sat, you could see a black roof below, or a white painted porch, or, from where they lay now, a car: a little MG, sporty, pretty, red seats, totally different from the middle-aged sedans usually transporting families to Maine. A screen door they couldn't see banged and a young woman in a short black dress raced to the car. She was holding a purse between her teeth and trying to get her masses of dark hair into a rubber band and get herself into the car all at once.

"Wo!" said Chris. "That's something else."

"Hnh," said Izzy, suddenly slightly dowdy in her cotten underpants and Chris's torn teeshirt.

The MG threw a lot of gravel and dust up into a cloud which it left behind to hover by what they could see of the house. Fifteen minutes later, it was back. "The dust has just settled," said Izzy disapprovingly. "A really dry spring, I guess. Oh!" she said. "It's a man this time!"

The man, short, dark and handsome, walked slowly from the car toward the front door and out of sight. "Let's figure this out," said Izzy.

"It's easy," said Chris. "Elementary my dear."

"Well. They didn't go very far. Just the Harbor."

"Right. Five minutes there. Five minutes back. Five minutes to what?"

"I don't know. What?"

"Switch off. They're working one job. He worked the morning. She's working the afternoon."

"You're a genius boy," said Izzy. "No wonder you get scholarships." They didn't bother to check his theory later that afternoon. Just assuming they were right they went down the hill, so Neville could play on the pebble beach and they could fish at the public dock when the tide turned. It was too early for schools of mackerel, but they were hopeful and used a jig anyhow. With it, Chris foul-hooked four pollock instead, which was more than enough. "I'm not bored with pollock yet," said Izzy. "You appreciate things when you haven't had them for a while." She hadn't caught any because she had spent most of her time keeping Neville from eating snails and rocks on the beach.

They were about to start back up the path home when Joe from down the end of the road (but mostly to be found on the steps of the corner store drinking beer) pulled up in his pickup and called to them, "Like yer new neighbors?" eyebrows up like he knew the answer.

"Who are they?" said Izzy.

"Girl's a looker, ain't she?" Joe said to Chris. They had known each other since before either one could drive or drink beer.

"Who are they?" Izzy repeated.

"City folks."

"I could tell that," said Izzy. Joe was making her mad with his taciturn-native locker room talk. "We're sort of city folks too if you want to go into that. What are they doing here?" She knew Chris had been coming to Maine long enough to have a sort of intermediate status, even before the two of them had actually moved here.

"Got some kind of little shop in the Harbor. Right next the hardware. One lean-to room where old man Tibbett used to keep stock. That Bo Tibbett could squeeze pennies out of a prune. Jesus knows what kind of rent he's got them paying. For something about the size of a good six-hole privy. Big sign up says 'FloryDory Silver and Leather.' And that's all I know, dear," he said to Izzy. "Be seeing you," he said to Chris. "Keep your eyes peeled." He winked with the whole left side of his face and drove off.

"Subtle fellow," said Izzy to Chris as they climbed the hill.

She frankly could care less about those three: Asshole Joe and two quickbuck touristtrap wheeler dealers. What she loved was Neville in her arms, Chris beside her and the way the house embraced them all—its three—and offered its every corner like a present, a familiar gift for them, the same thing opening over and over, for their new eyes. Their eyes did change, she knew. Nothing simple like green to hazel, brown to blue, or near- to farsighted—though she thought the latter was how it went as you aged (and age was still a distant surmise, something parents did), but changed by all the things they saw.

They settled in for a good summer. Chris had just barely enough work at the pottery to feed them if they ate a lot of pollock. They didn't have a boat but could borrow one sometimes. They took turns carrying Neville in a backpack so they could hike, but mostly they basked in the sun on their ledge and read or watched Neville. He was always up to something so they put their chairs at opposite ends of the ledge and divided the clear space in two, Chris in charge of the baby at one end and Izzy in charge at the other. In the late afternoons and on Sundays, a restful breeze full of patchouli and pot wafted up from the cottage below.

On Sundays, Chris insisted on overseeing the end of the ledge overlooking the porch where their neighbors always sat in the sun to play cards. The first time, Chris and Izzy had assumed they were playing strip poker, and that neither one of them cheated enough to keep their clothes on. The next Sunday, however, it became obvious that they were as naked at the beginning of the game as at its end. This suited Chris fine. The woman had a tiny waist and beautiful brown breasts and seemed to win, cool as a cucumber, every time. Chris hardly even pretended to read on Sunday afternoons. Izzy didn't really think she liked the neighbors, but Chris was ready to meet them.

"You don't know what you might stumble into," said Izzy when Chris said he thought they should just go knock on their door.

"That's what I'm thinking," said Chris.

"Don't be stupid," said Izzy.

"Or we could ask them up for supper?"

"What? And feed them pollock?"

"Well, I could make something special," said Chris.

Chris didn't really do the cooking, Izzy did. She had gradually learned about various herbs and spices and had a whole shelf full of tins and bottles that could transform pollock into various dishes with foreign names. Chris did know one special recipe for hash brownies, which he proceeded to make. He then arranged some on a paper plate that he intended to carry down the hill as a neighborly gesture. "You know, I think she might be a model," he said. "Even a famous one, I think I've seen her picture. That could be a piece of luck for me."

"Brown boobs doth not a famous model make," said Izzy.

No matter. Less than an hour later, Chris was back at the front door and saying, "This is Izzy. Izzy, this is Flora and Horace." Izzy wasn't mad anymore, thanks to the hash brownies, and giggled because she thought those were the absolute funniest names she'd ever heard. But Flora and Horace giggled too for all the same reasons and Horace said "Izzy! Is a belle or ain't a belle?"

"A belle, my belle," said Chris, because he knew she hated that joke.

"Isabella Ferdinand Columbus de Christopher," said Izzy, extending her hand grandly. So they all cracked up again and passed a rather pleasant evening together in which Chris and Izzy learned that Flora grew up on Beacon Hill and that she had been a model for a few years while she was in college and that she had worked for Richard Avedon (Chris almost passed out—perhaps with admiration) and that she had slept with the two Kennedy brothers that were interesting (Jack and Bobby, that is). Horace did not claim any such illustrious past, but he was the present owner of a large sailboat on which they lived in the winter, in St. Croix. They had it out for charter until October, which is why they were renting the funny little house (two times the size of Chris and Izzy's). And Flora's father didn't like her to be idle, so he had set her up with a silver and leather business to see if he couldn't get her interested in capitalism. They all laughed at the prospect.

A pleasant enough evening. While Izzy put Neville to bed, Horace went out for wine and potato chips to eat with the pollock, and Flora agreed to model for Chris.

Richard Avedon's model! Jack and Bobby's lover! Chris and Izzy had to admit they were impressed. They had once had a friend named Amy who claimed to have slept with Peter, Paul and Mary, but that was harder to believe. One look at Flora and the league she played in was apparent.

Now Flora and Horace waved up at Chris as he oversaw their naked poker on Sundays. He had explained that that was where he had to sit in order to do his share of Neville-watching. They certainly didn't mind and Chris's camera saw even finer sights. Izzy got through *In Cold Blood, The Autobiography of Malcolm X, Valley of the Dolls, Quotations of Chairman Mao* and *The Electric Kool-Aid Acid Test* in spite of Neville. Then the summer was almost over.

"You know," said Chris, as they began to think about packing for their last year in the city. "Flora says they have to get out of that house September first, because the owners want it. She wondered if we'd rent them ours." Izzy didn't feel as close to Flora and Horace as Chris did.

"I thought you never wanted to rent our house to anybody. What if they burned it down?"

"With them it would be different. We know them."

"We sure do," she said. "Enough to know that every night and Sunday especially, they might not be able to figure out how to put out a fire."

"We'll ask them not to build fires."

"Uhhuh. In September not build a fire. You know how cold it gets. Sure. But it's more your house, and you're the one that's always worried, so why not?"

"Besides." This was the clincher, Izzy could tell. "They're going to pay us a lot of rent and I can get that Nikon long lens."

"O.K.," said Izzy.

They went over the house with Flora to show her how things

worked. She was sweet as could be and understood exactly how Izzy felt about all the special things in it. They gave her the key and drove off with more cash than they usually saw in two months.

At the beginning of October, they had a very nice letter from her. She wrote how much she loved the house, and how especially beautiful it was in September. They were going to find some really nice surprises when they came back, she said. The boat was ready and it blew her mind to think she was going to be in the Virgins soon. And with her round, almost childish script, she sent her love.

October. November. Chris worked on his photography all the time, it seemed. He had his first show and Izzy was not really surprised that he sold two pictures of Flora wearing only cowboy boots. They were supposed to remind you of pinups, but they weren't at all. Very subtle. Very tasteful. The picture of her own pregnant belly received some favorable comment but nobody bought it, which suited her fine. The idea of hanging on somebody else's wall seemed strange to her. December . . . Surprises? Izzy wondered what Flora could mean. It sounded like presents of some sort. January, February, March. A gray, gritty April, May. Finally June.

They had to break their own door down again. This was getting to be their regular routine. And the first breath of air inside was almost the same—a little patchouli added, a little pot maybe, but oddly, for Izzy the cumulative effect was of less, not more.

A pile of boxes, studded with sticker ribbon rosettes, in the middle of the living room floor? The surprises? Chris looked in one. "A Braun juicer, great! We can really use that!" He went over to open the first window and the offshore wind eddying in the door behind Izzy and Neville was sucked past them and out to sea. Izzy shivered. She felt drained.

"And look at this casserole! We never had one this good."

"Uhhuh," said Izzy, looking for what was wrong. She did not have to look far. There was a note pinned on the mantle: "I made some trades, just little stuff we needed for the boat," it said. "I know you'll love all the things I left you." It was signed, of course, Flora with x's and o's.

What did Flora leave?

  1 Braun juicer, cracked in back and missing one filter but otherwise perfect.

  1 white Dansk 3 quart casserole.

  1 marble mortar and pestle.

24 leather pocketbooks, 8 black, 8 red, 8 green.

  7 velvet display boxes with 3 odd silver earrings for pierced ears and 1 pin of intricately twisted and flattened silver wire.

  1 empty Perrier Jouy painted champagne bottle with a rose-colored candle burned way down.

  1 10-inch stoneware jar without its lid.

  2 nesting wooden salad bowls and 2 small salad servers.

16 large, exotic (not from Maine) seashells.

  4 sets of printed double bed sheets, wildly floral and dirty.

  1 large jar with strainer top for growing sprouts.

What did Flora take?

  1 sweetgrass basket, old and ratty, but the grass still smelled sweet.

  1 handpainted sugar bowl.

  All the tins of spices and all the jars of herbs. Every single one.

  3 small handwoven bunk blankets shrunk tight and heavy and perfect for three little beds on a cold Maine night.

DIRTY PICTURES

They were about to die but they had not yet met each other when they were sent to the Pleasant View Nursing Home. Vivian was sent by her daughter ostensibly for the uncontrolled touchiness she exhibited all day after being asked to change out of her nightgown every morning and for her grouchy lack of control every evening during the dinner conversation. She was also sent because her son-in-law could afford to send her. Lucius, on the other hand, was a different case. He was what they called a 'scholarship patient.' Medicare paid for most of him and he was small.

She was huge. It was particularly apparent in her nightgown. No one could be expected to put up with it. So every morning her daughter fought to get Vivian decent, so that it would be safe to leave her, in case someone rang and she had to go to the door. She had bad feet and was slow getting places; there was a chance whoever might ring would have already left before she got there, but Vivian's daughter was very keen on her image and wouldn't want her mother in a nightgown at the door. Vivian wore a tasteful black dress all day and when the grandchildren would come home from school, there she'd be at the door, dressed and ready to grouch at somebody, anybody who would be fool enough to come in. The older ones solved the problem by not coming home until dinner, but the younger ones had to because their mother said

18

so. Their mother was often busy herself and couldn't be there; she was glad to have the house covered, as it were, by Gaga.

It was unclear what Vivian GaGa did in her black dress all day, but when everybody came home for supper, she made life miserable for them. Maybe she read the rhyming dictionary. If she didn't have a real complaint such as that it was too hot or too cold or too loud or too soft or too wet or too dry, she would make one up and rhyme it for emphasis. "Hoity toity boidy" she said to her granddaughter who was trying on a new blouse. "Hoity toity boidy, hoity toity boidy."

"Mom," said the granddaughter. "Stop GaGa."

Or, Vivian, seeing her oldest grandson, David, kiss his girl goodbye when she dropped him off for supper, would mutter at the table, "Palsy walsy galsy" until someone would finally pay attention to what she was saying and tell David.

"David, she's talking about you and Gwyneth."

"Palsy walsy galsy," she would say maybe once again, and you might have thought there would be a twinkle in her eye, but there wasn't.

"Mom, make GaGa lay off Gwyneth," said David.

"Thinneth Gwyneth? Gwyneth thinneth, Gwyneth thinneth," she said loud enough to drown out the "Hush, Mother!"

"Doody woody foody," she said mashing the gravy into the potatoes with fork and spoon simultaneously. "Doody woody foody, doody woody foody." And then she ate it. She was no good with both hands.

"GaGa eats worse than you do," David to his youngest brother.

"Did you hear that, Mom? Make him quit picking on me. He's always giving me shit."

"I won't have that language at the table," said his mother.

"Language!" said Vivian's son-in-law. "Look at your mother!" Everybody did and she was a mess which they already knew. When everybody looked at her she started to cry.

20

"Oh, Mother, don't start that!" said her daughter as gently as she could with her headache.

"That's enough. I can't stand it." The son-in-law stood up without finishing his potatoes. "She messes up the whole table, what's more the whole setup! You should have seen this month's bills at the club. You must spend all day there running up a bill like that."

"That was you and your business dinners."

"Not half of it wasn't. And you think I'd bring accounts home to this?"

"Well, and a nice little luncheon with GaGa will do for me!"

"We're the only people got to eat with GaGa," said the little kid who was her rival in mess.

Vivian just cried on. "I want to go away," she said. They looked at her because she seemed coherent.

"Bye bye baby bye bye," she sniffled, to put them at their ease.

So it was decided that night under the covers that everybody would be much happier, including Vivian, if she lived a little farther away. The Pleasant View Nursing Home was in the next town, and the waiting list was not too long for paying patients.

Lucius came at it from another direction entirely. He was so sweet he was always bringing people home to his sister's house, children mostly, and she was always afraid that anybody so nice must be strange and might do something strange and be in a lot of trouble. That he used to like to bring home children and play them old 78's and try to feed them used to upset everybody except the children and Lucius, who thought it was hilarious to eat ice cream out of the carton. "One for you and one for me," he'd say, spooning it into the kid's mouth and into his own. They they would put half a carton back for next time, listen to music and play dominos.

"The domino theory was all wrong because countries are all different sizes and shapes, and if a big one falls against a little one, it will mash it flat," he explained, having carefully arranged the pieces in a snake-like procession which he let his ten-year-old listener set to toppling. "That's why little ones have to be feisty and wary and ready to slip out the back door when they see trouble."

"Little whats?" said the kid.

"Little countries, little anythings. Little kids."

"Don't you think they're looking for you at home?" said Lucius's sister, coming into the kitchen.

"Yes, ma'am," said the kid and hurried for the back door.

"You come back soon," said Lucius.

But they never actually came back to knock on the door. And Lucius would get lonely and go out looking for another friend as soon as his sister left the house in the morning. She was not interested in his conversation even when she was there, and she was the only one he wouldn't tell his theories to. He would talk to anybody else.

"At least you don't offer them candy, I hope," she said as this last little kid went out the door.

"They like ice cream."

"I can't afford all this ice cream. I can hardly afford you."

"Who could afford you? You cost me a friend every time you come in the door."

"So I'm thinking I better lock you in before the vice squad gets to you."

"Vice squad mice squad. What would they do with me?"

"Lock you up. Put you away."

"One jail's good as another I always say."

"More like the loony bin for you."

"Runs in the family. You're just not smart enough to know you got it. You've never been smart."

"You think you've got anything up top?"

"Smart I've been."

"Smart you're not any more."

So Lucius was admitted more or less on the basis of his years and as a preventive measure, and, since he really thought one jail was as good as another, and he had a captive audience (because a lot of his neighbors were not particularly ambulatory, and the pretty little nurse's aides reappeared regularly to make his bed or otherwise tend his needs, and looking like cotton candy ready to listen), he was happier than at his sister's.

From his station by the front window, he had the pleasant view of the old four-story structure that this airy, vacation-style lodging had replaced. The old building was used now for administration and hospitalization and had an enclosed sliding board for bad-weather emergency escapes from its top floor. It opened into a charming, therapy garden tended by some of the patients who were up to independent work. Lucius enjoyed this part of the view, but it was not the reason he left his small, neat room and went every day to sit by the plate glass window in the lounge. What he really enjoyed seeing was the parking lot with its comings and goings, admissions of new patients, changes of staff and visitors for other people. Generally speaking, if patients had to leave, or die, it was out the back door. Or, at least, that was what Lucius assumed; because, although he had never seen a back door, he could count, and the continual influx of new older citizens to this very finite structure implied an exit which was not necessarily the same as the entrance he oversaw.

One happy, sunny Sunday he saw Vivian emerge weeping from a large station wagon filled with a smiling family. He saw David hoist her out and two other children carry her bags and one little boy take her fingers in his and hand her a plastic baggy with a goldfish in it. With her stature, Vivian stood out in any crowd, but it was the size of her sorrow which impressed Lucius.

She heaved such sighs as the tears ran down that he saw her soul as a great windy space like the plains, or a valley or the sea. She made no attempt to wipe away the tears, and he saw that her character was so great that she felt no need to be ashamed of grief. Her happy family was trying to cheer her up, but she just walked through them as if they were nothing. He deeply wished to rush and offer to help her, to carry her bags perhaps, but he could see she was well taken care of by her family. He watched them register her at the desk. They were going to leave her now that she had stopped crying. No, they were going to walk her down the "A" wing to her room, while the little boy ran out to the car to bring in the forgotten goldfish bowl. "Sweety sweety," said his grandmother.

"May I carry your goldfish for you?" said Lucius standing up from his chair as she passed.

She looked at his face which had once been touched by a stroke; one side of it was radiant with his smile while the other side was very sad. She could see all his moods at once and how sweetness pervaded them. She shook her head, touched but still immobilized in the slow passing of her dreary life. "Sweety sweety," she said again, going slowly on down the hall.

"Weird old man," said the granddaughter to David, but she said it a few feet away and on Lucius's bad side, and his feelings weren't hurt. He envied Vivian her handsome, cheerful family, and then he feared dreadfully for her health, certain that only some hideous affliction more dangerous and more incurable than years, must have brought her there. He sat down and bided his time.

He did not have long to wait, because the dinner bell rang at five. It rang at five either so that the patients could have finished digesting before dreaming, or so that the day staff could leave at six. "This is Vivian Hill," said the nurse to the little group at Lucius's table. "She just joined us today. I know she'll be very happy here with you."

"Lucius Hecht," said Lucius, standing up and extending his hand. "Pleased that you could join us." The others nodded or dithered quietly in welcome and Vivian did not seem to know what to say.

"You look, perhaps, a little sad, but you'll get used to it," said Lucius. It was unclear which of the expressions slowly

washing across Vivian's face would stay. Shyness, grateful-
ness, hunger, pleasure and then sadness settled in. Lucius felt
he had much more interesting company than before, and as
Vivian ate quietly and copiously, he watched the undulations
of her abundant surfaces, imagining himself almost a flying
fish among the waves.

He asked for two extra ice creams after dinner and took
them off towards the TV lounge. "They'll only melt, Mr.
Hecht," said the aide.

"I won't give them the chance," he replied, pocketing a
spoon.

"Look what I brought us," he said to Vivian, sitting down
next to her before the TV. She seemed pleased but still not
exactly voluble. "Sweety sweety" was almost inappropriate.
She came up with "Oh my."

Lucius thought there must be a bigger voice in there, more
fitting the instrument. She was playing it with a mute or the
damper pedals. Something was there she wouldn't let be
heard.

"But I could only get one spoon so we have to share." She
looked at him a little wide-eyed, yes she lifted her eyebrows
and stretched her cheeks out in a smile, and her eyes shone.

"Here, one for you," he said, "and one for me." She swal-
lowed hers and laughed, a great, booming laugh that rolled
over the room and made even the ones who were deaf look her
way. So they had met, and there was no good reason to say it
was too late. Too late for what?

"I think I saw them feeling each other up," said a disgusted
little nurse's aide.

"We'll have to keep an eye on them. Their families might
not like it," said the supervisor.

Little was seen of Lucius's sister, and the six members of
Vivian's family divided their Sunday visits evenly, so she saw
one of them at a time, and no one had to come more than once
every six weeks. About the third Sunday, the little boy came
and looked in the fishbowl, which had been placed on the top

of the turned-off radiator so the fish would have a view out the window. "Where's the fish?" said the boy.

"Bombs away," Vivian shrugged sadly.

"You dropped him out the window, GaGa?" he said in horror.

"Flew the coop?" she suggested.

"He's no bird, GaGa. Somebody stole him."

"Steal from the rich and give to the poor," she said drearily, letting the tears well up. He was afraid she might start one of her big crying fits that he was too small to deal with.

"I'll bring you another one, GaGa, tomorrow. I'll come extra." She looked happier. "Sure," he said. "Sure, that's a good idea. Don't be sad."

So Monday he ran in with a new goldfish and took the time to install it, while his mother ran some errands in town. "Watch out for him this time," he said. "Or her, it's hard to tell." Vivian did keep pretty close track of it, enjoying its darting movements and the way it caught the light, but she didn't see how it got away.

David had to come next and brought his camera. He was doing character studies for a school project, and someone had said his grandmother was a character all right. He had ten shots before he had even reached her room. She let him take some pictures of her clicking her teeth like castanets. "If you had two sets, it would be better. Maybe you could borrow some, GaGa." That was too much for Vivian, and she installed her own teeth firmly. She would have retreated into her old grouchy rhymes if Lucius had not appeared at the door with his little, blue, portable record player.

"Oh pardon me. I didn't know your family was here."

"Come in, come in, come in," she said.

"Great, yeah, come in. I was just taking some pictures, and I could take yours too," said David.

Lucius smiled and agreed and set up the record player on Vivian's radiator next to the goldfish bowl. "Your fish is gone again."

"I didn't want to say it," said Vivian.

"What will Shorty think?" said David. "What do you do, eat them?"

She clicked her teeth at him ferociously; they were impressive inside her face, and he didn't dare take a picture. He turned to Lucius, instead, and snapped a few of him letting the needle down carefully into the groove. This took great concentration, because Lucius shook when he concentrated, and he had to concentrate more not to shake. "You need an automatic," said David.

"When I can't play my own music, young man, it's time to quit," said Lucius, sitting in the arm chair with his good ear near the record player. He closed his eyes and picked his nose quietly, and David had a wonderful idea, a genius idea, one he expected might make his fortune. He didn't say anything about it but began to pack his camera up almost immediately, so he could go home and develop his thought.

"That was a quicky quicky," said Vivian.

"Sorry, GaGa. I just thought of something. Maybe Shorty can bring you another fish tomorrow and stay a bit."

"This is the last one, GaGa," said Shorty the next day. "You've got to hold onto this one better."

"Sweety sweety they're so pretty. I try my best."

Lucius came shuffling in, doing a little soft-shoe number, flopping his sloppy slippers. Vivian and her grandson clapped and he bowed. Then he danced on across the room, a repetitious little step to some interior big band. "If *you* don't get a *let*-ter then you'll *know* I'm in jail," he sang to the goldfish.

The little boy made his grandmother promise to watch the goldfish better and left soon. Lucius was already sitting in Vivian's armchair, resting from his dance. He often spent energy rashly but couldn't regret it.

"Ever swim at night when you were a girl?" he asked.

Vivian nodded. They were watching the fish together.

"It's like that now for me, at night asleep. You dive down and it's dark and you can't tell up from down, which way to go to surface. When the night goes on too long, you've turned wrong. You're not coming up for air."

"Oh sweety sweety," she said. "Take a deep breath before you go down."

By the next Sunday, the fishbowl was empty again. When Vivian's daughter came in the door, she wrinkled her nose in disgust. "What is that awful odor?" she said. Vivian shrugged sadly, because she didn't smell anything particular, and she was a little sensitive about occasional failures of her digestive tract—though she didn't remember anything recent. Her daughter went to get a nurese's aide to help her tackle the problem.

"It's just age," said the girl in the uniform, as she reluctantly left her more important task to check Vivian's room.

"This isn't age. This is dead," said Vivian's daughter.

"Well, they all smell alike to me," said the girl petulantly. "Work here long enough and you get used to it."

Vivian was looking very tearful. "Oh, I'm sorry," said the girl. "I forgot you weren't deaf."

"It's behind the radiator," said Vivian's daughter, sniffing it out. "Get down and look."

The girl knelt down. "Geez, you're right. It really does stink. I'm not putting my hand under there. Hold that lamp down here so I can see."

It was the various fish, in serial stages of decomposition.

"Suicides," said Vivian. "And they were so beautiful. It was the goldfish bowl they couldn't stand. It killed my pretty fish." She started to cry, because she couldn't help it, but she didn't want those other people to comfort her. The nurse's aide plumped up her pillows vigorously, and Vivian's daughter poured her a glass of water that Vivian only looked down into, as if for the fish, and splashed her tears on its empty surface, "Just where could my pretty goldfish live?" she wept.

"It's too late for that, mother."

"They shouldn't let them have pets," said the girl. "They get too attached."

But to cheer her, Vivian soon had an extra visit from David who wanted to try out his big moneymaking idea. He was going to sell ads to the *National Lampoon*. He had spent all week rifling through old magazines for good material. He first intended to do an ad for Scotch exploiting Lucius's ancient good looks and his bad habit. The old tie-silk bathrobe he had found in his father's closet and his mother's long white scarf for an ascot were presented to Lucius on permanent loan, since it was unlikely they would ever be missed. Lucius appreciated their quality immensely, but even more he appreciated the bottle of Chivas Regal and the handsome glass which David had brought. "That's on loan too?" he asked.

"Not at all, Mr. Hecht, a gift from me to you for helping me with these pictures." More likely a gift from his father's liquor cabinet, but that didn't matter to Lucius.

"You should have brought your grandmother a glass. I only drink in company."

"This tumbler will be fine for me," said Vivian, fishing ice cubes out of her water pitcher.

"Now GaGa, you're going to have to take it easy. Today I'm just going to do Mr. Hecht."

"Don't you worry young man. That's all we do around here is take it easy." Both she and Lucius were excited by the elegant costume which he had already put on.

"I want you to relax over there, by the window. Sip your Scotch, gaze out at the view. Just relax. I'm going to take a lot of pictures. We'll put the bottle right here to show the label. Don't mind me. I'm going to just shoot until I get what I want."

It didn't take much waiting. Lucius was a quick relaxor and had not had a drink for a long time. In fact, in twenty minutes he had dozed off, but not before a long, profound gaze out the window during which he alternately picked his nose and sipped his Scotch. Out of all the shots David took of that scene, surely there was at least one up to the standards of quiet elegance required of a good Scotch ad—life's simple pleasures.

Vivian daydreamed with her Scotch, too. "Do I get a costume for my picture?" she asked.

"You sure do," said David. "It's going to be great. You're going to need a fancy negligee."

"Your mother's getting me a new nightgown. You could help her pick it out."

The nightgown came in an enormous box. It was luscious and gauzy and enormous itself and had a lacy peignoir. Vivian giggled but really admired it. She put it on immediately. "That's splendid," said Lucius when he saw her. David was ripping all the covers off the bed, even unzipping the plastic, down to the bare mattress. Lucius stood by the door keeping it mostly shut, glad for a little mischievous excitement.

"This is a good mattress," said David. "But I'm not sure about the proportions. It ought to be a double. GaGa, see if you can lie on just one side of it. Put your arm up over your head, and bend your knees just a little."

"I'm going to fall off."

"No, don't fall off. That's good." He climbed up on the bureau with his camera. "Now, dream your best dreams for me." He snapped a few warm-up pictures to get her used to the flash. "GaGa, that's terrible! Why are you crying?"

"Don't cry, Vivian," said Lucius, who went to hold her hand as she sat up. "If it's still the fish, you know, that's not what's important!" Vivian was not consoled, but eventually she always stopped crying. David took a lot of pictures of the two of them, who had forgotten him, but he did not think they were going to fit the slogan "It's a third of your life, why not spend it on Beautyrest?" He had some hope for the first shots before his grandmother had started to cry, but gradually realized he had another scene, and that, with a montage, he could do the Cardin perfume "Behind every great woman there's a man."

"Would you two mind changing positions a little bit?" he asked.

Vivian's gaze which was still rather moist and full of whatever dreams had made her sad, turned from the sweetness that held Lucius's expressions together towards the eye of David's camera and stopped there, bitter and resentful. "What do you want?" she said.

"You don't have to do it if you don't want," said David.

"I think we should just go along with the pictures," said Lucius. "It's something to do."

"There, that dissatisfied look is perfect," said David. "Now see if you can't look more luscious, too."

"Never hear of the eye of the beholder?" asked Lucius.

"Let me do a couple of shots of Mr. Hecht behind you, GaGa." They moved around but weren't really enjoying the scene anymore. David gave up. He didn't like the amateur feel of it all. He probably needed professional models to pretend they were old people. But the idea was sound.

"I have one more terrific picture in mind," he said. "But it's going to take a lot of arranging, and we can't do it until it is all set up."

They looked curious. "More costumes?" asked Vivian, smoothing her peignoir.

"No, but we're going to sign you out. We're not going to do them here."

"Both of us?"

"I only need you, GaGa, but Mr. Hecht can come."

"Oh mystery mystery mystery," said Vivian.

The first thing David needed was a "before" picture. He went through album after album of family photos, looking for Vivian sliding. If she had ever been to a playground, the camera had not gone with her. He found some beautiful ones of her wearing a sunhat but still squinting at the bright day ahead. He found her laughing in a flower garden. He found her wading at a picnic, smiling down at the trail of her skirt in the stream. He found her going for a trip with a neat hat pinned on crookedly and a coat over her arm. But there wasn't a single one of her on a sliding board. He felt it would be cleaner technique to use a real picture of the child, Vivian, but, of course, there was no reason for it to be the same person. In the ads the people were a hundred years apart. Any little old-fashioned child would do. Broadening his field, it was easy for him to find a beautiful child, pigtails flying and skirts held firmly down as they fluttered up with the speed of her descent.

Next, he needed allies within the institution. The petulant nurse's aide assigned to the goldfish cleanup was much more interested in him than in her patients and was easily persuaded to join him in the parking lot on her day off but wearing her uniform. "Just bring your other things to change into afterwards, and we'll catch a movie," was sufficient bribe.

"Are we signed out?" inquired Lucius, as they emerged at Vivian's bad-footed pace into the parking lot.

"Yes," said David. "I did it already."

"What did you put down?"

"Pictures."

"Nobody calls movies 'pictures' any more. The super's going to think that's weird," said the nurse's aide, who wore her niftiest pink-striped uniform with "Monica" sewn on the handy pocket.

"They can take it how they want. I just meant we were going to take pictures. Who's to know these two don't need to apply for passports."

"Oh, that's a good one," she giggled loudly. "Where are they ever going again?"

"Where *are* we going?" asked Lucius quickly, before Vivian could respond with tears.

"Just over here," said David, as they crossed the parking lot and went into the little therapy garden, gently autumnal with its sprawling mounds of chrysanthemums.

"Oh, this is beautiful here." Vivian stopped and looked all around her. "This would be a wonderful place to stay."

"Someone works hard to make these plants grow like that,"

said Lucius. "I see people out here sometimes."

"I want to stay right here for a bit." Vivian headed for a bench.

"Oh GaGa, not now, later."

"Well, you tell me what we're going to do and make it more interesting."

"We're going to do 'You've Come a Long Way, Baby,' and you're the star."

So Vivian looked interested and Monica got them in through the back entrance of the hospital building and into two wheelchairs. "We both can walk fine," protested Lucius.

"It's better if you don't look too ambulatory in this place, or else someone will wonder," said David.

"I'm wondering already," Vivian giggled, as they took the elevator up.

At the quiet end of the hall, where it said "Exit," David made Vivian put on her old bathrobe over her tasteful black dress and exchanged slippers for her shoes. "Look, this is it," he said as he pushed open the exit door. "It's a slide."

"No, sir. Not me," said Vivian.

"There's nothing to be afraid of. It's made for sick old people," Monica offered helpfully.

"I'm old but not real sick," retorted Vivian.

"Looks like fun to me," said Lucius. "Where does it come out?"

"In the flowers," said David.

"In the flowers?" said Vivian. "Well that's a different kettle of fish."

"I though you'd like it." David was pleased. "You're such great old characters."

"You go down first, sweety?" Vivian asked Lucius.

"But wait until I'm down at the bottom to take the picture. I'll have to set up just right in case we can't get a retake." So David hurried back down and out, worried that they might get caught and he would be unable to have even one shot of Vivian's descent. He set his camera and whistled his signal.

Lucius looked a little pale and apprehensive even on his good side, but smiled bravely as Vivian said "Just take a deep breath sweety sweety."

"Toot toot tootsy goodbye," he started to sing. "Toot toot tootsy, don't cryyy." He was disappearing down the chute and she didn't want him to leave her and she started too soon, before he had even rolled out the end into the flowers. Vivian's great mass of devotion, bathrobe flapping, came hurtling down the slide, an emergency for which even David was not prepared. She flew out into him feet first and with all her marvelous weight practically annihilated him and his camera, so that there was a question whether or not he even got the picture.

And Vivian and Lucius lay there in the soft autumnal flowers deep in their own dark, not broken, but unsure of where the surface would be found.

FREE GREENS

Edith had to deal with Glenn's effects. It was time. There was no close family—none to want his things, none who might come to a funeral. No one of his university friends who did attend the brief service seemed a likely recipient for any particular treasure. It was almost a surprise that they were there, visits during his long illness having tapered off, perfunctory and embarrassed, rare. Ten or fifteen men, solemn with their own mortality, were present to shake her hand or brush her damp cheek briefly with theirs, but she knew she would never see these people again. They had been colleagues and she was not in the league.

So the botany books went not to the botanists but to the library, all except the ten copies of the one Glenn wrote and the special edition of Louisiana Flora signed by all his students when he could not finish the semester and, fuming, left the class in the clutches of an ignorant and pontificating graduate student. He interested people, she thought, but no one except her really knew him; Edith and Glenn had kept their knowing for each other.

Mourning for so long had been hard but, perhaps, this eased the pain now. She had put most of Glenn's clothes into boxes before he died, to practice his death, to get used to it, but she had not sealed the boxes, and this afternoon she took out a thin green sweater with empty elbows that still had his man smell in it, untouched by all the sweet insistent masks for incontinence, and a new plaid shirt she had bought him for a get-well present. They had both forgotten the shirt, not even unpinning it. She took the pins out so it would shake loose and hung it in her closet next to some baggy corduroy pants. The sweater she pulled on, so she could keep the house wide open this cool, late afternoon, so the sick smell would go.

In the mirror on the closet door, she saw how much she looked like Glenn in his sweater—before he was ill. The same coarse blonde hair, well, yellow gray to be honest. And the same deepset, sharp eyes, but his were blue—had been blue, and hers were brown. Underneath the loose sweater her body was lean and neat, the body of a woman who simply never needed a baby because she looked at her husband and saw herself reflected, but improved, and she knew that, in a lot of ways that was how he saw her too. Despite Glenn's interest in species, which are, after all, defined by reproduction (he never did quite discover a new one that could be named for himself, but she had no doubts that, had he lived longer, he would have), being the last of a bloodline never seemed to bother him. It had scarcely occurred to Edith, but now she realized she would have liked to be less alone.

She dragged the clothing box into Glenn's study, most recently the room where Glenn's living became reduced to just not dying and not dying until finally he did. She looked around to see what might be useful for the Goodwill people. A nasty digital clock that beeped and told time only in certain lights. A magnifying glass, a half-tasseled pillow, a ruler, a large pink conch, a broken projector, a repairable lamp. Oh God, she thought. I should have a garage sale. That's what people do. But she wouldn't know where to begin. And what was she going to do with this room when it wasn't Glenn's study. If she made it a guest room who would she have for guests?

His desk had served for all the equipment of illness. Glenn had done his time in hospitals, but as little as possible, returning home to a rented hospital bed placed where she was standing now. That had been one of the moments of deep mourning for her, when she realized absolutely that now forever she would sleep alone in their double bed without the lovemaking that had continued late into his illness, starting over and over in the face of death, holding it at bay one more time and only gradually becoming another sort of intimate attention, until she was the one who did all the touching—the bathing, the wiping.

Edith lay down on the couch, her feet against one end, her head against the other. She was exhausted. The lump under her cheek was the VCR remote. She took it in her hand and pushed the button distractedly, rolling back against the cushions to look at the screen. "Oh God, Oh God," she cried and burst into tears. Because there it was, on the screen, pushing in and out of a delicate, ruffly vagina, Jamie Gillis's dark, passionate penis, pumping and glowing, and why was she so touched? It wasn't even her favorite scene, it was one of Glenn's where Jamie gets Misty or vice versa, where manipulation becomes passion, but together she and Glenn had laughed themselves silly at the sexy, unpassionate parts. She did not remember ever stopping at this scene. It must have been the last time Glenn had watched—like a letter half-written, or a page turned down in a book for her, and there was this penis, and there she was weeping, no screaming, loud and alone for all the good fun gone. She stopped it too, in the middle. She ejected it and threw it in the box for the Goodwill. Then she put all the other cassettes in there, too, and went to look for the brown tape and taped the cardboard shut and dragged the box outside the front door. The rest of the afternoon was interminably dreary. Edith finally drank half a bottle of sherry, ate two pieces of toast, and went to bed.

Up before the sun, as usual, driven by her own anxiety about missing a minute of her life, Edith, despite her headache, tried to be capable again the next day. She did something that she had read might be appropriate for her at this stage.

She drove up to the Animal Shelter and chose a puppy; only, faced with the animals, she did not actually choose a puppy but a large cross between a lab and a shepherd who seemed to have manners and some ideas of his own about the world and what to do in it. He had been found with a collar identifying either him or his abandoners as Boudreau so she called him that. They stopped on the way home to buy dog food and a bright blue collar and leash, because it was via Boudreau that she was going to prove to herself that she could live without Glenn, getting out of the house and into the world again, slowly, gently, with easy, uncomplicated love—before taking on the drone work for which she was trained, or, if it should happen, the complications of knowing another human being.

The entrance to her driveway was a little humped bridge over a culvert, the sides of which had been planted with ajuga and impatiens. The roof to the carport had been removed to let the wisteria hang through. But the empty framework was dark wood and resembled less the usual garden house than the entrance to an oriental shrine. There was a courtyard where Glenn used to rake the gravel in patterns. A miniature concrete pagoda stood in the center beside three mature bonsai trees and another he had been starting, which looked scraggly rather than venerable. They had brought the bonsai with them when they moved here, just before they began to think Glenn might be sick. Now everything needed work; it had been months since Glenn pulled himself around the yard on his hands and knees culling the plants he didn't care for. The summer's growth threatened to cut out all the autumn sunlight that fell through small leaded panes into their living-room. Groundcover jasmine was starting up the stucco walls for the dark wood beams. It was one of their delights to believe they possessed the only Japanese Tudor house in the world; they knew at least, that they were uncommon in Baton Rouge.

The gravel aroused Boudreau's great interest. Edith could see where some neighbor cats had taken it for a catbox. How much work there was to do in these beds. And she wasn't sure she would really like gardening that much without Glenn. She noticed she had no real impulse to pull out the goatweed before it sank its roots too deep, becoming too stubborn to move. She leaned over, nonetheless, next to the dog and yanked a stem; it looked delicate but was already unyielding. She would have to find the trowel.

Boudreau's second day with Edith they took a walk in one direction and returned the same way. Her neighbors nodded and smiled, but she hardly knew them, even the one who brought her a casserole after Glenn's obituary was in the paper. She certainly wasn't ready to chat yet, so she merely kept open the possibility of friendly acquaintance by keeping her new dog carefully off their lawns. The next day they looped another way and met four or five children who said Boudreau was the fluffiest labradog they had ever met. Edith had very little small talk for children but watched them pet his thick coat and agreed that he was beautiful and nice. Soon, one morning early, just after sunrise, they found a third way that circled the outside of the neighborhood. Halfway along, up by the main road, was a bus stop with a covered bench. An old black man was sitting there, wearing neat denim overalls and a striped railroad hat. She could tell he was old by the tight, smooth, chestnut skin that had shrunk close to his bones. Like old Sol's when she was the little girl allowed to dig with him in her grandmother's garden. That was easy love.

"How you be doing?" he said.

"Oh, fine," she said. "Really fine."

"That black dog bite?" he asked, watching the dog sniff his way slowly from lamp post to bench, in the direction of his yellow work boots.

"Oh, I don't think so," she said. Then she remembered one of the purposes of black dogs and added "Not unless he had to protect me." She realized, however, that, on the basis of their very brief relationship, Boudreau probably had no more loyalty to her than to this friendly, handsome old man, and asserted her authority by saying "back Boudreau back." Boudreau did not move back but on the other hand, he stopped moving forward and wagged slowly and noncommittally.

"This is going to be a beautiful day for yard work," she said, because any such black man in this neighborhood would be there for yard work—except she had never really seen a black man like this. His overalls and striped hat were impeccable, a costume. He seemed to have just come on the set dressed for a part in a railroad movie. No smut, no grime, certainly no garden grime. She was embarrassed that she might have placed him wrong. She knew if he had been white she would not be standing there with him. She would never have remembered the gardener from her childhood. "That's what I'll be doing. What do you do?"

"Comes in twiced a week help out Ms Fontenot."

She really wanted to ask about what he was wearing, but said "You take the bus?"

"No. Walks," he answered. "Long road cross that river bridge."

"Huh," she said, more and more interested, more and more puzzled. It was five miles at least, probably farther. "Huh! All the way from Port Allen?"

"Has to get up long before the sun even think about it. Good walk from that little house I got. Don't has to work you know. But I likes to help out Ms Fontenot. Bring her a little something time to time. She need a little help and she appreciate something from time to time."

Edith saw an egg carton poking out of his plastic grocery bag. For Ms Fontenot she assumed. The country people with their big gardens often brought the folks they worked for greens, sometimes eggs. She longed for something fresh from the country but she was growing uncomfortable, thought she should ask no more questions. She sensed she was forgetting something. The codes were a little confused but even the simplest perception of who the two of them were in the world—he the sitter, she the passerby—meant that she should be the one to stop the conversation and move on.

"Here, Boudreau," she said. "Have a nice day," she told the railroad gardener.

"Yes, miss. Hope you has a fine day too." Edith and her dog walked away; Boudreau was a slow and attentive ambler but Edith liked speed. She yanked at his leash a little and he sped up.

"What in the world, Boudreau?" she said. "Did you ever know a man like that?" She stopped talking out loud, because, though the question was about her habits of thinking, she did not think she was quite old enough to be losing her habits of being. But she remembered so long ago how it felt to be a little girl whose best friend was a gardener with an old bureau drawers in the garage where he kept tins of Redman chewing tobacco and tulip bulbs. He used to like her to help him carry the bulbs and drop them in the holes. The two of them were always getting muddy and were made to take off their shoes to come in the kitchen. When she finally started school she had an enviable collection of tiny cloth tobacco bags with drawstrings and sweet-smelling tins that he gave her, which she had gradually traded away to her new companions for one childhood pleasure or another. Long long gone, she thought.

Their driveway was a few streets over. They crossed the little humped bridge that only had water under it after rain—not now. Edith ignored the goatweed and admired the flowers and groaned at the sight of the pile of boxes that Goodwill had still not come for. She had done that all herself. She felt strong.

She thought of Glenn, his absolute consistency, his sameness to himself that only intensified with illness. No quirky anger seemed to bubble up from the past to make their lives miserable at the end, and it always felt to her that he even kept his fantasies within reach of their life together. The X-rated films (most of which she didn't like, but just said so, and went away to do something else) seemed an example of this—some simple, not very dangerous pleasure in a wider experience of the human species. Sometimes he would call her, "Come here, you're going to like this." And he was almost always right. Generally, it was to watch what happened when a stranger came in the door.

As she had mentioned to the man in the railroad cap, the day was a nice one for gardening—except the earth was hard as brick bats from a drought she had not really noticed because of Glenn's dying. Edith hated scuffed knuckles and gave up on the weeds. Instead she hacked down a few banana trees to let some light onto her kitchen porch and through the window. The season was past for avoiding the sun.

Still, more sun on the kitchen floor, or on her back when she sat to eat her sandwich, was not enough to fill her long, empty days, and at best, walking Boudreau was pleasantly boring. The Goodwill truck finally came for the boxes and she began to call and ask for job applications but never sent any in. She tried to listen to music while she worked around the house but it made her cry. When she worked outdoors, she left the door open and tried listening to their music faded by some distance. She was still trying to get on top of the garden.

The old man was at the bus stop, not every morning, but regularly. She always stopped for his "How you be doing?" and was comfortable with him for longer talks. He lived alone now outside of Port Allen with a couple of goats, a big garden, maybe a dozen chickens, maybe six-seven rabbits. His house had been paid long ago but he hadn't any car. He had a nice pension from the railroad, had traveled all across the South. He kept very busy. He liked to walk in the morning cool because it made him feel good, but afternoons when he was tired and the sun hot in the sky, he took the bus. He had raised two families but they were all gone—most to Chicago, a couple of boys doing well in Texas, coming to visit Christmas. She noticed he had a little tic that she attributed to age—his tongue always moved in and out over his lips at the ends of his sentences, while he waited for her to respond.

Despite that somewhat disturbing symptom, she enjoyed his company for the few minutes a day and the few days a week he was there. His "How you be doing?" always delivered with an appreciative smile, as if she looked to him like someone doing fine, raised her spirits and she could feel her body prickle with her answer, "Fine."

One day, she simply could not contain her admiration for a huge bunch of turnip salad on the bench beside him and asked "How much do you charge for nice greens like that?"

"Oh, they free greens," he said. "Ms Fontenot she sure love her greens."

"Would you sell me some?" asked Edith.

"I brings you some," he said. "Be here Thursday way you always is and there be mess of greens for you too." He smiled broadly and she smiled back trying not to pay attention to the tic his tongue had. Age was very frightening to her now and almost the last thing she would want to think about.

"How about a dollar's worth?" she asked.

"They be free," he said.

"Well. I'll pay you a dollar," she insisted and sped off with Boudreau.

Thursday, of course, she was there with her dollar bill but he wouldn't take it. It was not as if the two of them were part of any interlocking family-servant system in which little gifts were exchanged and reciprocated one way or another over the years. Though she was sure they were some kind of friends, she did not even know his name and would have felt funny asking. Edith was uncomfortable and wished she had never admitted to coveting the greens but they looked beautiful, and the man was stubborn, so she took them and thanked him lavishly.

"I be bringing you some eggs next week," he said.

"Well, if you let me pay you for them."

He smiled and nodded. So she went off to try to do the needed garden work without shedding any tears, intending to bring the money back on Tuesday.

And Tuesday he wouldn't take the dollar any better than the week before. At his warm insistence, she accepted the eggs he had carried the five miles for her and looked forward to their thick country yolks.

"What you be needing next time?" he asked.

"Nothing," she said.

"You sure you doing so fine?" he asked. "How about nice little chicken? How about rabbit? You looks like a lady could stand some rabbit. Build you up little bit. With just them greens you never put on flesh."

Edith was not skinny. She was proud of her body's leanness. She had always felt very much in control of it, the way she could use it for pleasure, but didn't say so out loud. She just said, to her great surprise, "My husband and I, we don't eat so much meat."

At first, Edith's dawn anxieties had ended almost the second she had her feet out of bed, into her shoes and out into the pale light. But this changed as she began to realize that without Glenn, she seemed only to have ways to say no and do yes. It seemed insulting to reject the man's gifts. She didn't want to hurt his feelings, and besides, she liked the country produce, but her blood was pumping harder than her almost aerobic walk warranted. She tried deliberately to slow down, she became the ambler and Boudreau the fast walker, but still took the route where she knew she would find the old man. This time she was determined to say no and mean it and do it. The whole thing seemed so complicated—not at all as she remembered Old Sol and Little Edith. She liked him for his gentle way of talking and the things he chose to tell her—how proud he was of his boys in Texas, even his tongue tic was less upsetting, almost fascinating—but you don't stare at symptoms of frailty, any more than you turn down simple generosity, which made things difficult. Boudreau wagged his way up to the railroad man who always gave him a pat or two now, and Edith saw another brown bag on the bench. She willed it absolutely to be for Ms Fontenot.

"How you be doing?" he said.

"Fine," she replied.

"Come on over here and look in this here bag."

She hesitated. Boudreau was sniffing it.

"This not for you, black dog. This for your momma."

O.K. So she would look at it. But she was not going to take it. He nodded toward the bag beside him, meaning she should come closer and open it.

"Undo the bag. Take a look." He was really pleased with whatever it was. It was going to be hard as ever not to take it. She moved closer and unrolled the neatly folded top. Then she picked it up and looked in. Inside the bag were two plastic wrap packages of hot dogs. What the hell? Edith thought.

"How that look to you?" he asked.

"Fine. Well, I mean. I don't understand."

"Bought them for you fresh last night. You like them?"

These hot dogs made her *really* uneasy. Sharing the fat of the land was one thing. Buying her something was another.

"Well, that's nice," she said and then she changed modes. "But you take those right on over to Ms Fontenot's and put them in her frigidaire. Then you can give them to her or you can carry them home but I can't take them."

He looked sad, staring right at her the way he always did and moving his tongue while he thought.

"You don't like them?" he said. "Looks to me like you the kind of lady like them fine."

"Oh, well. That's not it," she said. "That's a nice present. It's just that my husband and I, we'd never get through all those hot dogs before they spoiled. You better take them home."

"You take a little now I brings the rest later."

"No," she was firm. "You take that home." She and Boudreau started off on the rest of their walk. "It won't spoil if you put it in the fridge," she called back, because the railroad man did look dejected, even lonely.

Thank God it wasn't rabbit, she thought. Refusing fresh dressed rabbit would have been almost impossible. But hot dogs! Whatever was on his mind? It seemed funny and her handling it with such address reassured Edith. So she was not even anxious the next morning she expected the man to be there.

"How you be doing?" he asked.

She smiled. "Fine." There was no bag on the bench beside him and she was relieved. Boudreau went for his pat.

"I been thinking," he told her, working his tongue a little as usual. "I been thinking you might be looking for some help."

Edith shook her head. "That's not something I can afford right now."

"You just tell me when. I come free. I don't need no money."

She stared at him, shaking her head some more. "I couldn't let you work for free."

"You just tell me when. I even bring a little money. You just say how much."

"I'm doing fine," she insisted. "I have plenty of money."

"Then I just come give you little help."

"No," she said. "No. My husband likes to do all that himself. He's the gardener."

"You just tell me when he not there."

"No," repeated Edith. "No," and began to back away, pulling Boudreau.

"Watch," he said. "I can do this." And he moved his tongue back and forth until she saw that something had prevented her knowing it was deliberate and not the least frail all along. All the gifts from his garden and the two packs of hot dogs were becoming plainer and plainer and making her blood burn. She half-wondered if she had needed Glenn there even to have certain ideas, if her way of forgetting Glenn was to go back to a consciousness that preceded him, before she knew she was a woman, before she was responsible for her perceptions or how she was perceived. The man was so different from her ideas that she had not really seen him at all. She felt she was being offered something she had to turn down for a thousand complicated reasons while still admitting it was a good gift.

"I'm sure you can," she could feel the fear on the edges of her smile. She did not know if she had taken Glenn into herself to use him for making her own limits or if now, acknowledging the offer, she was leaving their sameness behind forever. "I know you can. But no. I'm doing fine." She felt confused and stupid and limited and sad because she wouldn't walk that way anymore. And one morning after the holidays, when she had to go out in the car very early for some medical tests that required fasting, she saw him walking toward the bench and she guessed his Texas sons had come for Christmas because he was wearing a ten-gallon hat.

LOOK OUT FOR HYDROPHOBIA

It smelled sweet and funny when they came in the door. The air inside was too heavy to get up into the blue sky outside. It filled the empty rooms, unresisted because the furniture hadn't come. "What is that, honey?" said Diane, breathing deeply.

"Exterminators. We don't want someone else's bugs."

"You're so smart!"

So she just made sure the furnace was down and went around opening windows. The smell was not as bad upstairs as down, but she opened them all and came down, a breath of fresh air herself. Freckled and happy, redheaded and gay, she snuck up behind John who was looking out the bay window at the fire hydrant in his lawn.

"Boo!" she said.

He did jump. He always did. But he recovered quickly and laughed. "That's the greatest thing," he said. "Our rates will go down."

"As much as our mortgage went up?" she said hopefully.

"That's asking too much."

She looked at the apparatus in the middle of the small, green patch of lawn and wondered why the former owners had let the pansies die around its base. It wasn't the fault of last week's cold drizzle. Pansies put up with a lot of cold, and under today's blue sky should be smiling like pansy faces always do. But they were more brown than green, and the one or two flowers hung down.

"I'll get some new flowers. And, what do you think? I wonder if I could put a birdbath on top. It's kind of ugly just standing there."

"You know there's got to be a law against that."

"Honey. We can't park in front of our own house. Did you realize that?"

"We have a garage, silly."

"But our friends will all get tickets."

"So. Maybe they won't eat us out of house and home then. Knowing your friends though, they'd collect tickets and free meals, too."

"We're so far away they're not going to come, anyway. That's the one thing about this house."

"Oh, it'll keep us busy. You won't even notice they're not around. And as soon as the furniture comes, we'll get George back from mother, and you'll have all the company you could want. Besides there's work. We'll start by stripping the walls."

"I don't mind this yellow wallpaper in here. I think it might go with our chairs."

"But look where it's rubbed off. They ought to have put in a chair-rail. We'll just do it over. You can start painting tomorrow."

"I could wash the windows right now. That would be nice, wouldn't it." Diane went back toward her new kitchen with the center island and hood range and butcher block work surfaces to see if the people had left any Windex. But no. "You want to go out and get some stuff and we can work this afternoon?"

"Get out of there! Shoo! Aaach! Git! Git!" John was roaring. "Bring me something to throw, Diane," still roaring.

"What is it? What's the matter?" Diane raced to the front door where John was charging out.

"I want something to throw. Where is it?"

"There's nothing in the house, John. What do you want to throw it at?"

"Shoo! You bastard, git!"

The dog calmly lowered its leg when it was done and trotted off down the street.

"Turn my back for a minute and my fire hydrant gets pissed on."

"Oh, for heavens' sakes, just a passing dog."

Diane thought it was slightly silly, but she wouldn't hurt a flea, especially by laughing. The only laughter she permitted herself was for shared fun, little games together. They had a lot of those, still such a playful couple even though their little boy was old enough to begin school; hence, the new neighborhood with its bigger houses, better school, ungraded so their precocious George could speed through the traumas of childhood and get on to those of adolescence, at his own pace, not held back by the cruel average, the shifting elementary exclusions kids devise to deal with difference. Poor George, with his flaming hair. It would have been better to look like John. "There's not an ounce of me in that kid. Are you sure I'm the father?" John used to pretend to joke. At least, George was not as fat as she had been. No one would ever think of calling him a pink elephant; even though he had her memory, her facility with trivia; even though he remembered too much, batting averages, jingles, jibes. No one would ever drop "Elephants never forget" on him. Skim milk, string beans, cottage cheese, lettuce, carrots, apples, yogurt, zero cookies, zero candy, zero soda; an enormous amount of negative nurture, preventive eating would shield him, in a way that extra layer of fat never had for her. Maybe nerve ends are actually more plentiful in fat.

And she retained these fictive dendrites with her infantile fat cells (trim and shrunken now, but ready to reach greedily for any passing extra) which would explain her tendency to be ridiculously hurt by some of John's jokes. Most recently the friends. She was tired of that one. She couldn't wait to get her cooking things and start to cook in the shiny new kitchen. She wondered how the woman who lived here before had gotten any pleasure from it and left it so clean. Maybe it was just a real estate ploy, like John said. "You put $1,500 into a new kitchen, you'll get back $3,000 in your asking price." They would have gotten $5,000 extra from her, if she'd been the only buyer. Thank god for John, as she could never get over the feeling that it was a terrible put-down not to give someone what they thought their possession was worth; especially, if you really agreed, she thought you should tell them. Their real estate agent wisely never let her in the house with the owners.

John was still watching against the return of the dog.

"I'm hungry," she began.

"We ought to go. And have lunch and get the wallpaper steamer," he replied. "The more we do before our furniture comes the better. Did you shut all those windows?"

"Oh," she said. "Do you think it smells better?"

"I'm sure it does, and I hope the bugs were dead before you got here."

"I'll run do it," Diane hurried from room to room approving of the improved smell but not of the soot on the sills. "Look at this," she said, holding her finger up to John's face. "What a pain. It's the kind that smudges, too."

"Well, so much for open windows," he observed. "We'll save on heat, anyhow."

They backed out of their little entranceway and drove off along the avenue, past the nice, big, run-down houses and, on the corner, the nicest, biggest with a porte-cochere and a tasteful sign, "Funeral Home." That was the one Diane really coveted, with all its smoking chimneys. But she knew that, much as she loved space and air, that house was more than she could handle. She would have had to produce an army of children to give life to so many rooms and she would have to be an army of servants to clean up after the messy process. Not the birth process, the living. Giving birth was quickly mopped up, but the rest went on forever with ever increasing gear and decreas-

ing rationale to handle it. She realized she was not at all looking forward to the van's arrival with what John called their
furniture. They did have beds and chairs and tables and a sofa,
but mostly what they had was stuff, stuff that she had had to
drag out of the cracks and crevices of their little sold house—
Q-Tips and cotton balls and one pain pill, in case someone had
one pain, and broken sets of cards whose lost member might
be on the verge of appearing, two rooks and the queen found
rooms away from the chess set and now in some other box,
with linens or liquor, anything but games, and the Legos from
every ashtray in the house, packed with their ashtrays. Then
there was the closet full of fingerpaintings that she had longed
to lose but unhappily remembered too well taking her own
childhood artwork out of the trashcan, and the resignation on
her mother's face when given it a second time, "Don't you
want it, Mother?" Some hurt could be prevented.

She hated everything about the kind of hamburgers they
bought for lunch, but by the time she realized hamburgers
were all they sold, John's order was in process, and the girl at
the counter just looked hurt instead of perky as Diane mentioned some of the things she wished she might have. She tried
to make up for the overripe cardboard taste with too much
mustard and catsup, and succeeded in making a mess, which
she had to wrap back up when John said he had ordered them
to take home. "That'll make it our first picnic of the spring,"
she said and took some extra napkins. John ran next door and
rented the steam machine from the paint and decorator store
while she got into the car.

They were almost at their driveway when he began to honk.
Diane looked for danger in all the wrong directions and then
saw the old lady walking her old dog. It was on a leash and up
on the little wall that held the yards off the sidewalk, and she
had stopped a few steps ahead of it. It was a him and had quite
a good shot at the fire hydrant. Diane averted her usually
friendly face as the lady looked in amazement at the honking

car and its rabid driver turning in. "The bitch," muttered John. "Who does she think she is?"

"I think I get it about the dead pansies," said Diane, to mollify and show sympathy, instead of saying she hoped she didn't have to meet that old lady face to face but was sure she would.

They took in their sleeping bags and pads to sit on and had quite a cheery picnic on the sunlit floor while they talked wallpaper and paint.

They settled in very well. The van had to show up with their furniture no matter how Diane felt about it, and when it did, they pushed things around and arranged them; they looked wonderful if a little sparse, in the big house. Her kitchen utensils she arranged handily and began to think about real meals. The other boxes of stuff she pushed into a room they didn't have any particular furniture for, though they were calling it the family room. She took things out as they were needed and sort of hoped that they would sift into the new environment in a decipherable manner, find their own level. She had gotten everything they owned this far. She hoped it would take care of itself now.

George, whom she had missed, came back from his grandmother's, looking a little fatter, maybe, though he'd only been gone a week. He was all sweetness and light, so glad to be home where nobody said "Hush."

"But don't you get a lot of treats, cookies and things?" asked Diane, pinching his arm tenderly to make sure he was still not plump.

"Yeah, but she wouldn't let me sleep with my hamster. She said when he wasn't in his cage he woke her up playing the piano, and then she said I might smush him. You should hear Morton in a piano."

"I hope I have the chance someday. But, you know, maybe you'd better not let Morton loose in this house. It's so big here, with all kinds of hiding places, he might get away from you."

"He always comes back for breakfast."

"Well, it's yours . . ."

"I trust him."

John, knowing her interests, bought her a pressure cooker for a housewarming present. "It's the only safe way to preserve things," he said. "You can put up fruits and vegetables in the summer. And the saleswoman said it saves enormously on cooking time." Diane was terrified of the thing. She had known someone whose mother had scalded half her face with applesauce when the valve clogged with foam, and suffered agonies and looked weird forever after. How much of her own youth had been taken up accustoming herself to her freckled face! She would look in the mirror one day and see a white face with orange freckles, and the next day she could see only an orange face with white freckles. It had finally settled into one surface now, and she could no longer make it perform the optical illusions she remembered, except for that of camouflage. She could look in the mirror and feel sure she had no nose, or lips or chin, or even eyes, because as she was looking with her eyes she forgot to look at them. But if the pressure cooker should explode and strip her of her protective coloration, then she would have to look at herself again to see who she was and whether she was different! No. She was terrified and put it in the closet.

The things in the boxes did take care of themselves pretty well. George took out whatever he needed, which was a lot: cars, paints, Legos, clay dough, motors, old batteries, new batteries, crayons, marbles, plastic people, worn plush animals, Legos, more cars and trucks. Miniature traffic jams appeared all along the baseboards, between the rugs and the walls. They moved occasionally through the house with full sound effects. Diane unpacked very few clothes; she rotated a couple of sets of underwear and socks and shirts and things and neither George nor his father noticed they were the same. She wondered if she was being economical, or if they would eventually run through the same number of socks in the same amount of time. She pretended it was an experiment, in case they noticed and questioned.

George pushed the other boxes into a maze for himself and Morton. Diane could send him there with a clear conscience whenever her ears or head or back were tired, which could be after fifteen minutes of George. The hamster seemed to put up with anything, and though her son was impressed with its talents, she thought it might be an idiot.

They painted and papered together at night. The walls seemed to thicken perceptibly. Summer came and Diane kept the windows open and made an effort to keep up with the soot deposits. She made George blow his nose every morning because she noticed a little black rim to his normally drippy nostrils. "That's what nose hairs are for," she explained. "That's why you don't breathe in through your mouth."

John worked all day, which suited her fine. He handled security deposits at a bank and had probably reached his level of achievement, give or take a few raises and titles. He was not, at any rate, hustling. There were no evening meetings or business dinners or trips out of town. On the hot evenings, they would sit on the stone stoop of their new house. John had collected a bag of pebbles to throw at stray dogs who wandered too purposefully in the direction of his hydrant. Dog-walkers were very strict with their charges when John and Diane were sitting out. The old pair, woman and dog, that he had honked at, walked now on the park side of the street and Diane felt them stare as they went by, though she never looked at them herself. George said she was a mean old lady, very strict with kids, and that her name was Mrs. Bullitt and she lived in the upstairs apartment of the funeral home. All the time Diane was feeling Mrs. Bullitt go by, she was relieved that John had become more calm and reasonable. She could see him start to tense whenever a dog would round the corner and trot in their direction, anointing saplings and curbs in a preliminary fashion, but he no longer yelled.

George divided his time between Morton and Diane, but

Morton liked to sleep in the day. The only thing Diane could do well while George was talking was cook. There was often, almost always, a beautiful evening meal that she and John ate very peacefully after George was in bed. Then John would explain in detail all the security transactions of the day. Diane understood very well the logic of senators' wives being appointed to their defunct husband's senate seats. She was certain that if a Great Dane or a Doberman Pinscher dragged John off into the night, she would be able to step right into his job with very little difficulty. After dinner, Diane baby-sat sleeping George and washed up, and John took long walks in the dark, deserted neighborhood, to work off the calories, while she worried about whom she could leave George with if she had to take John's job.

To encourage independence, she sent George to the day camp on the far side of the park. At first, she walked there with him and was very impressed with the facilities this park had. They even had a little enclosure with some animals the children could pet and care for. There were a few chickens and rabbits and even two lambs and a goat. George liked it immediately. The third day that she walked him there, the director told her "Georgy certainly is verbal!" which both gratified and angered Diane. She was pleased, of course, that his precociousness was noticed, but could not understand George's putting up with being called Georgy. In all her life, and she was the mother, she had never belittled him that way. "You let her call you Georgy?" she asked him when the director went off to greet someone else. "She's nice," he replied and Diane went on home. From then on, she just helped him cross the street and let him walk to camp by himself, if that was what he enjoyed. After a while, he even learned to cross the street alone on the crosswalk by the funeral home.

She had been right that it was too far away for her friends to visit, so they never knew what an accomplished cook she was becoming. Part of her experimentation, of course, lay in reducing ingredients to just the right proportions for two people.

But she found that not all recipes work well in limited quantity. She would sit out on the low back steps and eat leftovers for lunch. In the middle of the day, the housewives opened up their back doors and let the dogs go out alone for a while to snuffle around the garbage cans and see what sort of tidbits they could turn up. Diane could hear them coming before she could see them, because the metal tops would clatter off the cans to the cement alleys and roll back and forth, a sort of fanfare announcing that she soon would have guests for lunch.

They ate well, John and Diane and the dogs.

Diane was putting on a little weight, but, because of his long walks and the energy expended on his various worries, John remained taut and handsome. George accepted the fact that there was a difference between kid food and adult food. "It's too rich for you," Diane told him when he offered to help her out with the spoon she was licking. Basically he had very little interest in food. Either he would talk all the time he was supposed to be eating and Diane would have to remind him to have a little yogurt, or whatever, or else he would bolt his dinner and rush back to see if Morton had found a way out of his Lego castle, or if he wanted to join the traffic jam, riding a truck in ever decreasing circles around the kitchen floor.

"Time for bed, George," said Diane, but he kept revving up and scrambling around. Knowing his immense powers of concentration, she didn't really expect him to pay any attention to her. The sun had set but it wouldn't get dark. She kept on stirring her sauce so the egg wouldn't curdle. "Go brush your teeth, George," she insisted as he hurtled by on all fours. The next time around they collided and she nearly lost her sauce. "The hell!" she shrieked. "Out of my hair! Out of my hair! Get in that bed!" George studied the atmosphere in the room as he retreated slowly. "It's not dark," he said.

"It will be! Upstairs!" she ordered. "I'll come kiss you."

George tried to make conversation when she came up with her kiss. It was hot and she tried to push the windows open wider. "Bet you don't know what that stuff is comes in the window," he said.

"Soot," she said.

"It's people."

"Don't be silly. What an idea. Who gave you that idea?"

"Sure it is. It's from the funeral home."

"Oh," said Diane, beginning to believe him. "Oh. That can't be true. Who told you that?"

"Kids told me."

"You don't believe everything kids tell you, do you?"

"Not everything."

"Well, don't," she said and gave him a Kleenex to blow his nose and kissed him.

"Been drinking wine for your lunch?" asked John, who was in the kitchen getting a beer when she came down. There was a half-empty bottle of burgundy on the counter.

"It's in the stew," she told him. "Why do you always ask that when you know the answer?"

John looked at her in surprise. She had gotten a little sharp. She usually answered with a friendly laugh. She returned his look and could see her bad temper made him more suspicious. Of a dumb two cups of wine in the stew he was about to eat. And walk off while she washed up. Supper was ready and the table set, so they sat down to it, and she ate ravenously, more than her share. Still there were leftovers.

"Well, why not?" she muttered as she poured herself a glass of wine out on the steps at noon the next day. She and the dogs finished the paté, and as the dogs didn't like tarte aux pommes, she ate that and they had cheesecake for dessert. After another glass of wine, Diane took a long, pleasant nap and awoke wonderfully refreshed, hearing George's call through her open window. "Mom, come see," he shouted. She looked out but the porch roof was in the way. She hurried down the stairs humming a bit of the tune she must have been dreaming and had to laugh at the sight of George trying to pull the camp goat out of the hydrangeas. The goat had a large blue one in his mouth. "It's too big, it'll get stuck in your throat!" warned George. "Spit it out!" He was beating it on the back, but the goat only directed its eyes crazily over its shoulder and kept munching, making the hydrangea small enough to go down. "I have to shorten Lestoil's line so he can't get your flowers," said George helpfully. Diane saw that it was tied with a very complex knot to the fire hydrant.

"What in the name of God are you doing with that thing? Your father will have a fit."

"I said I'd keep him. He didn't have any place to go after camp. I knew you wouldn't mind."

"I like him, but we can't have a goat."

"Why not! It's only for two weeks until his owners come back from vacation."

"Well, if it's not forever. I couldn't take it forever. But what about your father?"

"He'll help Dad. He'll keep the grass short."

"He'll keep the bushes short too."

"Mom," exasperated, "Not if I tie him closer to the hydrant. Help me get this knot."

"I think he ought to be a backyard goat."

"He's a frontyard goat. He likes people."

That would be nice, thought Diane, if the kind of people who liked goats stopped to talk. And she began to picture John's face when he saw what had his fire hydrant this time. They decided to leave the goat there, and, because George's knot was too complex to undo, and they didn't have a knife, they walked the goat around the hydrant three or four times and finished off with a few twists so he couldn't reach the hydrangeas. The goat looked crestfallen when he discovered his limits. "Oh, don't look that way," said Diane, picking him a large blue blossom. "Just one more." She patted him discovering he was very silky.

"Lestoil loves to be hugged," said George. "Look." He put his arms around the goat, who looked immensely pleased. "You do it."

Diane put her arms around him and her face against the silky coat. "He doesn't smell wonderful," she said. She sniffed her arms. "And neither do I now."

"It wears off."

"I don't think I'll wait. Are you going to stay here?" she asked.

"I'm going to see if anybody comes to be his friend," replied George, sitting on the wall. Diane went off to take a good soak and put on perfume afterwards, though usually she didn't wear it. She found George still sitting on the wall when she came back. The goat was next to him and petting the goat was a girl whose age was hard to guess. She was considerably older than George, maybe almost adolescent, but nourishment seemed to be a problem. Her head seemed too old for the rest of her.

"This is Nancy," said George. "She's from the country and knows all about goats."

"How wonderful, Nancy, you're lucky," Diane observed. "Where do you live now?"

Nancy didn't answer, just kept on petting the goat.

"She's a foster kid and lives up behind the funeral home with Mrs. Bullitt. She says she thinks that black stuff is people, too. It gives her the creeps."

"You silly kids. Do you like it here, Nancy?"

Nancy still didn't say anything. She seemed to like it there with the goat, which she kept petting. Diane gave up on conversation and saw John's car approaching. At least, after the big scene, he would enjoy the perfume.

John bucked to a halt and stalled at the end of the driveway, because, in his astonishment, he forgot to put his foot on the clutch.

"What the fuck is this?" he shouted, lowering his head and going straight for the goat. Nancy disappeared.

"A goat, Dad."

"It's a goat, John."

"Well, why the hell are we cursed with a goat? Who tied that mess?"

"We did," said Diane. "It's just for two weeks. George's..."

"Well, it can't stay here."

"Why not? He's really sweet."

"You'd like him if you tried, Dad."

"George's teacher couldn't keep him in her apartment. The owners will be back in two weeks."

"Well, George can't keep him either."

"I like him too, John. He'll be good company."

"Good company! It's disgusting! A grown woman sitting on the front steps thinking about making it with goats. I could puke!"

"Might as well. Be good for you. How about the backyard, George? We could compromise."

"I don't know. Lestoil likes to see people."

"You can take him for walks or something. Let's put him back there. That's as far as he's going, John."

John had given up on untying George's knot and was hacking at it with his penknife.

"You'll wreck the rope. We can undo it. Go drink your beer," urged Diane.

"I don't want to see him when I come back out here," John told George.

"You won't," Diane said. She and George unwound and unsnarled Lestoil and led him to the back steps where they tied him to the rail.

"He won't mind it here, too much," said George. "There's garbage."

They went in the back door and found John looking in the oven. "Where's supper?" he asked.

"I thought we'd go out," said Diane.

"Honey, I'm exhausted. We're not going out tonight. Where's all the food we bought?" John always went shopping with Diane. It wasn't that he didn't want her to spend money. He just wanted to watch her do it.

"We ate it."

"All that pork and chicken?"

"That was paté."

"We ate all that?"

"I have to eat lunch, you know."

"You're going to get fat," said John, looking at her. Then he noticed that, as well as plump, she looked really sad. "Now," he comforted. "Don't. A little padding's nice." He came close to give her an appreciative pinch. "You go around smelling like that all day?" he asked, sniffing the perfume. "The goat like that? Or the mailman?"

It was all she could do to keep her knee out of his groin. "It's the kind you like."

"Tell you what," he said. "I'll run out and buy us a nice steak while you feed George. Then you can just whip us up something nice and we'll relax at home."

So he went out to find something special and Diane poured herself a tumbler of sherry so she could get on with the relaxation.

George went to bed before dark again, and they had a California cabernet with their steak Béarnaise and pommes de terre en lichettes and coupe Melba. John disappeared for his long walk, his constitutional, while Diane put away the leftovers and washed up and crumped. She didn't even notice him come in and barely noticed his making love.

"What a pity," she said out loud and woke herself up in the middle of the night, thinking about Nancy.

Diane's heart just broke for Nancy as she saw the girl more and more during Lestoil's two weeks. She seemed to be just at the lonely edge of adolescence, bony and puffy at the same time. She did not have any crowd for shelter, the way most kids her age did. She liked to talk to George and sometimes Diane could get close enough to hear about mean Mrs. Bullitt, but usually Diane's approach silenced Nancy, who petted the goat, or buried her face by its ear and whispered. As long as Diane was out of the way, Nancy didn't mind going into the house with George to get a drink or to play trucks with Morton, though she clearly preferred the goat. Diane finally thought of something she could do for her, and one day gave Nancy a couple of her own smallish shirts from a box in the family room. She was getting fat for them, anyway. Nancy took them and looked almost pleased. Diane gave her a little something every day and then one day, looking at all the boxes still half-packed, she said, "Just take what you want, you know. I don't need this stuff."

Then Nancy didn't come back and they didn't really know why. Lestoil's time was almost up and they were going to miss him, except John.

It was one of the hottest days of the summer and some of Lestoil's acquaintances came by about the time George and Diane got up from their naps. Most of the goat's friends were older than George, who basked in Lestoil's reflected glory and magnanimously offered them all cookies and lemonade. When Diane came out the back door with a tray, they said, "Let's go around front. We got a hydrant key!" So they moved the festivities and the goat to the front yard.

It took their combined strength to jerk open the rusty hydrant. They took turns running into the powerful stream and pushing as far as they could towards its source. Diane did not think she would be the strongest, but she was. She could go into it the farthest until she was afraid it might tear right through her—but it knocked her down first. She wondered for a half-responsible moment if they were having a dire effect on the general pressure, if everybody else's showers were dying, but swore as she struggled to her feet, not to waste her time worrying about other people's comfort, and joined the band of kids first over the stream, then under, splashing their personal rainbows out into the hot afternoon.

Her red hair lay like tiger lilies along her neck and sprang like the horns of three devils from the top of her head. She could feel it. Sometimes she was an orange person with white spots and sometimes she was a white person with orange spots. The bold stream was washing the soot off all of them, the boys dancing, the girls prancing, glancing off their slick backs into the sun. They were all the free things—amazing anarchy, amazing grace, diving over and under the stream. There were many more than the little clutch of original visitors. George and Diane held hands and ran at the water, one over, one under, and the stream could not tear their hands apart. Mrs. Bullitt and her old dog came along looking mean. George, undaunted, hollered, "Hey, where's Nancy?"

"Don't be wise," said Mrs. Bullitt. "You know."

Diane looked at her, challenging her with all the dignity of sodden curls and transparent clothes, to face her on her own terms, and dare speak that way again to George in her presence.

Mrs. Bullitt pulled her sweater, worn like a cape against unexpected weather, a little tighter as she shrugged.

"And what you don't know won't hurt you, big charity lady. Except sometimes. You'll see." She buttoned her sweater with self-importance while the slow old dog crapped in the gutter.

All the loose dogs came and yapped at Lestoil's heels, as he bucked back and forth with the kids through the water. More kids came and ate all the cookies. Someone turned on a radio loud. And people Diane had never seen came out and sat on their steps. The air smelled of steamy pavement and goat musk, and the droplets of purified water like the evaporation off bleached sheets flapping in the wind.

A cop car came up. "Uh oh. Well, it couldn't last," thought Diane. The cops just looked on benignly for a few minutes.

"Maybe they come for Mrs. B," said one of the kids. Diane and George laughed.

The boy looked at them queerly and said, "You don't know how come? You don't really know where Nancy's at?"

Diane and George shook their heads.

"Hospital," he said. "Got throwed back down the stairs for

stealing. They're sure going to get her for child abuse. At least, anyhow, she sure won't make more money off foster kids."

"My God," said Diane. "Stealing what?" It couldn't be, there was no way it could be her stuff, that stuff she'd given her.

"Your stuff," replied the kid.

"But I gave it to her, every bit of it."

"People knows that, too. She got better enough to talk. That's why Mrs. Bullitt so mad at you."

"Her mad at me? That poor kid!"

"Yup. She's mad and she's mean!"

There were still kids jumping back and forth, breaking the stream and shrieking with pleasure. The cops showed no sign of stopping their fun, but Diane's was stopped anyhow. She turned away from the crowd and stared off down the street. "I'm going to go see Nancy," she said. Here came John's car. She started walking slowly off in that direction and was face to face with it when it stopped in the entrance to their driveway. "My god, you're obscene!" he shouted, looking at her light clothes plastered to every curve and crevice. "Put my jacket on." Diane looked at his mouth, expecting it to foam.

"That's him!" shouted Mrs. Bullitt. "That's the one!"

John was trying to make Diane put on his jacket and she was trying to keep it off and go where she wanted. They weren't paying any attention to the cops until one put his hand on John's shoulder. "O.K., let's go," he said.

"What?" asked John. "What the hell. I didn't do anything. She's the one turned it on."

Diane looked at him furiously. "I sure did. It was great. I wish I had two or three and got arrested for turning them all on."

"Come on, mister." said the cops "We already waited ten minutes for you to get here."

"What the hell did I do?" said John.

"You know," said the cops.

"What did he do?" asked Diane.

"You don't want to know, lady," said one cop.

"Indecent exposure," said the other.

"Pisses on every fireplug in the west end," shouted Mrs. Bullitt. "Every night. Like clockwork."

"John?" said Diane.

"That's not a crime," said John.

"Sure is," said the cop.

"While I was doing dishes?" said Diane.

"I seen him," said Mrs. Bullitt. "Every night. Like clockwork."

"Since when is that a crime?" asked John.

"Since she seen you," said the cop. "Get in the car."

"Are you coming, Diane?" John asked, feeling the grip of justice on both arms.

"Nope," said Diane.

"You'll need to get bail," he told her.

"*You'll* need to get bail," she said. "I need to do something else."

COTILLON

Georgia was always passionate and she had been encouraged. Her mother was already a widow when Georgia was born, and sometimes this was given as the explanation for certain moments in Georgia's life. Her father, dashing Dr. Leary, had no predisposition to death; it just happened while he was mowing the lawn, though he could well afford not to, that he died. He left enough wealth for one lifetime of leisure (that would be Mrs. Leary's) and enough working genes to produce a bright and beautiful baby with brown curls and the kind of blue eyes which usually darken but did not. They turned laughing, willful and assertive.

Mrs. Leary named the baby Georgia so that she could call her GiGi and immediately provided her daughter with the only critical need for rebellion she ever could find. When GiGi felt she had come of age (about ten years later), she announced that from then on she was to be known as Georgia. It took her almost ten more years of concentrated battle and intervening tragedy to win, but by the time we knew Georgia, everyone had forgotten GiGi except her mother and the people who had nothing to do but tell stories.

Not every child would have been the perfect solace for a widow, but Georgia was. It was so easy to make her laugh, and her tears dried the moment she was given what she desired. She was wonderfully precocious and dominated conversation, making what might have been a painful social reentry unnecessary and even impossible for Mrs. Leary.

Georgia was not spoiled because it never occurred to her that she would not have what she wanted. Her mother's wants simply coincided with hers. At school she was known to be a little hot-tempered but generous with her smile. Her prettiness was unavoidable and her intelligence adequate, but her grace was as pleasing as that smile.

She danced. Neither she nor her mother would have wished her to suffer the heavy calves or grueling hours of serious ballet, but as long as she was in school, she danced once a week classically and once a week in the manner of Isadora Duncan.

Sometimes Mrs. Leary's wisdom was questioned as she and Georgia advanced at a rapid pace through youthful pleasures. Maybe the daughter's tastes seemed quickly jaded because the second time around, Mrs. Leary knew what to eliminate and what to include, and Georgia did not have to dally long at any particular age. She went to Cotillon a year ahead of her friends and was often a wonderful success, not only because of her natural aptitude for dancing and smiling, but also because she was almost the only one shorter than any of the boys. She dressed as she pleased in something new every time, and whatever her mother put on her lips was both subtle and lush.

Although the position was customarily reserved for the mother of some young, impoverished person of a good family who needed financial aid to go to Cotillon, Mrs. Leary, comfortable as she was, became the paid social arbiter. The woman who taught dancing did it to earn her living and had very little judgment about who should and should not be invited to join the classes. Mrs. Leary did this with consummate ease, because she could see there really were no choices. She may have turned her little salary back to help whatever poor child might otherwise be unable to come because she was not greedy, only eager to be at Cotillon with Georgia.

She had by no means grown old, though many of her contemporaries had. As they escorted their children to the porte-cochère where Mrs. Leary oversaw the decorum of each entrance, she was startled by their gray skin and streaked hair, their sagging silhouettes.

When faced with the inevitable compliment, comparing her with Georgia, she quietly replied that it was gross exaggeration she was hearing. She herself never dealt in exaggeration, nor, indeed, could she need to because Georgia was superlative.

Georgia, looking in the mirror, said "Mother, I don't look like you. What are they talking about?"

"They have already forgotten your father, dear. It's such a pity. There was no need for his death. What a pleasure he would have taken in his little GiGi and her growing up, his little image turning into a woman. But you just keep watching that mirror, dear; that is my brow already and that is my nose. And you have my breasts, too. No woman in his family ever had breasts. People aren't wrong about us. For twelve, GiGi dear, you're well developed."

"Georgia."

Georgia found she was not as happy as she expected to be though Mrs. Leary was in her prime. Dancing so well was a disadvantage no one had thought of. Georgia had even developed a tendency to lead, which, the dancing instructor explained, could only make it impossible for her to be a harmonious partner. "Use her for demonstrations," suggested Mrs. Leary. "She could be a great help to you, and it is such a pity to waste her wonderful abilities."

One of the greatest difficulties in running the Cotillon was persuading any of the young people to move at all. Some evenings, resistance to pacing out squares or ells was almost insurmountable. Because there was very little activity that required chaperonage, the chaperones directed their best efforts towards propelling the boys in the direction of the girls, or, more effectively, the girls in the direction of the boys. "Watch out, here come the cowpokes," said the boys as they maneuvered themselves to the service side of the punch table, where they got in the maid's way.

"Help me get these girls to dance," said the instructor to Georgia. "We will dance with ourselves at first."

The girls, who had all clustered watchfully in front of the chairs but across the room from the punch table, tended to turn their backs and look expectantly at the nearby wall when the instructor gestured her invitation. "We shall simply have to take them by the hand. I will dance with you. Listen girls!" she said very loudly. They each politely turned one ear but no eyes in her direction. "Georgia and I shall lead the dance. In a moment, we shall separate and choose a partner, and then we shall dance again and separate and choose new partners. Do you understand? Then when we are all dancing, we shall each go and choose a boy to dance with. And there won't be any punch served until after everyone has danced." The boys, who were not being addressed, clearly understood, because they moaned. The girls gave no sign of comprehension but managed to inch a little closer to each other without moving.

"Here we go!" called the instructor, signaling that the orchestra should make music. She clasped Georgia firmly in her arms and began to waltz. Mrs. Leary beamed from her position in the little crowd of girls, whom she was encouraging. "You see, you see, what wonderful fun it is!" she said. The girls smiled politely at their impassive feet.

Georgia radiated pleasure and energy and her partner did not remember to let her go immediately. As they waltzed past Mrs. Leary the second time, Georgia smiled sweetly at her mother, who remembered how strongly the instructor smelled of perfume and smoke and even sometimes bourbon, and admired the discreet way in which her daughter held herself. "You see what fun, girls," she said.

"Now!" said the instructor, who whirled gaily off towards the shrinking crowd. Georgia did the same. She grabbed the closest hand and pulled. "Come on, now!" she commanded. The girl did not budge, and Georgia whirled a few waltz steps down the line to pull on another hand. "Dance! Let's dance!" she called. The hand vigorously withdrew. "At least you can move!" laughed Georgia. She pirouetted down the line beginning to taunt them with her steps. "Look, you can do it!" She dipped and twirled and they didn't. She spotted her mother again, "Come on, mother, we'll show them," she said.

"Me!" said Mrs. Leary, mortified. "Not me! However can you think I would dance?" Georgia was pulling on her, just the way she had pulled on her ex-friends. "Let go, GiGi!"

"Georgia," she insisted, not letting go at all. "I can't bear to dance with that stinking lady. Let's show these little asses how to do it!"

Someone said she heard that and the astonished answer "GiGi!" and the emphatic sound of Mrs. Leary's palm on Georgia's cheek. When they looked up from their feet because the danger had clearly passed, they could not tell whether Georgia was going out the door willingly or being dragged by Mrs. Leary. It seemed she was perfectly happy to be going out the door but not with Mrs. Leary.

The upshot of the scene was that Georgia was permitted to attend the weekly tea dances in the summer. It was understandable that she preferred young men who could dance to boys who wouldn't or to smelly ladies or simple cows for dancing partners. Mrs. Leary insisted, however, that it would be assumed that they were truly mortified if they did not continue the Cotillon, and Georgia, who foresaw tea dances for comfort, resigned herself to what seemed a lifetime of monthly Cotillons with the bitterness she accorded the Curse, which had also just made its appearance.

With the Curse came the possibility of intervening tragedy. There was, in the course of events, a great deal of whispering about Georgia; although no one would say loudly whatever was whispered. All anyone could audibly say was that she became prettier and prettier and was expected to make a brilliant marriage rather too young, but she had better be careful. One day, however, in the gym lockers, after she had been on an unusually long Christmas vacation, it was remarked that Georgia's nipples were brown.

"I didn't know they weren't always brown," said one kind soul. "She has brown hair."

"You have yellow hair and you don't have yellow nipples," said another.

"Why does it make any difference?"

"It makes her like a colored person?"

"Imbeciles! She's been pregnant."

"Pregnant? You have to get fat."

"Not for a couple of months you don't. Or even longer for people with hips like hers."

Everybody looked surreptitiously at her neighbor's pink nipples, as if they were authorities, and Georgia wasn't there at the moment.

Whether because of her inherited but well developing social acuity or because of some youthful attempt to deal with either the universe or morality, Georgia neutralized the effect of her brown nipples by becoming the kind of Episcopalian who went to Early Communion with nine or ten dowdy souls and Evensong with even fewer. Her sincerity was infuriating, and it relocated the current of criticism.

The following year, she attended a boarding school which happened to have an opening for a social director of Mrs. Leary's precise level of gentility. Out of sight, out of mind; no one knew how Georgia managed, but not faced with her presumptuous beauty, no one was compelled to care either.

It was in the year she made her debut that she flew through the windshield. No one could blame the boy who was dead, and there was almost more sympathy for Mrs. Leary than for Georgia. The poor woman spent many days weeping beside her daughter's bed, waiting for her to wake up under the bandages. Finally, desperately seeing the coma as an expression of willfulness, she began to call her daughter Georgia, imploring her first to stay alive, then to wake up, then to be happy she was alive. When they took off the bandages, it was perfectly clear that there was no little GiGi anymore. One side of her mouth was pulled straight, and across what had been Mrs. Leary's brow, there ran a deep furrow.

We were the next generation and our thoughtful mothers, remembering long sad evenings of looking at their feet, organized a little pre-Cotillon group, five girls and five boys. After school, in our ordinary clothes, we walked over to Georgia's house where we were given Cokes and the information that we were not there to play football. Most of the other girls did not seem to mind, and horsing around in the kitchen squirting Cokes kept the boys busy while Georgia passionately turned the shelves inside out looking for a record with an unescapable beat. It took too long, but she was determined to find the right one. We five girls were all deeply in love with her and made ourselves very helpful. The shiny cord of tissue that bound her face into a jagged frown and all the explosive exclamation marks that spread out across her cheeks assured us that inside she was a beautiful person. We finally unearthed the record and returned to the kitchen where we found our irrelevant friends sponging Coca-Cola off the cabinets under the supervision of a white-haired lady in a black dressing gown.

"Mother, don't be bothered now," said Georgia. "Let them have a little fun."

"Who are these young hoodlums, anyhow?"

"You know them all." Georgia proceeded with introductions, omitting our own first names and giving only the maiden names of our mothers. Two of the girls were so intimidated by this procedure that they half-curtsied which made the boys snigger.

"Well, I can see that I do," said Mrs. Leary. "Every one of them should know better."

"You'll be happier in the front room, mother. We'll be playing the Victrola back here."

"I just came back for a little nip of tea."

"One of the children will bring it to you."

"I suppose I should get back to my Patience. I'm winning."

She disappeared to our audibly rude relief.

"Now we'll take partners," said Georgia, ignoring our manners and setting the record over the spindle.

Two of us grabbed her by the hand as she turned to face us. We were too old to say "Me, Me!" in fact, too old to grab her by the hand, but once it had happened we held tight and glowered at each other conveying the message that the other alone was at fault. I felt Georgia's hand, which had gently replied to my grasp, loosen and my frown began to fix on my face as my mother had said someday it would. "It will get stuck," she said. "Think bright thoughts." Nothing bright would come unless a pain is bright or fresh, new tears rising are bright. Why had I ever taken her left hand and not her right? Then I would learn to dance in those beautiful arms and be held close to that most lovely, most unmotherly body, close to its inner beauty.

"We are here for you boys and girls to learn to dance with each other," she said, and I had the satisfaction of seeing my friend's hand drop to her side as well. "If any of you are special friends, you might as well dance with each other." The girls began to move towards each other and I could see I still had a chance of being the odd one who could dance with Georgia. "Well, that is fine for you, girls, but what about the boys? Boys never dance together."

"No sir!" said the boys. "I'll say!"

Georgia could see that very little was going to happen that she did not cause, and she had learned at least one thing years ago in that ugly bed. She was patient, and she frowned at us reassuringly. "We'll just do it by height. So much simpler." So it was settled who was to be whose partner for the rest of the year; unless we grew unevenly, and no one minded because it was simpler. One of the couples got so used to dancing with each other that, eventually they got married. Meanwhile, Georgia said we were her bright stars, the hope of her evenings, the leaders for her Cotillon, and we must learn to dance and enjoy ourselves so irresistibly that everyone else would want to follow. She dashed through the steps and we trod along behind, not lightly.

We didn't mind it. We had Cokes when we first arrived and ice cream before we left. We even acquired some maneuverability. Georgia's inner beauty, which was lost on the boys, never faded for us. And sometimes she did dance with me to show a step correctly. Those were moments when, despite my large feet, it occurred to me that it might, indeed, be possible to have everything one wanted. And the sadness of being let loose at the end of a dance was never quite contradictory.

We became somewhat proficient at the box-step waltz and even the hesitation, the fox-trot, the shag, the samba, even a little jitterbug by the time we were ready for Cotillon. She would not teach us the hucklebuck, though we were sure it existed and that she knew it. We were her hopes, her shining stars, her irresistible pleasures; everyone would want to do what we did so well, but we were not yet beautiful.

So we arrived at our first Cotillon and politely shook Mrs. Leary's hand at the door. We had not come with our partners because we were too young for dates, but we came just like everyone else, a little group of girls, a little group of boys. The boys went to the punch table where they got in the maid's way and the girls went to the chairs but didn't sit down.

Georgia was wearing red, strapless with a waltz-length skirt, and she was standing with a very handsome, slim man. Someone knew that he had wanted to run a dancing school, too, but no mothers would let their sons attend. Instead, he dressed department store windows and was Georgia's partner for demonstrations.

Georgia announced the procedure. He and she would dance a dance based on what we were to learn that night, a waltz, which was only a beautiful box step, then ten very talented young dancers who were standing right there with them, who in fact were their friends, were going to join her on the floor and were going to waltz also, to show them how easy it was and what wonderful fun; because, although it might look hard at first, it was really easy and they were all going to love it. And the punch would be served after they had learned the box step. She called out our names and told us to stand in the middle until she gave us our signal.

Totally discouraged, I watched Georgia spin elegantly onto the floor in the arms of the window dresser and wave us to follow. With even, dull tears collecting behind my throat, I saw the others begin to go out and obediently moved myself. Everything was holding back the tears for me, the loud pressure of the music, the bright lights already dancing without the little skim of misery across my eyes. Then my partner came close and attentive as he was supposed to; we were not supposed to hold hands and certainly wouldn't, but he whispered very near my ear and very loudly, so that I could feel the wind from his breath, that she didn't have to bother to say that about the punch. There wasn't even any in the bowl yet. And when I began to laugh at that all the tears unstopped and ran out all the time I was laughing until, although I almost couldn't, I was so relieved to dance, to be dancing when it was our turn.

THE MOTHER AND THE WHO

Gail looked at her neighbors on the bleachers. Women her age were jouncing grandbabies while they waited for the concert—sometimes simultaneously babies and grandbabies (baby uncles and baby nieces, maybe, which she wouldn't know because she didn't know who they were). She was waiting uneasily thinking about assimilation: about herself and about people who could painlessly turn things directly into themselves; their metabolisms were like that. She thought they were untormented and too fat, with adaptive padding for the survival of the fattest on these bleachers. Eating more might eventually comfort her, but she was way behind in terms of comfort now. Only a friend's knees to lean back between over the gap, only someone close—sharing a cold beer, gently pulling the ends of her blond Afro—could help now. No such friend had been there since her yellow hair was long and smooth.

She was looked at, too, more or less, considered probably transient, another teacher (another mother?) passing through. Her permanent gave her away and even a breeze might carry her off, she was so light.

But she was wedged in neatly, had made a little space for herself where the concert had packed them in, doubleknit human fabric. Hers, she thought, must be the only natural fiber in the crowd. Even her kids had been told they had to wear something "dressy" to play—Megan the violin, Greene the viola. Would it ever begin?

She unfolded her magazine for something to do. It was *The New Yorker*. She knew she had reached a new stage when she stopped resisting its controlled and classy pleasures, the same year she heard the Beatles and Dylan called "classics." The mailman had delivered two copies before her bed and rolltop desk had followed her to the country. With six weeks notice, her subscription made a smooth transition to Indiana, but she and the children owned so little that only a move by someone else in their direction would motivate the movers. The magazine never lasted a week anymore, though she read everything. Baseball? The Race Track? The copy to pictures of ladies' togs? Ads for getaways, hideaways, spots off the beaten track were all she had left to read now. Suggestions that she read no further if she could not keep a travel secret were as funny as the bitter cartoons. She had gotten away and there was no one she could tell a secret.

She was probably not passing through. Megan and Greene were establishing themselves with a vengeance, not to budge easily again, putting out feelers into teams, groups, clubs. Once Megan's age (surprised now that she was no longer), Gail had planted the rooting branches of spring flowers. When they died, her mother said that kind of roots, waterroots, were too fragile for soil.

So be it. She saw the analogy. She was cut off (but not cut down as the grave stones say) in full flower by some sharp collusion of time and space, the way her spring branches had been scissored for a moment of celebration (an ovation? a vase of birth, marriage, death?). She was blooming without roots, her supports her children, fast-growing bindweeds.

Finally they appeared, Megan and Greene, in a line of others, all bearing instruments and looking up for familiar faces. They didn't see her. Her neighbors waved hoohoos and babies were held in the air to see bubby or sis. She supposed she might have waved her magazine but felt too out of place.

Megan's long feet showed under her dress. Six months ago at another concert (in another civilization?), she had been proud of the deep and dangerous ruffles snagging her toes. Now Gail was sure Megan's knees were bent to hide the sneakers. Not until she had tucked them on the chair-rungs (first violin!) billowing her skirt over them, did she grin. Concert mistress. It bode no good that Megan sat there. And Greene first viola! They had always played buried in the crowd where they went to school before. Many neuralgic evenings correcting papers, her mind wandering with their approximate melodies, Gail had thought to make her fortune patenting a silent violin.

The teacher walked among them helping with difficult pegs and deaf ears, tuning up. Hope prevailed. Gail's emotions set off like harmonics, one string quivering because of another— the opening bars of last May's concert (her dreaming of the land, renewing rural roots), the same thing ugly (her, in the sticks booklearning hicks), combining in the dominant desire to be the giver of good life to her children. Some awkward attempt at tuning—the memories, the anticipations—recalled that whole closing ceremony, which she, last spring, had taken for opening, caught in a moment of delicate disharmony. The poignant modulation of notes, a pastoral slipped out of key, had spread vaguely then among the listeners and out the doors propped open to catch the breeze scuffing up dust on the baseball diamond but passing not coming in. Lightning; thunder; no rain. She would go out with the uncertain melody looking for the storm.

Coming here was no mistake but the answer to her country dream. She had not foreseen the fresh air's becoming empty and raw by November, but the kids' color bloomed and they might get some rabbits (if Greene could be convinced that it was O.K. to eat their predictable excess progeny).

Their bus driver, Mr. McKenzie, had offered them a buck and a doe. "Don't take but two," he told them. "Rabbits, sometimes it don't seem like they need but one, but you and me know better, right?" he said to Gail when she took the children out to look at them.

Mr. McKenzie sat now in the middle of the front row. He must have come early for the occasion. His grandson, Davy, was probably in the orchestra, and definitely in Gail's last-ditch class. It was getting to be now or never for him to learn to read. Davy seemed to know "education" was necessary to be a farmer these days, but Gail knew he still hoped that reading was, like osmosis, a passive enterprise. He was better at other things. Smiling, for instance. Gail recognized his smile in his grandfather's. Mr. McKenzie sat beaming toward the kids from his bus route, all set to enjoy whatever came out of the instruments they banged aboard on clumsy, dark mornings and rowdy afternoons.

Mr. McKenzie's rabbits had Gail, Megan and Greene at a standoff. Greene said he didn't care if other people killed rabbits, he didn't expect he would eat his friends. Gail thought it would be a good lesson in reality. Megan was looking forward to a bunny fur rug. Mr. McKenzie laughed at their indecision, but was keeping a pair for them, expecting Gail to lay down the law, or, at least, the majority to rule.

Most of the orchestra came in on the first note. Those who didn't caught up slowly, playing a gavotte she recognized even through extra rhythms. "The music teacher has taste," thought Gail and looked at her program. The next piece was a medley of commercials; Gail retracted her thought. Toward the end, there would be some other classics, finishing with "Eleanor Rigby."

The children lit into the Oscar Meyer wiener theme; the gaiety of their attack sunk Gail in gloom. She had only dragged them to the end of the world to find simple country living dominated by values she thought she had escaped. The audience ate it up. They laughed and laughed and the orchestra played well. They smiled at each other recognizing "The Pepsi Generation." "Barry Manilow," thought Gail. "I should have known it." She was sick that her children's musical understanding might peak with the Pepsi Generation. She vowed yet again to make it up to them.

Something fell on her and started to cry. He was dragged back by an arm before Gail knew what happened. "What I tell you not to jump," said the woman behind her, shaking the child to get the rest of the cries out. "Now you set there and listen at it." Gail felt the hopelessness of her teacher dream too. What chance did grammar stand? Discouraged, her thoughts lapsed into the melodic line, but she was more unsettled by her difficulty locating it. The conductor waved her arms trying to pull Water Music out of the children, she drew them towards her to gather loudness, she pointed her finger to call for emphasis, but it sounded as if played from many little boats at once, downwind, on rough water, heard over the marshes alive with squeaks and rustles. A tour de force—the conductor bowed proudly and all the children bowed.

They played "Amen," and the chorus sang it. It was the song she had marched to as "Freedom," the one that once lifted the roof of the A.M.E. church they set out from together, one black woman leading in her voice like thunder, and Gail had ceased to worry about starting to march without emptying her bladder; though if she were kicked or only fell in the crowd she knew, she might die of her own poisons. There was strength in the chords that she did not know from any other part of her life. "Freedom. Freedom," inexorable tonic progression accommodating every voice. Why were they still calling it "Amen" here? So be it. This is the way it is.

And now Gail wished for a private pleasure (here in her finally chosen, peaceful Freedom Land such as it was), a confession and absolution of guilty nostalgia. It was given with unexpected sweetness. The children could not hear the connections in Handel. But in "Eleanor Rigby" (undersung by the hazardous unnamed notes of their strings), they were heard and tenderly rendered. It was made for their approximations. Gail and the happy teary-eyed others (whom she could not have thought of as Beatles fans) stood to applaud.

"What did you like best, Mom?" asked Greene in the car.

"Eleanor Rigby," answered Gail.

"Those old songs are the greatest," added Megan.

"None of those guys knew Paul McCartney was a Beatle, Mom. They think he's just Wings," said Greene.

"They're too young. Things change so fast."

"Can I use your typewriter, Mom?"

"Tonight? It's late, Megan."

"I have to, Mom. There's not much time left."

"Why didn't you do your homework before we went, dumbunny?" said Greene.

"It's not homework."

"It's definitely too late then."

"Mom! You don't want me to be like Dorfie Merchild, do you?"

Gail always took their requests seriously. She tried to remember Dorfie Merchild.

"What about him?" said Greene.

"Nine days later he died for no reason whatsoever."

"Of course I don't want you to be like Dorfie Merchild."

"Then I can use it?"

"For an hour. But that's it."

"Can I use some carbon paper, too?" Megan was first out of the car and across last summer's old sopping grass and November's mud. Gail and Greene went more slowly.

"It will be crunchy tomorrow when the bus comes," said Greene.

Agreeing, they went in the door Megan left wide and found her sitting at Gail's desk, still in her parka, interleafing paper and carbon. Greene, who hoped to start growing, ate two bowls of granola and went to bed. Gail looked at the Cincinnati paper for a movie or something. She felt like going to town even if it meant two hours on the road for two hours of flick. She wished she could afford the day-late *Times*. The crowded city fantasy would improve with little facts from familiar sounding corners to support the bizarre, the quirky thing, unbelievable except that it was New York.

Megan tapped and cursed and balled up papers for an hour and went upstairs with a pile of unfinished work. Gail found her still printing hard and deliberately when she went up to bed herself.

"Go to bed, Megan. What is it?"

"I'm done. You'll see tomorrow."

"This prayer has been sent to you for good luck," Gail read over her shoulder. "What's that trash?"

"Don't read it now. You'll get one tomorrow."

"I don't know if I want one."

Megan set the table and delivered her letters, two of the twenty. Greene read his. "I don't have twenty friends," he said.

"I do," said Megan.

"I certainly don't," said Gail. "You don't really believe this stuff, do you? Chain letters are against the law anyhow."

"This is even if you're not superstitious, which I'm not."

Greene asked, "Why are they against the law?"

"The mails, I guess. Think of the pile-up if all of a sudden everybody is sending twenty meaningless letters to people who send twenty more. The whole system breaks down."

"Then I won't send any of them but ten in the mail."

"Don't even do that," said Greene. "You know when my calculator starts running dots by because I multiplied too high? That's what would happen in the post office. And it would be your fault."

"It would not!" insisted Megan. "Somebody else sent it to me. I just don't want to be like Dorfie Merchild!"

"It doesn't matter," said Gail. "These things always fall apart. Somebody forgets. Or somebody like me gets them and they wouldn't send a copy for the world."

"Or like me," said Greene, looking at his sister and tearing his letter down the middle.

Megan began to cry.

"You'd better not start that stuff," said Greene. "It's about two minutes until the bus gets here."

"You stayed up too late, Megan. That was stupid."

"It's you that's stupid," said Megan, putting on her coat, wiping her nose, not forgetting her books, her instrument or her letters.

The bus lights shone down the dark road and they went out. Gail never drove them, though the regional high school where she taught was near their junior high. She always needed these extra minutes to recover from the muddle of dreams. She sat down with coffee and looked at her copy, but focused between the lines. Where did it come from? She let the words sharpen:

This prayer is sent to your for good luck. It has been around the world nine times. You are now to receive luck. This is no joke. Sam Elliott received $50,000 but lost it because he broke the chain. Wile in the Philippines General Welch lost his life six days after he received this letter. He failed to circumstance the prayer, however he received $775,000 before his death. Do not send money. Do not keep this letter. It must leave you within 96 hours and with 20 copies. This was written by St. Anthony do Carliff and comes from Venezuela, a missionary from South America, and must move around the world. This is true even if you are not superstitious. Take note of the following: Comset Dian received the chain in 1953. He asked his secretary to make 20 copies and send them. A few days later, he won $2 million. Pasquale F. gave it a try and won the jackpot. Dorfie Merchild not believing the chain threw it away, nine days later he died for no reason whatsoever.

Had she ever copied one? Yes, in about 1953 also, as a precaution, and the mails had not collapsed. She speculated on the injustice of Comset Dian's winning $2 million when his secretary sent the letters. The combination of receiving and desir-

ing to send was effective. Strange that the only good luck was
money and never in foreign currency. Surplus cash was universal good fortune, but had the almighty dollar required
translation, and at what rate of exchange? Could the letter she
copied have circled changing word by word, like gossip, into
this one that killed Dorfie Merchild, even if he was not superstitious? She was between lines again, thinking for no reason
whatsoever of Pascal and blunt instruments, about truth's being such a subtle point and our instruments too blunt to touch it
accurately. Still, he had been certain truth, if not God, was
there. And Gail tended now to think that too was superstition.

Megan was generous. She would share her good fortune.
Besides, when it arrived in a white envelope on the sidewalk
by her feet it was not cash.

"Hey! Tickets for The Who!" she yelled.

"Like wow," said Greene. "How many?"

"The Who?" asked Gail absentmindedly.

"This is just the greatest group going, Mom."

"I know who The Who are. They've been around since my
time."

"They crash up their guitars and stuff," said Megan.

"Really great music even on a record. The Who in concert!" Greene was impressed. "How many, Megan?"

"Three," Megan told him, fanning them out and looking as
if she might consider inviting somebody other than her brother
and mother to go with her, to take her. "You can come, too,"
she said to her Mom and Greene.

They turned it into a festival, this conjunction of her past
and their future adolescence. She was not yet standing beneath
them, looking up at the eruptions and aggressions on pimply
faces, but Megan's passing Greene meant they were both
about to shoot out of sight, these two little kids to whom she
had devoted her life since her own last adolescent twitches. To
go to a concert together to celebrate this passage, would it be
like touching together their Beatles, their Dylan, their Wood-

stock even—everybody on the grass together, generations making new generations (on grass together, or suckling grassy milk, the impious beginning of the country dream, perhaps, downed fences and the lions with the lambs dreaming it could be like that forever).

Megan started telling everybody she knew. Greene made her shut up because somebody wanted those tickets bad. The Who had been sold out almost before it was on the computer in September. They heard of a few other kids who had tickets. Davy McKenzie had slept all night at Sears for his.

They decided if they had to drive all the way from Brookville anyhow, they should make a big deal, splurge, eat in town. "But we still have to get there early, to get seats," insisted Greene, who seemed to know a lot about things.

"We've got tickets," said Megan.

"Yeah, but we haven't got seats."

Gail drove around the small downtown looking for where to eat. By the Music Hall, they found something called a deli where the meal was hectic and delicious. "You always eat garlic if you want to deal with a crowd," said Gail. Their orders were not written down but loudly relayed to the kitchen. They didn't really expect to get what they had asked for, because there were too many people all getting the same treatment. To their surprise, the right thing came in overwhelming plenty. When it was time to pay, Gail asked for a check. "You tell Izzy," the waitress told her. They told Izzy and for everything they said he rang something on the cash register. His statement at the final bell seemed reasonable to Gail who paid whatever it was.

They drove down towards the river. There was already a crowd at the Coliseum. "See Mom," said Greene. "I told you. People camp out before things like this. Davy McKenzie skipped school."

"We're small. We can slip through," said Gail.

They parked in the garage, somewhere that seemed both deep and high. "Remember the level," said Gail. There were so many people that voices dominated strangely the roar of the garage. They moved with the crowd past the stadium. Gail could see that she was old and her children very young.

The crowd began to concentrate its direction. There was only one way to go. The children, with her hair and her lips, the excuse for her presence, unfaithful copies, were slipping through more efficiently than she, leaving her to fend for herself. She knew to eddy and sway with a crowd but was unable to feel the rhythm of this one, felt only its swelling and a certain logical vulnerability for being out of step. She said to herself, "They're just kids. Each one of them you could talk to if you wanted." Megan and Greene had wormed their way into a narrower ramp approach and were always at least one person ahead of her. She kept trying to pass through to them. A generalized tumescence pressed her. The crowd was thickening and stiffening. Then Megan and Greene were at an impasse looking back and she reached them.

"This is it until they open the doors," said Greene. "They're late."

A hard blast of music, familiar, "My Generation," filled the air. "Starting without us," someone said pressing hard against her. The crowd's push behind became as intense as the amplified Who coming towards her, and she tried to control her fear by turning her attention to her children. They looked strange to her. Who were they? More here who weren't her. She tried to shove them ahead to get away. The crowd squeezed forward through the ramp, moving where there was no place to go. She had to get her children out. She had to keep them close. A reservoir of panic began to burn loose inside her and she felt the crowd's waves now, caught in its murderous frictions.

"Mommy, I'm drowning. My feet don't touch," cried Megan.

"There's no air," said Greene, grabbing Gail's neck and starting to climb.

Gail grimly pulled her head away. "Use your arms. Don't slip under."

"I'm stepping on someone," screamed Greene.

Sphincters gave out. Shoes were lost. When they had burst through into the Coliseum, they wanted to go home, but still were pressed into the music. No one was being let out. They were caught in the hard wild sound, engaged in the surplus that could only end in destruction of finely tuned instruments as if they were blunt.

Jackie Armstrong was always picked up first. He said "hi" to Mr. McKenzie who had been his protector since he was just a squirt in kindergarten. Mr. McKenzie shaped his life. School time, chore time, school time, chore time. He sat in the back of the bus now because he had expanded up and out so he could handle any big mother by himself, but he would never pick on a squirt.

Mr. McKenzie hardly said "hi" back. He didn't turn his head. His face was gray even in the yellow light before the door swung shut. "A heart attack," thought Jackie, who had seen his own grandfather die. His mother invariably proposed that explanation the two times each year the bus wouldn't start or had a flat, as dawn approached and Jackie watched the road from the kitchen window. "He's too old to drive. One of these days he's going to start around a curve and just never quit turning."

"And there we'll be splat in the middle of the road. Right Mom?"

"Or the river. Or whatever. He's a dangerous driver."

"Mr. McKenzie can drive these roads with his eyes shut. Even dead probably."

Jackie looked hard at him before walking back to his seat. His eyes were shut for sure.

"Feeling O.K., Mr. McKenzie?" he asked, as the bus started off.

"Pretty good. How about yourself?"

Jackie didn't look to see if his eyes opened. The bus turned down the long curving mile toward Megan and Greene's house in the valley. It was dark. Sleeping in, Jackie guessed. "Ain't nobody been up late like that at The Who going to be up for school do you guess, Mr. McKenzie," he said.

"Once you get started you got to keep on living," said Mr. McKenzie. He honked his horn.

"How they going to get on the bus straight out of bed?"

"Wake 'em up when you can." He honked until a light shone and then let the old bus roll off. "My Davy's dead. Been to the morgue all night to see him."

"Davy?" said Jackie not breathing.

"My grandbaby," said Mr. McKenzie. "His little mother she's sure shook up. I been there for her. That's how I know them little kids ain't dead with them others."

"Davy," said Jackie looking at the vinyl seat beside him and thinking about the wads of bubblegum Davy had stuck up under it for the years they'd had the back seat. Davy could have chewed any of it was soft enough and known it was his.

"What kind of mother want to take little kids to a place like that? Them things driving us nuts got all the time in the world."

Jackie didn't even say "Davy."

"What they got to live with now I hadn't even thought. All this night and I wasn't even thinking who it was walked on Davy."

POSSUM TRIPTYCH

Faith.
Many Possums later

A man, a woman, three babies and a dog went up into the pasture. The babies (as such) were has-beens, and they gradually walked farther and farther ahead; so that the dog was running back and forth to share his obstreperous presence. His tongue dripped happily, his tail was high and he liked stopping to worry the flesh of the hillside, tearing off turf to show its bones.

The babies missed each other now that they were scattered to the winds. They kept the faith and pretended they were children again. They were still young enough to do somersaults trying to remember what it had been like. Every now and then they could bring back an old laugh.

No, they weren't babies at all. Her children were two women and a man. It was just something she thought to trick herself into an old happiness—the same way they went after that laugh.

This walk they were taking—had they decided to go anywhere? The dog had. He had found a spot and was digging under a brushpile on the crest of the hill. The woman hoped this was not the end of the walk, because she had intended they go into the woods where there might be mushrooms.

The thawed ground had lost its deep wetness. The past week, the sun had seemed almost too hot, the foliage too new and delicate for shade. Where the woods were sneaking into the pasture she saw first one child then another then another fly into the air using the spring of saplings, not going as high as they did when they were small, and the trick hadn't frightened her since the youngest was seven or eight, but they still looked back to see if it had worked, and smiled and waved.

The briars in the fencerow had flowers, she smelt them on the breeze and could smell the cold earth at the edge of the shade turning the last whiff of snow over to the sun. The ache today was something healing. What a strange world, she thought. They're in your body and then they're gone.

The dog barked madly, dug and pounced. "Git it! Git it!" called her husband, closer to the action because they walked like Indians; he cleared the path and she would come behind. Really, he said, she was just too slow.

"Git it! Git it!" he was yelling and she could see that it was just a way of participating. No need to tell the dog to get something he so completely had, shaking whatever it was until it was a blur and pieces of it seemed to fly off into the air. The idea of such complete collapse, such edgelessness upset her; even if in principle, she would have thought dogs are dogs and life is just taking these chances. Whatever it was should know better than to camp out inside the dog's territory. But, though only seconds were passing, the thing seemed to go on endlessly disintegrating. And the violence of the pieces flying made her shriek as if torn herself. "Stop! Stop it! Stop him!" She yelled. The dog certainly did not obey and her husband didn't interfere, but something began to go wrong with the dog's pleasure, and he finally gave the limp body a few last shakes and set it down. He never did care much for dead things. He sniffed the ground disinterestedly here and there, as if he might find something more but didn't, and trotted over for her approval. "O.K. O.K. A dog's a dog," she said and patted him. Tail high, he bounded off to catch the children so they would pat him too.

"God, look at this," said her husband as she reached the scene of the crime. She saw a very dead, but whole, possum. And scattered in the fescue there were finger-sized naked pink things—tiny dead possums! "Oh that's so awful," she said. "Why can't he stick to groundhogs? Look at those amazing things." At least it wasn't bloody, just sad. "Don't start," her husband told her. Just what she was thinking, crying could be a full-time job if you got started, and she bent over the naked babies who had a sort of blunt look to them, like miraculous tiny pigs, and their eyes were sealed behind translucent bulging lids like birds still in the egg. What she really wanted was to show them to her own children—something of a leftover urge to pass on wisdom: now children, this is what a possum is like before it hatches. —Comes out of the pocket, Mom. —Yes, well, you know what I mean. But something kept her from picking them up, some sense she would be interfering in the dogness and the possumness and the half-happy ache of the spring day. On their way back, they would look.

Conversation on the high arch of the tree that blew down years before and spanned the stream wasn't tadpoles or dam projects or who pushed whom the way it used to be. It was where you could live the way you wanted, where there were jobs, a long discussion of apartment prices, roommates and lovers. The old willows there had some sodden oyster mushrooms, not worth picking now; she should have come two weeks earlier and walked alone. She climbed up and sat in the sun next to her husband and children. The stream was full but clear and bright. No one solved any of the problems of the world in the next twenty minutes, but for the time being they all seemed in abeyance.

"Hadn't we better cook?" said someone. "If people are really coming at six o'clock."

They started back. "Wait until you see the most amazing

thing!" she said. "But you mustn't cry." She put her arm around the shoulders of the youngest.

But when they got there, you know what had happened: there was not a possum in sight. No big gray mother and not a single pink corpse. The dog ran round and round his old mayhem sniffing for souvenirs. He found more than they, clues at least, and started on the brushpile again. She dragged him out of it. "Leave them alone," she said. "You leave them alone," and kicked him softly in the hindquarters to make her point. But how could they have been so completely fooled, the dog included? It certainly looked like death, of the worst kind. Stone cold death. "You don't suppose buzzards or something came and carried them away?"

"You're still being fooled, Mom!"

But how could unborn babies know how to play dead?

Hope.
In Funny Places.

Everyone else believed the mothers but she had been there, to the forbidden place, and knew better. The sun was gone, a big eye blinded. Not even stars yet. A lightning bug maybe. The sky was still pale but there were no shadows left when everyone ran to hide. The air was electric from the summer, old heat rumbled in the sky with a slow light far away, new heat ran in their veins and they could feel the electricity in their own speed. Numbers chanted by fives told how much time was left. Enough barely to slip one way through the privet then double back behind base into the perfect and forbidden place where no one (they were the believers) ever hid. The mothers all said "and stay away from the septic tank. You know what's in there!" Of course there wasn't any. It wasn't true like a lot mothers said. There was no smell even. Their bathroom smelt worse. There was a big pipe made of something like brown china sticking out of the ground to about her middle. And it stuck into the ground about the same. At the bottom there was a manhole cover she didn't think she would open. Maybe the mothers all thought they were that stupid. Actually, she couldn't get it open. She had tried but you can't lift a manhole that you are standing on too.

The brown china rim was still warm from the hot day. Her left leg slid over it first, leaving the right and her hands far behind as she touched with bare toes, then let herself all the way down and heard a sound—Hahhh with no voice. Ahhhshh it said. She was all the way in and there were eyes there too. Yellow. Green. The color of what day was left in the sky. She said, very quietly as It reached ninety-ninetyfive-ahundred, "Hahhhh yourself, ahhhsh." The possum was silent. It was very small, the size of a squirrel but, with its telltale tail, no problem, it was a possum. "Ready or not, here I come." She could hear It start to thump off from base, the big china pipe caught the ground sounds. Thump thump thump they almost rang. She could have touched base then, but this time she wanted to be looked for until they were all called home to bed. She wanted them to look for her until they gave up.

She had just begun to feel this power and she liked to use it. Dust clouds followed her tearing down the gravel roads on her bike. She could swing from branch to branch in the trees and curdle their blood down below with her bellow. But she had another power too that she was liking. She could get into things and be completely with them. She could do this with rocks and trees and water and grass. It lasted seconds sometimes, or hours. The sky lit briefly and she waited for the rumble with the possum. When it came, it was barely more than silence, buried deep in the cicadas' high song.

Possum and girl studied each other. The possum had the advantage of seeing well in the dark but the girl had lived longer and knew a bit more. They were still and staring. The girl spoke first, under her breath, like a possum. Hhaash. HHhaaahh. Brer Possum he say nothin', she thought to herself. Then she thought, no, wrong one. It was possum lost the hair on his tail to Brer Bar's teeth. And it was little possum can climb a big tree. And if you tickle a dead possum, he'll burst out laughing. Both were solemn still but she reached her hand to his hairless tail and touched it near the tip. Around her finger went the fingery tail like a baby's grasp. Ahhh, she said with a little voice; ahhh, it said in a whisper.

Then she lifted her hand and the possum came too. She held him high where she could look closely into his startled eyes; perhaps they were permanently startled, he gave no signs of fear, but hung quietly wherever she dangled him. Of course, she never moved fast, and when she spoke to him, her whispers were scarcely different from his possum sound. She was certain it was a him, for no apparent reason. "Old boy," she said, "You've got a friend now. Maybe you'd rather have your mother, but she lost you and you've got me now. How about that?" Perhaps the possum could handle only one activity at a time and was satisfied to hang there without replying. She wondered if she could touch him with her other hand. When she did, behind his ear, he lifted his lip in something like a smile, revealing, but not using his very sharp teeth. "There you are, old boy. There you are. You can have the rabbit hutch in the garage and I'll feed you every day so we stay friends." The rabbits had belonged to her brothers and her cousins and she had only shared in the family dog, who was really her father's. The possum would be hers.

There were more sounds around her, someone looking in the privet hedge. She silently put the possum down and picked him up and put him down and picked him up. When he was down he moved a little, looking under some dry leaves beside her toes, but he seemed in no hurry to go anywhere and caught hold of her finger whenever it touched his tail. It was very dark now except for the heat lightning and a few stars through the trees above her. "Allyallyinfree," yelled It. "Allyallyox-enallinfree." She didn't budge, and then she heard one mother call and then another and then her own. Still she didn't move. It seemed they had given up without announcing it, almost as if they didn't care. Suppose she was lost, or had fallen in. This annoyed her and she sat in stubborn silence in the septic tank with her only satisfactory friend. Her mother called again, everyone else had gone home. "I'll give you until I count ten." She could hear the numbers going by and listened as if they were of no more account than It's "five-ten-fifteen-twenny". Then her mother indicated that an absolute limit had been reached. She blew the police whistle she kept in case her voice wore out. It meant there was no negotiation possible.

She stood up and hung her possum over the edge of the china pipe while she tried to climb out. "O.K. O.K., we're coming," she called, to silence the whistle. Scrambling out with just one hand was much harder than slipping in; it took a while, and she couldn't walk too fast because of the new friend on her finger. "You had better hurry it up," said her mother, spotting her in the shadows. "It's way past your bedtime."

"Look what I found," she said.

"I'll be darned," said her mother. "Where did you find that?"

"If I tell, everyone will know my secret hiding place."

"Just me," said her mother. "And I'm not in the game."

She didn't tell anyhow.

"What do you think you're going to do with that possum?"

"Keep him in the garage where the rabbits used to be."

"What happens when you go to camp? I don't need anything else to take care of."

"I told you I didn't want to go to camp."

"But you're going. What will happen to the possum?"

"I don't know. Probably I shouldn't go."

"Well, time will tell. Sufficient unto the day. Put him in the garage and come to bed."

It didn't take long to make him a nest and lock him into the hutch. He looked ready for sleep in something soft and that reminded her of her own cool sheets, so suddenly she was sleepy too. Before she left, she gave him a name that she was ashamed of later when she wished she was someone extraordinary, who had always had original ideas. She called him Pogo, because she was just a little girl who read the funnies.

She had to make a list of ten favorite things for the camp she didn't want to go to; four of them had to do with Pogo.

1. Talk to my possum
2. Tickle my possum
3. Ride bikes
4. Climb trees
5. Eat watermelon
6. Spit seeds
7. Swim
8. Read
9. Walk in the woods with my possum
10. Give my possum his vitamin pill

This was, in fact, a censored list. She had split the watermelon-eating and seed-spitting into two, because she knew no one would understand how much she liked taking other people to see her possum and watching him bite them. She was the one he loved, the only one. He hung by his tail from her finger when she rode her bike sometimes. She was training him to use the handlebar but he wouldn't learn. He only liked her finger. And he liked his vitamin. There was always a bottle of shiny, smelly capsules in the corner where they ate breakfast, and mornings now she took one extra and rolled it for him in a ball of dogfood. Each time his sharp teeth pierced a pill, his eyes popped open twice as wide and his hair stood on end with surprise, and pleasure she supposed; she always laughed. She had expected him to swallow it the way she did, in order to avoid the taste, which was exactly like the smell only worse. But he seemed to like it and pushed at her fingers with his cool nose to send her back for more. "One-a-day," she said. "One-a-day." They loved each other.

Then suddenly, it was the week before she had to go to camp. Her mother would hear none of her refusals, neither the quiet reasonableness nor the screaming meemies, which she could alternate with astounding speed. There was a stack of new underwear and shorts and shirts with name tags sewn in. And then her mother said, "You know you have to turn Pogo loose now. He has to go back to the woods."

The real tears settled in. "He never came from the woods. He can't live alone. He thinks I'm his mother."

And her mother said, "We all have to grow up, you know. Grown possums live in the woods."

"But he'll get killed on the road. They're always dead on the road. Half the woods are on one side, half on the other. They're always crossing and they're always dead!"

"If you don't put him in the woods, I will. I should think you'd like to do it so you can say goodbye."

So the night before she was leaving for camp, she took Pogo into the trees at the corner of the woods farthest from any road. Her mother wouldn't let her take the bottle of vitamins for him. "Too much of anything isn't good, he'll eat them all at once." She knew that was true and hid a little treat of three or four in some tree roots where she turned him loose. The possum had already perfected the slow amble of relatives he didn't know and he wandered off, as if he wouldn't really mind living in the woods. So really, she was the only sad one, being left by the most perfect friend she was sure she would ever have.

"I hope this isn't the end," she said. She had read that in a love comic.

The next morning, her mother put her on a yellow bus on the other side of town. She sat behind the driver. There was not a single person she knew on the bus and they all knew each other and kept chattering to prove it. She looked straight ahead at the road past the man driving. She felt separate from everything, even her own feelings and concentrated on the line stretching ahead and slipping rapidly under the bus. It would serve them right if she got carsick and threw up. But then she saw something lying on that center line, and she knew it was what it always was. The bus passed it and she hung out her window to look. It was a big one. "Get back in there," said the driver.

"Can't we stop and save that possum?" she asked.

"You got better things to do than saving dead possums," he said. "A squash possum is a dead possum. You got to go to camp and have you some fun."

But suppose it only needed somebody to tickle it. You never knew. She watched the long road the best she could with wet eyes.

Laughter.
The Love Left.

There were neat footprints of mud by the food dish almost every morning since the cat moved outdoors. In the first weeks, when they were getting settled, she didn't dare put the cat out for fear it would hate where they had brought it and run away back to the farm. If it could. You heard stories about dogs who did that. This, however, was a real outdoors cat: after intensive litter training, whose major product was badly scratched wrists, it still preferred brown carpet and closet corners. Out it went.

The dog was gone already. He was old and moving was too much. He went into a decline and dragged himself around and cried until only his front end worked and they had to have him put to sleep. The house was so empty.

It never took any time to clear the supper dishes. It had taken no time to cook or eat supper either. The house was meant for only two people, and maybe their small animals, so nothing about it took time. She did not want to slow her life down so that she and the house became a perfect fit.

She propped the door open to catch some cool night air and went out the back door with some scraps for the cat. Though it was fall, her accustomed clues were lacking. The trees were green and heavy and the air as damp as spring. She saw the first stars here a week ago when they had a cold snap, dropping the temperature precipitously into the fifties and making the camelias bloom. People said that her blood would thin out, so she would adjust to the heat and not be able to stand the cold. The first in the list of capacities to go, she supposed. What would be next? Did one lose the ability to bear smell, sight, hearing? Was that what age was?

There was no black night here close to the house. Streetlights and other house lights spread into the vines and grass and between the banana plants. She set the dish of leftovers next to the open door and sat on the top step. The cat took a choice scrap of meat into the darkness, growling.

There were no ghosts in this house, no familiar moments, no joy, no trepidation. All the wilderness was outside now: bayous edged into the city and tangled with slums. But from the porch, across the green-gone-sepia in the night air, the three houses she could see were shut up tight against flora and fauna. They were dark now except for the rooms lit by flickering auroras of television.

She was dying for lack of prairie winds, banging doors, bloodcurdling cries and laughter.

"Don't start," she said. "They were already gone."

"But they were everywhere in the house," she answered. And in the mare's ears pricked by the gate when the yellow bus passed without stopping. And in the pine forest they planted one cold spring, too early to see the poison ivy but too late to escape its blistering plague. And the wind blew and the doors banged, things broke and were replaced, and skin tore and grew back together.

Something rustled the neighbor's bamboo and moseyed into the shadows of their yard. Lower than a dog, rounder than a cat, and not at all the half-expected, dreaded, stranded alligator come to inhabit their plumbing, this was a familiar figure whose tracks she had already seen by the cat's dish.

"Hahhssh," she whispered. "Hahhhh."

The possum looked her way for a moment then went on foraging in the shadows. She watched what she could see of it for a long time until it seemed to disappear under the far edge of the porch. Suppose it lived right there with us, she thought. Her feelings might begin to change. She wanted to see if she could find where it went under the house. Where was the flashlight? Having seen one somewhere, she went inside to look for it, but their possessions had not completely settled in and found accustomed places. There were too many things to fit in this house. She banged around for a long time with some boxes in the bedroom.

"What are you doing?" her husband called over a TV sound of crashing, splintering, tinkling destruction.

"Looking for the flashlight."

"What for?"

"I saw the possum down in the bushes. I want to see where he went."

"Huh!" he said, partly interested. But whatever was coming apart on TV had not quite finished. "There's a flashlight in the car."

"Oh yes. You're right. Come see it."

The carport was out front and the flashlight finally turned out to be in the far back of the wagon. She didn't take the keys, so she had to reach back and catch it with the umbrella.

She supposed the possum was long gone as she went back through the house. The TV was off and she heard the refrigerator door open. Its fan was humming as she turned the corner into the kitchen and met the curious yellow eyes of the possum. Their gazes crossed and mixed at some chaotic edge to which she felt dizzily close, the edge where she liked to live. Then there was a horrible noise, "Git! Git!" her husband was shouting from next to the refrigerator.

She tried to hold on for a second longer before she fell, before their different fields were wrenched apart. Before the nearest heavy thing to hand had hurtled across the room and struck the possum's back. She crumpled in tears and he fell

down to die. Flat planes, walls and closed windows piled
down on her, pressing out her breath unbearably against the
vinyl floor.

This is death, she thought.

But the same flat smoothness set the possum on his feet. It
was no place to die, real or pretend. Or live either. He looked
sourly over his shoulder as he dragged his hindquarters and
hairless tail outside. To die. A ketchup bottle missed and
smashed in its own gore.

Is there a painless way? Had she held on just too long?

"You've killed him," she said furiously.

"I'm sorry," he said. "Really I am. I forgot about you and
possums. But don't you think he'll be back? Don't you think
he's in the bushes laughing?"

She supposed.

And she was used to loving.

THOSE ARE PEARLS

The year they lived abroad Iris discovered more about distance than she had expected. She read guide books and maps and quickly learned the back roads and the best marketstalls to shop. It was exciting and she was proud that she could easily do what everyone said would be so hard, "On scholarship money, with a little bitty baby!" She had pointed out that she and Ben could spend wedding money, because they hadn't bought any furniture, and that the little bitty baby was already two and a half. "But doesn't Margaret still wear diapers?" "Only at night," said Iris, "And she's trying. And she eats regular food."

Ben studied hard, as much on his own projects as for courses at the *Institut*, but late afternoons they would all go out in the tiny car to explore or meet some other students for a drink. Weekends they picnicked. Thanksgiving they celebrated on the long crest of the Luberon with plenty of wine, paté and a pumpkin pie Iris had made out of something other than pumpkin. Christmas they had decorated a tree with oranges and lemons, piercing them with a long needle, the red thread drawing heavy perfume onto their hands, into the room already full of the familiar evergreen smells. The colors were bright though the branches drooped. They splurged on a pheasant in the market, and it was so beautiful when Iris plucked it, soft handfuls of order, browns and iridescence, that she cried. But it was delicious, and she was still having fun. She described it all very well in her letters home.

New Year's Eve she wrote a long letter to her father, a holiday letter. Her mother had died not long before, and though her brothers were living at home or nearby, he particularly missed her, she knew. That evening they left Margaret sleeping soundly and slipped out to share a neighbor's little midnight supper. Iris was apprehensive leaving her alone. The stone walls were so thick in the *mas*, they would never hear if she cried; though they would even be in the same building. "She never wakes up, remember?" said Ben. It was true, but they never left her alone either.

They did not know the neighbors very well, and were flattered to be included. Iris knew it would not have been understood if Madame had stayed home with a sleeping baby. They went and found that the little *souper* was a feast with wonderful wines and champagne for dessert as the year turned past them and *fine champagne* for warmth before the fifty-foot trek home through the cold of the first hour of the new year.

They stopped a few steps from their door and looked at the bright sky. "Look, a gibbous moon!" said Iris.

"A what kind?"

"Gibbous. It's the proof that the dark side of the moon, I mean the dark bites taken out of it, are not the earth's shadow but the unlit part of the moon because the sun is shining on it at a different angle from the one we are looking at the moon from."

"Run through that again," he said, kissing her and beginning to take some small, dark bites so that she couldn't—although she was perfectly willing to do so, having finally remembered the word alone. She had never remembered it before, despite her father's repeated teasing, not quite once a month, but often enough that even the village idiot could have named that phase correctly. "Know what kind of moon that is yet, sugar?" Maybe, forgetting had to do with the times before she knew better that he showed her his strength, "Do you want to see my power?" slowly blotting out before her eyes the bright face of the moon, and making it return simply by pointing at it long enough.

For the sun, the arrangements were more elaborate, involving smoked glass, but no matter how hard he exerted himself, he could only nick it. She remembered how tired his arm was afterwards.

So she had finally grown up both hopeful and sceptical and this night in a strange country remembered the word unquestioned, maybe because nobody cared anymore whether she knew it or not. She was being kissed.

They went up to Margaret's room to check that she was all right. She had not moved, and Iris was suddenly afraid that she was not alive. She did not run to the bed (silly), but her heart began to pound with relief when, finally reaching Margaret, she leaned over and felt the baby's breath on her own cold cheek.

"She didn't mind that we went, did she?" said Ben.

"No," said Iris and let herself be persuaded to drop her clothing in a path between Margaret's room and theirs. The damp chill began to interfere, and she dove for the saggy wool mattress piled with their two down bags, just as someone banged on the front door. "Christ," said Ben looking for his trousers.

By the time they had replaced enough clothing, the sound was no longer of a fist, but of wood on wood, a full-scale attack. As they often heard in France, they had never been through a war; they didn't know what fear was, and they went down to see who was there. It was not another party, no midnight revelers, but two gendarmes. Do they arrest people before dawn for not having renewed their student visas? No, not even in France. They say to you that for reasons unknown, monsieur and madame are to call the American embassy in Marseilles, right away, and then they walk off into the night, leaving you to find a phone. Nobody has a phone in the country. It means a descent into the town to find some all-night bar.

It means wrapping up the baby and bringing her along. She never minds. She is good. She won't cry, the good baby that you never were.

The trip was silent, that way Margaret could sleep and they need not formulate their fears, not knowing if naming a death would make it come true or hold it off. Which name would they choose? They felt they still had a choice, that they were involved in preventing or causing calamity. Nearing town, Margaret decided she didn't want to sleep but to practice talking. "Where we going?" she said. "Why?" They were forgetting to answer her and she kept wanting to remind them. "Where? Why?"

"Here, baby, shh," said Iris as Ben left the car. "Ben's just going in here." He would call, because his French was better; hers was still easily thrown into confusion by gestureless telephone words with static. She could see him in the bar, buying the *jeton*, making the call; she saw his posture change as he heard whatever it was, and she saw him coming back. She could tell how bad it was from the way he moved.

He got into the car and she didn't ask anything. He said, "It's your father. Your father is dead."

The unfaithfulness and treachery of death! How could he have died without her being present? The long letter she had spent that afternoon writing, as if they had been talking but writing him things she would never have said, about homesickness and discoveries as well, beginning to write as if they were people who knew each other rather than her usual gay recounting, as if nothing hurt or mattered, was too late to mail now. He had gone.

"He had a heart attack." She didn't cry. "We have to find some place that we can call your uncle from." When she started to breathe again, a few tears came, just slowly as if accompanying some long old sadness returning, and as gradually dried up.

Ben decided to try Martin, because his landlady had a phone and would understand the urgency if they paid in advance. Iris

let him figure it out. She felt she was just going along for the
ride. Martin looked a little embarrassed when he let them in.
The cause was shrouded in a gray blanket on the bed that occu-
pied most of his apartment; only her cherubic face showed.
"Je vous présente mon amie, Hélène," he said, and they all
said *"Enchanté"* formally, even Margaret, who was becoming
bilingual by repeating everything she heard. Iris let Ben explain to Martin and repeat it in French for Hélène, and she felt
a certain self-pity grow with their sympathy. Martin said he
was sure his landlady would not mind waking up for a hundred
francs, but that the whole crowd had better not go. He would
take Iris and stay to help her.

Martin placed the call and waited with her for it to go
through. The landlady made Iris a little tisane to calm her,
though Iris thought if she were any more calm she would pass
out. Martin asked questions about her father, his age (he was
fifty-three, too young); what he did (he was a good doctor); if
she had known he was sick (she didn't think so, but began to
wonder). He translated for the landlady who was shaking her
head. Once again, Iris felt near tears, touched by sympathy in
a way she could not touch herself, but puzzled by the joking
phrase "left in the lurch" she heard herself think.

The call came through and Martin handed her the phone.
The voice that she would hear had to cross the ocean floor
through cables hundreds of fathoms deep. "Thy father lies,"
she thought taking the receiver. "Those are pearls which were
his eyes. Nothing of him" but she stopped herself, conscious
of selective and faulty memory, as what had any Ferdinand's
loss to do with hers? She put the phone to her ear. "Hello?"
The sea-change was that the voice of her uncle, purged of its
particularity, could have been the voice of her father. Her
older brother, she realized, was developing the same rich tim-
bre, the slightly strange phrasing. She would not get it because
she was the daughter. "Hello?"

He had died at cards with his friends; just before the turn of
the New Year, he stood up and said, "I don't think I can play

any more," and died. He would be buried day after tomorrow. No. She should not come home. They were taking care of the boys. There was nothing she could do. It would be silly. He would have thought it was silly. She began to realize it would be silly. They said goodbye.

She was disappointed and could cry for that. Iris had said very little, and the landlady understood even less, but wanted her to try a little more tisane. When Iris had drunk it and calmed down, Martin took her back to where Ben and Hélène were drinking wine and Margaret slept in the big blanket. Ben sweetly asked what she had heard and what she felt, but she hardly knew herself. She tried explaining in French, so that they could all talk together. It did not seem any harder than English. Maybe she had finally made some progress with the language. They sat together, drinking wine because she did not want to go home and dream. Eventually, they all were under the blanket with Margaret, keeping warm, and Margaret let them sleep late in the morning. When she found them all right there, she just lay still and talked to herself.

"Maybe you would come over in the afternoon and I'll make eggnog; so that Hélène will know what it is like," suggested Iris as they left.

"Are you sure?" asked Martin.

"I'm not," said Ben.

"It would really be better," said Iris.

"*Elle se sent abandonnée, peut-être*," said Hélène to Ben.

"*Oui, c'est ça, abandonnée*," Iris said to her.

When they came, it was not like the night before. Everyone said the eggnog was good. Maybe it was the big blanket that was missing. Iris was very depressed when they left. She had finally begun to cry, but still not as if it were connected to the fact of death. She just cried instead of laughing when she broke a glass and when she burned the supper.

They had decided what to do about her not going home. Ben would take care of Margaret while she would be alone to imagine the funeral and her presence there. After the first fury that he would never read her letter, she let herself believe that in the moments before he died—those moments she had spent writing—he had known what she had to say; that when he stood up to say "I can't play any more," he had understood the serious, finally not playful, writing. So she imagined the scene at their country home, under the tree where other ancestors lay. He had told her that he would be buried there, not in the cemetary plot with her mother. She knew the ritual and the sad faces also present. She examined them all carefully in her mind and buried her father.

A week later, a letter came from her youngest brother, describing the ceremony at the grave next to her mother's—in the cemetary, not under the tree. She realized then that the treachery was hers, that she was the only one who had known where he wished to lie. The irrevocably mistaken hours burying him in the wrong place returned to mind over and over during the long, snowy winter, an unusual winter, the gray winter they never have in Provence.

She had a dreary laziness. She did everything well enough but nothing wonderfully any more. Ben and Martin planned a trip for spring vacation: to Paris to stay at Hélène's. Hélène had timed a sick leave to coincide with the Nouvel An, but lived in Paris with her two children. Martin said she would enjoy having them. They could all squeeze in somehow. The plans were set and then Martin's parents decided to come and be shown the Côte d'Azur during his vacation. He was furious, feeling he could not turn them down, but was comforted that for once he would eat well in France; so Ben, Iris and Margaret went off to spend two weeks with Hélène.

Iris did well, she thought, living in French for the first time, but found it so fatiguing that she always was asleep before Ben and Hélène had finished talking. Margaret regressed and wet the children's bed repeatedly. Iris put a piece of rubber under her, but it was always elsewhere by morning. She washed the mattress and sheets everyday, but still the odor was penetrating the material. Hélène's temper was short on such matters.

She scolded Margaret until she cried, and let Iris know she should have better control over the situation. Luckily, Paris was interesting. Ben would go to the library or museums in the afternoon, and after Margaret's nap, Iris would push her in her cart up and down the streets just looking.

One Thursday, they went to meet Hélène at the hospital where she worked. Iris had never thought of the smell, to prepare for it. It was the same as that of St. Luke's, St. Elizabeth's, the Retreat for the Sick, all the little city hospitals where the child, Iris, had "made rounds" with her father on Sundays. She knew it was a frightening smell for some, but for her it was the smell of comfort, of his power. It was the smell she had been told was ether, which in her unguided readings through generations of hoarded volumes would be the smell of what held the firmaments on high; it was the whole, blue ethereal sky of someone's forgotten science which she had deeply adopted.

From the first breath, she began to burn, from the ends of her fingers, from the bottoms of her feet, from her toes, up the tops of her thighs, up her arms wrapped around Margaret, and she tried to take one more deep breath. It was, instead, a vigorous, blocked snort of her secretions, as if the hot tears were flowing from every tributary, and she had to bury her face in the baby's shoulder to catch the flood. Then Ben and Hélène took Margaret, because she kept trying to lift Iris's face with gentle pokes. "Why? Mummy, what?"

The tears felt endless. Twice in Provence they had seen the Fontaine de Vaucluse; once in the autumn in its pit they saw reflected the bright, full moon still almost invisible in the twilight sky; and then again they saw it spew the Massif's melted snows into a turbulent Sorgue. Now rafting recklessly, on a voyage without her tourist's instincts, curiosity, maps and handbooks, she was on water made in another time, rising here in another place, endless. But when Ben and Hélène took the baby she had opened her eyes and seen she could not cry forever. Soon enough to save their afternoon, she stopped, and they were in time to pick up Hélène's children at the *garderie* and go to the Jardin de Luxembourg for the marionettes. Judy was a fiend, beating Punch until he almost fell out of the stage. Hélène's children shrieked with laughter, but Margaret took it seriously and cried out with each blow. Ben tried explaining to make it funny, and finally, in his lap, she would laugh, looking at him to see when it was time. Iris was conscious of the others' fun, which she saw articulated in the curve of Ben's neck when he threw his head back to laugh, repeated in Margaret's mimicry, echoed and applauded in Hélène's clapping children, Hélène's clapping hands. She wanted to rest her eyes, still sore from weeping, and looked down past her own quiet hands to watch Hélène's foot forgetting its shoe and beckoning in response to the laughter all around. She felt no laughter to speak of herself.

They wandered in the Jardin afterwards. Iris felt much better, almost good. The tears had finally come so easily. But she still felt a directionless floating, as if she were the flood herself and also a minuscule, unplaced point somewhere in it, that could never know its own latitude and longitude. Ben and Hélène thoughtfully left her to sit on a bench and played ball with the children to wear them out, because they had to be very quiet in Hélène's apartment. They always took off their shoes and put on carpet slippers when they went in the door, to avoid fierce banging on the ceiling below and the coarse voice screaming *"Pas de tapage!"*

They fed the children when they came in and dressed them for bed. Safely distant, Margaret was now happily reenacting the puppet show, and she jumped around hitting Ben with her shoe. "Fall down, Daddy!" she said. He obliged with a loose-jointed collapse, and she jumped on him and beat some more, as the broom handle began to bang on the ceiling below. Hélène stopped laughing and told them to stop right away, because the woman downstairs was mad. She hated anything that was fun, that was pleasant, that seemed alive. Once she had thrown dishwater out the window on the children. She screamed at them from her doorway. She would call gendarmes to silence them if she could not do it herself.

Iris began to feel her spirits return. She cooked them a wonderful meal. (Buying the food and cooking seemed a fair trade for crowding Hélène's apartment.) She was angry when Hélène said it was nice, but cooking was really not worth all the trouble Iris put into it. She would have argued about who got to decide what was worth what, but her French was still too shaky for an argument. She hoped her silence was expressive when Hélène complained, as they did dishes together, that she had used every pan in her kitchen.

Next day, a beautiful day, Ben, Margaret and Iris drove out to Chartres. They picnicked at the edge of a grain field, where they could see the cathedral rise out of pale green waves, as the breeze across growing wheat carried the shadows of high, fair-weather clouds. They sat looking for a long while; the space, at the same time great and comprehensible, was what they had begun to like most in France. The harmony was nearly a consolation for all that was lost outside. Everything Iris needed might be in that sight, soothing, quickening, replenishing with a hope for understanding; a feast, a breath, a filling. It was hard to go on with their tour.

Then they spent a long time wandering about the cathedral, too. Ben found you could walk out on the roof, and Iris and Margaret went outside to wave at him from the garden. They both wanted him to come down right away.

They drove back to Paris after supper. Margaret had made a crisis when the café owner wouldn't let her have her own glass of water for fear she might spill it, but it seemed nothing could spoil that day.

It was late when they began to climb the stairs to Hélène's apartment. Ben had a key so that they wouldn't disturb anyone, and they were very quiet, Margaret deeply asleep on Iris's shoulder. They pushed the button to illuminate the staircase, but it only lasted for three flights. Ben had to find another switch in the dark for the next three. Iris just kept walking up, her feet accustomed to the rhythm of the stairs. She was in a hurry to get to bed, expecting at this late hour, some privacy for pleasure.

She was about to step up into the next flight of dark stairs, when the light clicked on. A huge woman faced her, filling the step to the next landing. With the light, the woman started yelling. Iris stopped. She knew who it was but only something of what she meant. It was probably the baby she was after.

Iris had never physically fought for anything in her life, but she immediately knew she would fight for Margaret. The woman lurched, grabbing the rail to lean closer. Iris saw a man behind. She heard Ben as he ran up, "We've got to get the baby out of here." He grabbed Margaret, still obliging substance, collapsed in sleep. They both hoped to carry her from this inheritance of nightmare anger into a bed of her own dreams. Ben turned his shoulder to cover Margaret, a football manoeuvre, and carried her past the woman and the husband in her shadow. The woman hardly looked at them, she was concentrating on Iris; when she stopped yelling, she left her tongue out, ready for the next tirade. Whose enemy was she? What did Iris have to hear that the others did not? Why should she have to pass this torrent of hate when she had never before been touched in anger? She had to pass alone without even Margaret for a reason, because she was living up there with the others beyond that woman. That was where she was going; she fixed the woman's eyes with her own and started to climb. She still could not understand the words except for two, re-peated again: *"Sale bosch!"* Mistaken words for a long-dead enemy? "Filthy German."

Iris moved as steadily forward as she had in the dark, feeling rhythm again through her fear. Then suddenly the woman swung at her and hit her cheek with her full hand. Hardly pausing, the other hand crashed against the other cheek. Iris kept looking and moving though time had stopped. She heard, in the silence between the woman's accusations, doors all up and down the staircase click open. She did not count on help.

She did not strike back. She held their eyes together and just kept moving through as if the woman were an apparition. The woman stepped back to wind up another blow. Because Iris was still moving, her hand missed and Iris felt that her neck was as strong as the heavy arm. The woman was stepping back now to keep up with her, and enlisting her husband, who had never moved forward and still did not. Iris passed through.

She kept the same pace now past the three doors on that floor; all were cracked and each shut as she went by. She heard the woman's last threats, bitter and sparse, for some future encounter, as she climbed the long flight of stairs. When she got to Hélène's apartment, the door was shut and she had to knock. Ben opened the door. He had put Margaret down still sleeping and begun to tell Hélène about the woman's shouting. Hélène was in bed looking drowsy, annoyed, concerned and charming.

"La vâche!" she said. "Le monstre!" "Was she so awful to you as well?" she asked Iris in French.

And Iris began to tell her, words coming with furious speed insufficient to her meaning, and she poured them faster and faster, without stumbling, in a torrent of surprise and anger which was new to her. It was like joy. She was saying "She wanted to kill me and I passed her alone!"

How long she told them that and in how many ways, she did not know. What stopped her was the realization that she was on her knees telling them and their faces were going blanker and blanker. When she paused, Ben said, "Don't. Why are you doing that? You know Hélène doesn't understand any English." He took Iris's hand and began to translate what he gathered had happened, and Iris realized that her anger and her joy might as well have been glossalalia:

I am a wide flood on a plain; a wind on deep waters; a shining tear of the sun; the hulking gibbous moon its fat face reflecting another day's light; the day before and after; passing through; coming back.

She shivered herself to sleep.

The remaining spring (the few more days of vacation, the drive south again, surprised that the sunlight intensified in so short a distance) and the early summer (already Provence had begun to dry) were pleasant, filled with picnic trips. They realized they had little time left in France. It began to seem the perfect time to conceive a child, and so it was.

They planned with Martin, Hélène, her brother and children, to rent a house on an island off Brittany their last month. Everyone had said it was impossible to really get to know the French, and they were glad for the chance. Of course, then it wasn't easy knowing them that closely. The house had one faucet from a rainwater cistern (little rain) and together they emptied dish slops and chamber pots off the quai into the high tide. The village was friendly, with grocery and dry goods and bakery and a butcher who had a steer (though sometimes a cow) led from the boat to his back door once a week. The fishermen, when not in boats, were in the numerous bars and seemed not unhappy to have strangers with them. Because Margaret was too little to leave alone, Iris spent most of her time with three children. Hélène's children, being four and six, were expected to take care of themselves, but seemed to like her company. At night, it was clear who should stay with the children, because Hélène's didn't need staying-with. Iris did not really miss the evenings spent in one café or another, because Hélène's brother concentrated on trying to shock her and bored her instead; Hélène, if interested in her at all, was so critical of Iris's child-rearing, particularly her attitudes towards toilet-training (Iris didn't know she had an attitude) and unemptied plates that Iris was uncomfortable with her. She enjoyed the children's open affection and when they finally slept, she was happy with a book, or when she finished all the books they brought to the island, with her own head, which seemed to her very interesting and full.

She loved the island itself, its tiny roads lined with six foot square potato "fields," its rocks and tide-pools, the inescapable sound of surf. It was sunny which made it possible for them to live together by staying outdoors and apart, though not possible to wash very often.

Near the end of their month, one of the café owners proposed a feast for them. If they would pay for ingredients, he would prepare *homard à l'armoricaine*, and they would have the café to themselves for dinner; afterwards the fishermen could come and drink with them.

Once again, it was clearly an occasion on which Margaret had to be left. Iris had to shut her eyes to the dangers, or really she had to remind herself that, once asleep, Margaret seldom woke up. It was a wonderful feast. The café owner found a six-pound lobster. At first dubious about the relation between age and tenderness, they discovered a better lobster never was, and it swam again in the Loire wine urged on them by their host, to increase their good memories of Brittany.

Afterwards, the high full moon gave such bright light that they could almost see the mainland. They wanted to camp out on one of the long arms of the island. Iris wanted to go too, but not without Margaret, so Ben found the tent to keep her from being mosquito-bitten. Iris carried Margaret, Martin brought his camping stove, Hélène and her brother brought the wine and coffee, they all brought sleeping bags and went out single file along the cart trail.

They all were watching the beautiful moon, and because they had had so much to drink, none dared say what they were seeing. Iris distinctly saw two moons and giggled to herself, but she also saw both moons begin to disappear. She did not want to take her eyes off them and stumbled. Everyone was stumbling, but the smooth path couldn't be missed, because of the knee-high stone walls at first, then the tight scrubs along it. Finally, she was sure enough that it really was happening to say "It's an eclipse!" And everyone agreed with relief that that was what they were seeing. But, having some pride, she did not say "It's two eclipses!"

There were two soft spots near the point. They made a fire

on a rocky outcrop in one and laid their sleeping bags around
it. Not far away, in the other clearing, they set up the tent and
put Margaret in it away from the mosquitos. They stayed
awake for a while, enjoying the wine and each other's company. When it was time to feed the fire or go to sleep, Ben
wanted to sleep out but they decided Iris should sleep in the
tent. She snuggled in next to the sweet-smelling creature with
its thumb in its mouth and its rump in the air and slept well.

She slept until just before day, and woke up remembering
loving dawn, how she used to sneak out to see the sun rise,
pearly-early in the morning, and how once, returning, she had
met old Gloria, who cooked for them, and how she said, "I
sees you out trying' to get more than your share the day
again," and kissed her. So shedding the sleeping bag, she
slipped out of the tent, confident of not awakening Margaret,
who had snuck off into a corner. "Such a mobile sleeper!" she
thought. She zipped the tent flap shut, smiling at her silly love
of the sunrise. She remembered a verse her father used to tell
her about a girl and the sun, when she was too sentimental
about dead birds or flowers. It was German, and though she
didn't know any other German, she knew this verse and its
meaning:

Ein Fraülein stand am Meere,	A girl stood by the seashore
Ihr war so weh und bang,	In such great pain and dread,
Es grämte sie so sehre,	What was all her grief for?
Der Sonnenuntergang.	Because the sun had set.

She turned and looked around in the milky light at the adjacent little meadow, the charred spot of old fire and the four
sleeping bags. One old French army bag had rolled to the edge
of the scrubby gorse; the three others were together, one
straight and snoring, self-contained; a leg emerged from the
bag that matched and zipped with hers and disappeared again
into the khaki one that showed a tiny foot. The protruding foot
was socked but that leg, its extending and retracting joint, its

embracing knee, was bare except for the short, thick hairs. Wide awake, she wished it mosquitos, welts and drips of blood, fiery itching. In her sentimental days, she had thought such a sight would make her stomach turn, but it didn't flutter, saving itself, she supposed, for morning sickness at the odors of breakfast. She looked a bit longer, feeling after her anger, sadness for a bereavement she felt she had known already.

But the sky was growing rosy; she wanted to see the sun rising over the pale sliver of the continent, to see if dawn here was different from dawn in America. If she had never left there, how long would she have waited for this dawn? Six more hours? Someone was seeing this one sun (from among those millions that hung, shining in the ether last night, only this one was making her morning gleam) first all the time, but still it seemed possible and important to be the first to see it. She was striding out the rabbit run trail, barely widened by other visitors to the eastern point. There was nothing useful out here; no potato fields, too much of the island's spine showing; no mussels hanging together, too much surge and surf; nothing really here but dawn, for which most people waited where they happened to be. She went as far as she could to meet it. It didn't burst on the sky, but sparked and lit the clouds on the horizon. Almost as fast as it appeared, it was disappearing again into a band of cloud. She wanted to feel awed, but she couldn't. The sun seemed fragile, not yet warming, passing now above the thick stripe of obscurity, lighting the top of those clouds, moving towards another layer of cirrus. It was the perfect morning for that day, and barring a suicidal swim into the gray face of the sea, into the sun's cold reflection, she could have gone no farther to greet it.

Soon the sky was full of an ordinary day's light, and she could hear the baby crying. She supposed someone else would hear it, too. But no, the baby kept crying and crying, wetter and wetter, blubbering disappointment and rage. Well, she thought, maybe loneliness is not yet its element. So she went back, relinquishing her own.

The sleeping bags, she noted as she passed, were keeping more to themselves, no arms, legs; the heads seemed aggressively covered. There was something uncomfortable about them.

Margaret was leaning on the screen, crying and sucking her blanket, and putting precarious strain on the tent with its shallow pegs. The sun reflected, quickly golden, on the snail trails where she had pressed her nose into the screen. Iris zipped the door out and crawled in, taking the baby in her arms, rolling into the tent in her embrace. The kisses were all mucous and ammonia. Iris thought that when the sun was first shining on some slippery combination of elements, when something was about to divide and become something else, that mucous and ammonia were the elements, the ether being already eons distant. They fell back asleep and Iris dreamed of shopping in France, walking to a shellfish stall with her *filet*, seeing the square baskets, their orderly rows of black and purple mussels, with the labels naming and pricing *moules* in different sizes, *huitres* in different types, baskets of *palourdes, télisses, oursins,* each arranged in patterns and named a new word she had to learn, separate in its bin. She stopped at the last basket and looked carefully. Here the creatures touched each other with every surface; every face was a common line. Their shapes were irregular, gibbous ovals, nearly square. They were translucent, and she thought there was another layer but could not see far through the sun reflected in the membrane faces. In the center of each was a dark spot. A tadpole in a frog's egg? They were cells, big and fat as the French sanddollars, but soft, clearly all edible. She was wondering how to prepare them and, looking at the dark nucleus of one, realized it was about to divide again. Were they sold by the piece or the lot? The little white sign stuck into one of them was an eight on its side; so it did not say. Was it one creature or many ones? The nucleus was changing more and more from a circle to an eternal eight. There was a dark, dank oily odor, black—the death of nucleus cleaving?—the café in the market? —the bitter French breakfast, because last night they had brought coffee but no milk. She awoke, cells, smells confused again in the heaving revolt of a body conscious of the only ways it might not be alone, fearful of the inevitable parturition, of the danger of nursing and loving, of yet another loneliness to come; morning sickness.

CHOOSING FATHERS

Elly said "Tall and dark."
That was the first thing out of her mouth.

Her immediate impression was that this was not the right answer. The interviewer had not actually said anything after "What is your first requirement?" and there was nothing overtly negative about her demeanor—Ms. Hanks was rumpled and wrinkled, with low breasts snuggling down toward a generous lap as if she had spent her life until now being sat on by children. You could see she had to be very professional with her questions to cover up her kindness. But still Elly was sure she should have said something more elevated, less shallow, less physical.

Elly herself was short and dark, in fact tiny and dark. She had been called petite; it was a compliment. She had been admired as elfin, as doll-like at least once too often. She had always had plenty of boyfriends but hated to rely on them. She had to fight her way to the front just to see things. "You are not so tall yourself," said Ms. Hanks. "Is this an overcompensation?"

"I don't want my daughter to be short."

"And why do you assume she will be a daughter?"

Ah, thought Elly, why did I assume that? My father's daughter, I will make my father another daughter—is that it? A sweet, loving comfort, and what will I get out of it?

Displacement. Yes and irresponsibility. I will have replaced myself—his treasure—with a new peek at the future. I won't be the only one in the world, there will be one more me to fulfill his dreams. "I wonder," she replied, "if I don't think of this as more like cloning. Is that an uncommon assumption?"

"Well, of course, there are those who would *rather* have a girl and those who would *rather* have a boy. And usually their assumptions will reflect that—often negatively—for instance, they think they'll have a boy because they want a girl, etc. But cloning? Never heard that one."

"I'd be happy with a boy—a tall one," said Elly. But then, would that be like erasing her own short father, his cocky grin, his puns, the chip on his shoulder, his scrappy resistance to the world? Little bantam poppa, she thought fondly, maybe you'll have a tall peacemaker for your grandson, a dove.

"Tall. I'll put down definitely."

"Short would be O.K."

"I see. No preference?"

"No—tall first and short second." This is *my* baby, she thought. I'll make it as I damn well please.

"Average?"

"Not average." Her worst prejudice was against the average.

"And dark? I see from your record that you are Jewish. Ashkenazy. We could approach the religious question now."

"Dark just appeals to me. I'm always drawn to dark men."

"But this is not romance we're talking about. You'll never see the man. Is this bothering you? We should discuss it, if so."

"No," said Elly. And she thought of a line of dentist's chairs like the plasma center—Musak and a man jacking off in each vinyl recliner. All tall dark men. All for her. She laughed—Musak wrecked the erotic pull.

"Laughter is a way we have of releasing tension when we can't face something, you know."

I know, lady, I know. I've read all that shit, thought Elly.

"Facelessness does bother me," she said. "And the turkey baster."

"Of course, it is not literally that. You can take a look at the facilities after the interview. And you do know that many women will choose insemination by a friend."

"Yes," said Elly. No. There was no one she knew whom she thought of as a possible father. "But I don't have any male friend good enough to ask at the moment."

"And the old clock is ticking?" said Ms. Hanks.

"Yes, it's ticking," said Elly.

Religion came up again. Elly was her father's only child. Her mother survived the concentration camps by seven or eight years, long enough to give birth to Elly and take her through her first two years of life. But she was never strong again and she died. Elly had some photographs of her thin little person, but could not quite remember her. Uncles, aunts, cousins, grandparents all had died in the camps, only her parents had made it out. She could see the toughness and luck that made it possible in her father, and knew her mother had given everything she had left to her, Elly. Elly knew life was a miracle.

Still, her religion came down to a strong feeling that she should honor her atheistic father's Jewish blood but was not willing to limit her choice to nice Jewish sperm. She thought she had inherited his atheism too and her own blood was enough.

There was a sheaf of papers to go over: questions she had already answered with a ball-point in the privacy of her kitchen. She thought some of them were intrusive and irrelevant and said so to Ms. Hanks.

"The more details we have," Ms. Hanks replied, "the easier it is to make a good match, based on similar details the donors provide."

"Well, who are the donors?" said Elly.

"Oh, all sorts of young men in need of a little cash. Mostly college kids."

Elly taught college. She knew her students sold plasma to pay their rent. Sperm had not really occurred to her.

She drove home after the interview, after having met the turkey baster. She had seen the little room where their encounter would take place and made an appointment for ten days later when the match had been arranged.

The clinic was in Cincinnati. Her college was an hour's drive away, through a spring landscape of gentle hills where the trees stood in windbreaks, just leafing out in delicate shade. A few thick, puffy clouds out of the faraway Gulf, riding a soft, damp wind threw scattered darker shadows that raced across the bright grass, playing fast and loose among the cattle, and there were more puffs trailing behind them. Maybe it would rain tomorrow, but not just now. Elly whistled. She sang. She rolled down her windows and turned her radio up loud. She pushed the pedal down and sped along. "So great! So great!" she said to the wind.

She patted her not-pregnant belly and announced "I'm going to be a mother!"

"And you're going to be the father!" she shouted to the clouds.

Instead of going straight home, she drove to Susan's. Susan was her best friend, but she didn't believe for a minute that Elly was actually going to do this. No matter how much Elly talked about it, Susan—who had a boyfriend named Harvey she was going to marry this summer, and a mother, and a father and brothers and sisters and a slew of cousins and nieces and nephews already—said the whole idea was too strange for her.

So Elly didn't tell her when she made the appointment at the clinic.

Susan wasn't there, but Elly went in anyhow. No one locked doors in this little podunk town. She liked that. Susan was probably at the library. Her house backed up on fraternity row and it was obvious that if she had any work to do (which she always had because she still hadn't finished her thesis) she couldn't have done it there. Thursday afternoon party music blasted straight through the high brick walls the alumni had constructed to contain the beer and boys and exclude uninvited guests. Elly did not remember parties having started on Thursday when she was at college. Friday was as much a wipe-out now as Saturday, Sunday or Monday. That really left her only Wednesday mornings to teach world culture (M-W-F, required and crowded) and she knew she wasn't getting across.

She helped herself to a beer and strung up Susan's hammock between the tulip trees. She could have gone home, but it wouldn't have been much quieter because she lived in the same block. Besides, she was in the mood for company and loud music, even if the only company was provided by her good friend's things and the music came from a party to which she was not invited. Elly shut her eyes and enjoyed it all. No wall was going to keep her from the party.

She pictured the whole front row of her class tomorrow, a group of variously average boys, their eyes glazed either by beer or by the *Iliad* as she tried to interest them in a 15,000-year-old war. Their ritual initiation to adulthood might be via the animal house, but they were certainly the solid good-citizenry of tomorrow. Moral, upright Trojans. (That made her giggle to herself. She supposed there would be plenty of those tonight!)

If they were Trojans, then she was who? Wily Odysseus trying to put something over on them? Surprise them with intelligence. Wake them to their blindness.

Oh well, syllogisms aside. She went to get another beer and in came Susan with Harvey. "Hi," said Elly. "I'll buy some more. You're running out."

"Great," said Susan. "But you'd better get it now because we ordered pizza, but we were counting on the beer."

So Elly had to go out right away, just a block and a half. Beer was more available than water really. Her announcement had to wait until they sat, all three, at the kitchen table and, with the Fabulous Thunderbirds playing backup, she said "I did it."

"Did what?" asked Harvey.

"Signed up. At the clinic."

"You didn't!" said Susan.

"I'm lost," said Harvey.

"I told you I was going to—for artificial insemination. You just didn't believe me."

"Don't you have to be married?" asked Harvey. "I thought there were laws."

"They don't care. Why should they care? It's not like adoption," said Elly.

"Elly. Are you sure you want to do this with strangers?" asked Susan.

"I kind of like the idea."

"But you know who gives the sperm, don't you. It's those fascist pigs over the wall there, when they're too broke to buy beer," said Harvey.

"Fascist pigs is a little strong, don't you think?" said Elly.

"No, I don't," said Harvey. "Damn swastikas on the door at Hillel. You know who does it. They think it's funny."

Susan said, "I don't think they mean any harm." She was the only WASP, but she took up for almost anyone anyhow. "They're just stupid—of course, stupid genes aren't what you want either. Do they do IQ tests?"

Elly assumed so. Anyhow, she had specified not-average in just about every category. She wondered if people ever asked specifically for below-average sperm. There was a lull in the music but the party voices went on. Harvey, Susan and Elly just sat and listened. No single voice stood out. There was some sort of consensus over there that the world was good and fun.

"I'm going to infiltrate them," said Elly. "I'm going to take their genes and turn them into something they can't imagine!"

"*In*filtrate!" said Harvey. "It works the other way, turkey."

"No, listen. Don't be crude. I'm going to take those mobile sperm and do something about their real inertia."

Susan had been thinking, partly about her general WASP guilt and the Hillel doors, partly about her more particular guilt that Harvey was going to have to have half-WASP children, and she said, "If you're really determined, why don't we do it together?"

Harvey turned red.

"No," said Elly.

"Well, really, if you think about it," said Susan, "it makes more sense. Harvey has already been tested for Tay-Sach's. No problem there. And what we could do is you go upstairs and put your knees up. Or however you do it. And Harvey can do his thing and I'll run upstairs with it in the turkey baster."

"One big happy family," said Elly. "And what happens when I want to move to California with Harvey's baby? Forget it."

"Forget it," said Harvey.

It was a little hard to forget and they kept coming back to it over the course of the evening. Was it as simple as thinking a person had a right to be close to his baby and the complications that would ensue? Probably not. Elly had the feeling that she wanted the father to be somehow more universal. Harvey was very particular. She found herself staring at his pores, and his dark lashes. Perfectly acceptable traits. Harvey blushed and looked off nearsightedly into space. Susan said, "Look, I'm sorry I brought it up." They all hugged each other warmly and Elly went home.

At home, though, she couldn't sleep. She didn't even try. She knew she was too wired to lie down, so she put on her baggy sweatshirt and jeans and sneakers and went for a walk. The town fell off into the night very quickly and stayed as a rosy glow in the moist air. The brick streets turned into macadam lined with tiger lilies and the ferns of wild asparagus and tight, neat barb wire fences. You could hear the cows munching grass slowly through the night over the distant party murmur. There were intermittent stars, pale as moth dust and the moon came and went. The road was straight and easy; she didn't need any more light than the cloudy sky provided. She was happier than she had been for a long time.

Then a carful of beery boys came careening out of town going very, very fast. She got in the ditch to watch it pass and the lights sped by her and off toward Indiana. The sound of the speed pulled something like her heart out of her in fear. God! Make them make it around the curve to the bridge, she prayed, over the hill you can't see over, through the four-way stop.

Out on the country road, you could hear that one car for a long way, roaring, downshifting, roaring and fading. No screech. No crash. But still, Elly's chest was tight with fear. There was so much death in her family! Far, far more death than life. How could she dare to hope?

How could *she* dare to hope? What made her special? That was what she needed to know now. Being the only child of a survivor? And who was this survivor? An average little man, a botanist who loved pink flowers that suddenly, one generation and not another, had a streak of white in their petals. A methodical man, who kept notebooks of pressed grasses that no one was ever interested in—to his astonishment, his dismay and finally his unmitigated scorn. "What do they know?" he asked. "What do *they* know?"

She was almost out to where the road curved down to the bridge. Here came the beery boys screeching and thundering across the loose planks on the old trestling. They gunned their motor up the hill toward her. Survivors, too. She stepped respectfully into the ditch again.

Their muffler had a hole in it and they were singing what seemed to be various loud songs. They were making enough noise to wake the dead and off they went again toward town, leaving her in the darkening night with all the absence. She turned back too. She never could think of what her family's deaths had been like. She did not even know what their lives had been like. Her father had told her years ago, when she first began to know what made her special, "Death always comes at the end of every life. But life doesn't have to show its face in all this death. When it does, that's the miracle." And the empty future, too, was full of deaths. It was very ordinary, death.

Elly could feel the sky beginning to dissolve: far apart, small drops at first, mostly she heard them on the leaves along the fences. The road out was so easy she had not really noticed the stars' disappearing. She could smell the dirt in the fields, the fresh cowpies, the warm cows themselves.

It began to pour and she had no choice but to get as wet as everything else. She remembered looking at Harvey tonight—when she thought he was too particular to be the father. And now she knew for sure what she half knew then: this was not the time to worry about losing anything, because she could provide a past with no help from anyone. Any daughter of her father's (and she was the only one) could pass on their blood alone. What she wanted now was something like this undiscriminating rain. She would take her chances with what the world had to offer—assuming that nothing is more delicious than holding your average miracle in your arms.

"I'm going to have a baby," she said to the night.

"And you're going to be the father," she said to the rain.

MAYDAY, JONES'S GARDEN

You're Supposed to Be Feeling Good

Did Karen Jones first see Jones's Garden in the company of nineteen other survivalists rounding the point of Hall Island under oar, or rather from behind the wing of a plane settling down towards Rockland over a brilliant sea? She was never sure. Forehead to the window of the plane, she had said to herself — One of those rocks is for me — with some of the old anticipation of King of the Mountain, and unexpectedly susceptible to the beauty of the Maine coast with its sunken mountaintops darkly dotting the blue water. The only islands Karen had seen were small stands of woodland where the cattle stood on hot days in the vast pastures, or that had been saved to slow the wind across the cornfields.

Then, pulling on her oar, in rhythm with the others, it occurred to her that Dave the straight, headman Dave, was the sort who would set her on this particular rock when he charted the dispersal of the group for solos. —Bet they save this one for you, Kare, said her beautifully matched oarmate. Matched in height, weight and even motivation by careful Dave. Karen was sent by her mother, the other girl by her father, and the

129

letters of application had told him almost to the erg how much muscle each would apply to her oar. Dave's business was to see that the boats and everything else went straight. So these well-matched oarpeople pulled together all day and in the evenings loved being so much alike. One thing about this other person, though, was annoying to Karen; she slipped so easily into the community. First she gave up makeup, then smoking, and she was very vocal about how close she was to giving up meat. Karen fiercely maintained her identity. As she looked at the ration of twelve matches in a plastic baggy Dave was handing her, she was glad not to have to make choices, having thought to bring her Cricket lighter.

—Have your water stashed away? Dave asked. Karen flipped the top of her knapsack to show the tops of five plastic shampoo bottles.

—Good girl, said Dave. —Remember to ration. Five bottles isn't much. Now somebody will be here for a health check early tomorrow. So you shouldn't have any problems. This is a great little island. The one I'd choose for myself. You'll see.

Karen looked around her at the scrubby hill. —Some garden, she said.

—Garden of Eden. True Paradise. Euell went bananas when he saw it. You'll be ten pounds heavier when we pick you up. I promise you.

Karen shrugged and looked down at her self pressing against the army shirt and bush pants. In fact, it had gotten hot, and she could not see her nipples anymore, except almost.

—My god, I almost forgot to give you your flag.

—Oh wow. You almost did, she said and went back with him to the launch.

—My memory must have been flagging.

—Ha Ha.

—Bad. Bad. Well, here it is. Where you ought to put it is the top of the hill. Then nobody will bug you, because they just won't land. They really respect your privacy hereabouts.

Fishermen know the rewards of being alone. Boat people all know about the solos, too. If they just know you're here they'll stay clear. So be a good girl and we'll be seeing you.

—O.K. Dave. Sure.

—Taking this solo in your stride, Miss Jones of Jones's Garden?

—Well?

—Good stuff, he said.

She stood and waited for him to wave. He did and she waved back as the launch left the cove and disappeared into the smoky haze.

Get that flag up now . . . With seventy-two hours to go, what's the hurry? Just use up the only thing you have to do all at once.

But anyhow, she did it. She found a piece of driftwood tall enough and tied the bandanna to it; then she wedged it between two large rocks on the top of the little hill. Sitting beside it, she unpacked her knapsack neatly all around the flag. Of the five plastic bottles only two held water. The Johnson's Baby Shampoo, vinegar and Flex Creme Rinse she pulled closer to her, thinking of clean hair, lit a cigarette and contemplated her aloneness. So this was it. The flag was up and there was nothing to do. The island was small; she had better save that activity. Her hair was not as dirty now as it would be in a few hours. The water would be cold. It was hot already. The heaviness was hot. The haze was like a curtain, a shower curtain for a steaming bath with filmy scenes of islands and firs and little boats around her. Aloneness was the thing. How was she to cope with seventy-two hours of this? Twenty-four would be more than enough to learn whatever she was supposed to learn. If it was this hot at nine o'clock what would it be like at noon? She stood up and took off her shirt and lifted the faces of her heavy breasts to look at the sun. They were white . . . They would be better brown. She pinched their noses. Then she kissed them on the lips. —Sweet thing. Sweet thing.

—God. You'll blow that, too, in the first hour. You need a cold shower. She walked slowly down through her filmy shower curtain with its Oriental decor of haze, rocks, flat water and the fading, crisscrossing lines of a wake where a lobsterboat motored back and forth nearby. The rockweed did not stay put on the boulders she had to cross to reach the water, and, finally, she had to lower herself onto her hands and slither feet first, in a kind of four-limbed walk so that her butt would stay dry, toward the patch of smooth rocks. They were less smooth than they seemed at a distance; so she did not sit down or even take her shoes off when she reached them. She had cooled down without the sea; baby barnacles crunched under her docks like the bits of shell that peel off a perfect hard-boiled egg. Looking out across the smooth Muscongus, she thought of slipping a hard-boiled egg with a little salt into her mouth.

—Oh shit, she said and sat down quickly to take off her docksiders and wickdry socks. —It's only going to be barnacles. She rolled up her pants enough to stick her feet in the water. Instantly, her head ached and her nipples pointed straight out to sea. —That's all I'm going to get is barnacles.

What she needed was a radio (that was what she decided about nine-thirty) for company or to keep her mind off it. Solitude and self-sufficiency. Survival. She was uncertain about her responsibility to communicate her experience to the group. On the final night did they sit around a candle and, each one, reduce seventy-two hours to a minute? Did anyone say —All I wanted for seventy-two hours was to turn on the radio and groove. Did anyone say —I put up my flag and took off my shirt and was horny for seventy-two hours? How did they get through it? They are all sitting in a circle, listening intently, and someone is saying how he saw it, chewing on sea oats, looking for gooseberries and mussels to eat, watching a gull fish effortlessly and unsuccessfully, how he was that gull. —Wow. That's how it was man, they all say.

What she needed was a radio. And what a bust with all the

radios around she couldn't have one. What a bust and what a pity.

Making Believe

(NOAA Weather Radio for the state of Maine has high prose standards. Weather is to entice.)

July is bringing another lustrous day of typical summer weather into our tri-state area, but a threat of thundershowers beclouding our prospects for the immediate future should bring relief for Sunday.

Forecast for southwestern interior Maine including Portland and vicinity. Hazy skies with a chance of late afternoon or evening thundershowers. Winds light and variable throughout the morning and afternoon shifting to northwest with the . . .

(The big 10-W switch flicks over and for miles around the air is shivering —You on Zak? Come in Zak. You seen our mermaid?)

When I Stop Dreaming

About the same moment, one maiden aunt and her younger sister were packing a lunch for themselves and the brother-in-law husband to take on a fishing trip. Ednah took the mayonnaise from the frigidaire which lurched into action, adding its shudder to the roar of the fan dragging the smell of bacon out of the kitchen and into the woods. —Oh my, said her younger sister, I dream of silence. I cannot abide this racket. I want to sit in my chair and listen to a few birds, not many, mind you, just a few.

—Why don't you go on out then? I can do this.

—Well, and why should you? Your last day. I'll just turn

them off. She switched off the fan and unplugged the refrigerator.

—Martha, you goose, what are you doing? Ednah was feeling the odors settle down into her white hair and over her shoulders.

—Many's the time, said Martha. —Nothing spoils and I rather like the smell of bacon.

It was cooked already. They fished it out of the pan and onto a brown paper bag to dry. With a serrated spatula from L.L. Bean's, they spread their homemade type bread with homemade style mayonnaise. They sliced very ripe tomatoes into a plastic container and separated leaves of lettuce between damp towels, which they wrapped in plastic. The now crisp bacon they put into a baggy. Those were their sandwiches. —They do take up more room this way, but I can't abide soggy sandwiches, said one of them.

—Should we buy something to have on hand in case we don't catch any mackerel?

—What an idea, Martha!

—There's not much except eggs.

—You are too practical. The problem will be catching too many fish, deciding with whom to share them, whether or not to filet them all.

—I could offer some to Mrs. Thibault when I pick up the lemon tarts and our blueberry pie.

—You are going now? Why don't I come and just poke my head in at the realtors' to see what they are thinking about my offer.

—I shouldn't do that if I were you, seem so eager.

—They know I'm eager already. What harm could it do? I would really like to have some idea before going back to the city. It is the perfect house for me, so close; I would even pay their price.

—That's precisely what you are not supposed to let them know.

—Well, I'll just come in the car with you anyhow. And if I

go to the realtors' I do, and if I don't I don't.

—That seems almost reasonable. I don't suppose it matters if you spend all that money anyhow. Money from heaven like that hardly counts.

—From heaven! From mental anguish. And it certainly counts. It is probably the accomplishment of my life. Those policemen will think twice before calling anyone a nutty old crab or a batty old bag again. And forty thousand dollars is not to be sneezed at.

—No, indeed it isn't . . . Let's go and spend some of it on tarts and pie and see what happens to the rest.

These two sisters were dressed in soft cotton dresses. They both wore stockings in spite of the heat. Martha wore deck shoes and Ednah wore saddle shoes with pink soles. Both were ample but solid ladies who did not jiggle very much when they walked. They took Martha's car to go into the village, rolling the windows down to dispel the heat and the odor, which was a combination of forest and machine. —Look what you're growing, sister, said Ednah.

Martha looked where she pointed and then leaned down to look more closely at the delicate mushrooms pushing through the carpet. —Oh my, I *am* slowing down, aren't I? She started the car and they went on into the village, passing the little white house sprouting a For Sale sign on its lawn.

—I can't think of anything more perfect, said Ednah.

—It is a sweet house. And it will be nice to have you near us.

—Close but not too close.

They bought the tiny chess tarts for their picnic and the blueberry pie hot from the oven for their dinner. Then they promised Mrs. Thibault some fish. —But while I'm here, I might as well pick up a little hamburger, just in case, said Martha.

—If you buy a hamburger, I am going to go next door and buy a house.

—You do what you want and I'll do what I want.

So the two parted for a few minutes and both took a little longer than expected.

The news at the butcher's counter was that there was a mermaid sighting.

—Well, what in the world does that mean?

—Some naked hippies more'n likely.

—Heard there was a whale out there, too.

—Yup, that was the goony bird boat seen that. She was spoutin for the tourists off Tenants Harbor.

—It sounds like an exciting day on the water, said Martha, as she waited for the beef to be ground. —Who saw the mermaid?

—Some fellows blessed with a powerful signal, I guess. They cut in on everything when they saw her. Lost half the weather report. Just some no account hippies running around half-dressed is what I think. Naked people on welfare all over the place this summer.

—I hadn't seen any.

—You don't see what you're not looking for.

—That butcher is such a moralizer, Martha said to Ednah when they met at the car. —Do you think that is what happens when you cut off your fingers?

—Couldn't be worse than my real estate agent. She wouldn't just call up and offer them the whole price. She said we'd made an offer and it was our duty to stick to it. I wanted it settled so it wouldn't tease me all day.

—You tease too easy and all day will be half over before we get to the boat.

—Isn't that about right? When does Hen expect us?

—Oh, about now. He wanted to tidy up and listen to the weather. The new forecast doesn't come on until ten. Then he was going to make up his mind whether or not we'd go.

—You mean there's a chance we won't? After all this. What could be the matter with the weather? A little muggy, that's all, no wind to chill us.

—The six o'clock said thunderstorms late in the day.

—But if we're going in the middle.
—Yes, I'm sure we'll go.

Making
Believe

for the Maine and New Hampshire coastal waters from
Eastport to the Merrimack River and twenty-five miles off
shore for Saturday the tenth of July, winds light and variable
ten knots or less this morning, onshore in the afternoon,
shifting

Time Keeps on Slipping
Slipping Slipping

Zak was hauling traps along the deep shore of Morse Island
with the Top Ten turned on full volume. The Eagles were playing something strong and cluttered, with a rhythm useless to
his work. He used a simple block and tackle powered by his
own lazy arms. The rewards did not justify speed. He threw
out a few shorts, kept a cull. He might not get many lobsters
but he could get Instant Weather, or with his CB, he could talk
to his buddies on land and sea. Or he could run those radios
low, standing by while the bass of his AM or stereo tape deck
outdid the motor in feeding his soul. He had a low soul, a bass
spirit (a deep being?). His heart throbbed especially for pis-
tons or a good bass section.

He worked in stiff waterproof pants and boots to keep the
stinking bait off his jeans. His naked torso was sweating from
minimal exertion and not evaporating; the air was already saturated. He ran the motor full throttle over to his next string of
traps, stopping abruptly, hooking his line with a lethal homemade bait hook, hauling it in, finding no keepers, spearing the
redfish into the bait boxes and letting the line slip away behind
him, leaving a brilliant pot buoy, bobbing for a moment before

the immense calm flattened his wake. Only running full-throttle through the haze cut into it, split apart for a moment the dense air which closed behind him, heavier now with his music and sweat. He quit.

When he quit there were still five or six traps stacked in the back of his big skiff. He had intended to set them today, but it hardly seemed worth the effort in the heat with the luck he had been having. He had his fork and hods, the tide was right, there would be more to be made on clamming today. He switched his set on Call.

—Come in Knucks . . . You on?

—By Jesus, what a loser. Where you been? Come in.

—I been right here. Come in.

—Been hollerin every goddam frequency I got. I seen a mermaid. Come in.

—No foolin. Come back.

—No foolin. Been hollerin all mornin. Thought you was dead. Come back.

—Not me. Just tuned in the rousin lobster music but didn't rouse no lobsters. Come in.

—I been thinkin mighty serious now of clammin. Come back.

—Sounds good. Come in.

—Knew we'd get us one someday. Come back.

—Yup. Come back.

—I'm pretty near there. Come in.

—Give me twenty minutes. Come back.

—Roger. This is over and out.

Making
Believe

A weak frontal system will be dissipating over the forecast waters with lingering fog over George's Banks and the colder shelf waters. A high pressure area located over the Great

Lakes should be moving off shore by early evening, preceded by some thunder shower activity. Winds south at ten to fifteen knots, changing

Still
Crazy

Jane was hanging over the edge of the cockpit locker stowing oranges against the hull. She kept them in place with a wall of six-packs and bottles of apple juice, and placed a few heads of lettuce, some green beans, summer squash on top of them. The less fragile provisions, potatoes, onions, carrots, apples had been stowed last night with the cans of emergency food. Sal was asleep in her carrying basket in the forward cabin. Dick just slipped alongside the Gypsy in the dinghy and started to lift the canvas bags over the coaming.

—I wonder what Hank's going to be like, after all this time, said Jane inside the locker.

—I can't hear you, Dick said, climbing aboard carefully, so that the bags of paper diapers, the extra charts, the sleeping bags would not be kicked over.

—Oh God, more stuff. We'll never get off. That better be it. Anything more to go in here? Jane had pulled herself back out of the narrow opening.

—No, that's it. What did you say?

—I was just wondering about Hank, what he's like now.

—He sounded pretty much the same on the phone, more pompous, maybe. But that could be the phone. Here, you go below and I'll hand you this junk. Then we'll pick up and go.

They went out under motor. The wind was almost nonexistent and on the nose. Jane stowed systematically and in silence so the baby wouldn't wake up. With luck there were at least a couple hours of peace, more if the motion of the boat were right. Thinking of the baby sleeping now and of Hank sailing from somewhere to the rendezvous at the end of this day, she could not shake the image of him burping his son on his shoulder or scraping pablum back up to an eager mouth which pushed most of it out again. Ellen had not left yet but she might as well have. Ellen's face, older, she had just seen, but she could not imagine Hank older, pompous? Ellen had stood in the door for a minute, unfairly, knowing who was in the bed. It was probably written on the chart she had in her hand, but Jane had no idea who this was in her white coat, in this hospital in this town.

—Hi Janey, the woman said.

—Ellen! There she was then sitting on the end of the bed squeezing the toes that stuck straight up under the covers. — How are you?

—How are *you*? I saw your baby, she seems fine. Does your episiotomy hurt?

—My what?

—Stitches. Your stitches.

—God yes, like broken glass.

—They'll bring you a heatlamp today, a little Florida vacation in bed. Was it bad?

—Awful. Well, they said it wasn't bad. Easy.

—You'll forget.

—Did you?

—Yes, but I'm in this business to remember.

—You're a full-grown doctor now?

—The resident in OB.

—It's been a long time.

—How many years?

—I dasn't count. What about Hank and the baby? Do you see them?

—The baby! That shows how long it's been. Roy is the Compleat Boy now. Last I saw him there were great big teeth growing in the gaps in his grin.

—You do see them?

—Not so much. It's hard for me to get away now, but

they'll stay here a bit in the summer. They sail down east. They'll stop here and take showers.

—Really? We grew out of dinghys too. We're going to try to cruise with the baby this summer.

A nurse had come in and gone to the other bed, checking that everything was in order, then she had pulled the curtain between the two.

—Looks like you're going to have company.

—That's good. I thought I would be able to read but my mind is frazzled. I brought *Don Quixote* but I think he got lost in the labor room.

—You threw it at the OB. It's the story of the day at the hospital. And when he picked it up and everybody was laughing at you, you kept yelling "Give me back my Quixote." They had some time convincing you you didn't need it anymore. In fact, that's how I knew you were here, you were you. Not just any Jane Brown, but this one.

Jane Brown enjoyed that last sentence in how she remembered the conversation. Even if what went before changed, it always came back to this: that someone had seen her, that she had not imagined all that scene she was forgetting with the pain, that it was how she was found by her friend. It was true, then, that she had asked the nurse when the contractions were too much to bear, at least, too much to read by, that being her previous model of misery, if it was almost over. —That's nothing, sweetheart. You felt nothing yet. You just getting started. Jane Brown was there. Jane Brown had been there. Someone had seen her and told someone else who could tell her about it.

When she had thrown the worn out book, had she come as close as she ever would to Don Quixote in his very clear knowledge of what he should be and do? Most likely, and now the pain with its knowledge was forgotten. That ecstasy had hidden. As he said, there were no birds this year in last year's nests. And when the question: why am I here? for what? for whom? descended she had to fish back in her head for someone to tell her that the maddest thing she could do with her life was to let herself die, just like that, without anybody killing her, but just finished off by her own melancholy.

—What are you doing down there? Nothing?

—Hardly. I'm stowing. (The rest of the question: when that kind of knowledge is forgotten, will a new one come to hold things together?)

—There's got to be a limit to how long you can stow.

—I don't know what it is then. There's still stuff loose.

One more thing she could not have found if she were looking for it: the air was hot, and, except for the night nurse and a crying baby, only she was awake. And the crying baby cried and cried until she knew whose it was, hers, because her milk had not come in, and it was starving. So she got up and walked down the long hall, very slowly, because of the broken glass between her legs; when she got to the nursery, she could not tell which baby was Sally. One was still crying and crying. No real Sally was crying as she was stowing. The starving baby in the nursery had not been hers (said the nurse); still, here came her milk now, in answer to what?

When I Was Just
a Little Boy

The Auk was reaching ever so slowly across the Gulf. She seemed harder to move than she was. The miracle was that she moved at all.

—Hey, Dad, said Roy from the hanging locker, where he was tangled in monofilament and spinning lures.

—Yes?

—You won't believe what I just heard.

—That seems likely.

—Some guy's going to see a mermaid.

—No kidding. That's great! Hey, that's really a good one. But I told you not to fool with the set.

—I didn't. I bumped it.

—Did you bump it back the way it was?

—Yup.

—Is the tape recorder still going?

—Yup.

—That's all you're supposed to do. Change the tapes every half hour, right?

—Will the part about the mermaid be on there?

—Unless you screwed it up.

—I didn't. We can listen to it later?

—When I transcribe it.

—Then you'll see I'm right. Hey, Dad?

—What?

—I can't do this. I need your knife.

—You can't have it. Bring the stuff here. I'll do it.

—I can't.

—Of course you can. Why can't you?

—It's all tangled up in the radio wires.

—Christ . . . You just leave it alone and come and take the tiller.

—Wait a minute.

—No, you do it now. This is a good time.

—The tape just stopped. I have to change it.

—O.K. Well, switch the channel and see what you're getting.

—Nothing. Doesn't seem like anybody's talking on the lobster channel today. Except the people about the mermaid. You're probably going to have just a lot of empty tapes again.

—Just my luck they'd switch to CB the year I finally get a grant.

—Why don't we buy a CB? We really need a CB.

—You may be right.

—Maybe it was a grant to buy a CB.

—May be.

—When can we get one? We could get one in Camden.

—Maybe.

Momma Don't Take
My Kodachrome

Karen, with no radio and an ice cream headache without
any ice cream, was in no mood for maybes, for revery, for
slipping into someone else's head and out again. The sea was
insufficient. She turned back to her island. Clearly the bram-
bles hid berries and god knows what else. She was not particularly hungry, but sort of understood that if all she was going to
get was berries (and barnacles) a great deal of time would be
consumed in the process, more, perhaps, than berries. She
thought of a motto to scribble on the next john wall she should
be faced with: "Eating Sucks." She chuckled a little over her
future puzzled readers, who had not faced survival, and then
wondered if she had made any noise laughing. She could not
really remember if she had said anything since Dave left; she
had the idea that it was all right to talk to yourself as long as
you did not answer, and so, silently crossed the rockweed to
the low rocks that hid the berry bushes.

The gooseberries were like jewels dangling in the scrub.
They were red and veined in the way magazines showed man-
made stones "star sapphires" — "star rubies?" Best, though,
they popped cordially, sourly, sweetly under her tongue. Always ready for a little fling, it clucked and sucked and she
devoured several handfuls of gooseberries before even coming
upon the blueberries and the raspberries, so ripe that they fell
off the bush as she brushed it. Dave was right about abun-
dance, but that it was healthy she doubted. Her mother would
have given her Kaopectate before, during, and after such a
meal, she was sure. It was packed in with her traveling things
but certainly had not occurred to Karen as a necessity for iso-
lation. Somehow, it had seemed a cure for a social disease
connected with traveling, not unlike her spasmodic picking up
people, something that could not be helped if one was in trains
and planes and stations and streets for any length of time.

—Well, Mother, you've got me this time, she said. —I'll have a hard time picking anybody up on this rock. She sat down where the sand came into the gooseberry bushes and picked a few more clusters of fruit, which she draped over her ears in the manner of the grapejuice-ad lady from the Finger Lakes. Unbuttoning one of her many baggy pockets, she took out a sterling compact which she carried for the mirror. A signal mirror was required. This was an old loose-powder compact her mother had been given when she was presented to society. On it her grandmother had had engraved "Know Thyself" which was the sort of exhortation Karen always expected to hear from the old lady, who, last seen was wearing her veiled hat and white gloves in the rec room at the nursing home, sitting bolt upright as if afraid of dissolving, becoming a puddle on the floor. Karen had kissed her and accepted her "Better Late than Never" gracefully as a sort of benediction. The mirror was very good and very clear, no powder had been near it for twenty years, at least, and it reflected the gleam of the berries over Karen's ears to her great pleasure and the little beads of glow (such a high-toned mirror it was) over her lip to her annoyance, but she licked them off without malice, even, perhaps, pleasure again? Aiming the little mirror for new vistas, she glimpsed the tip of her gooseberry-pink nipple blending with the berries dangling from her ear. She ate that bunch thinking the blueberries and raspberries together would be more becoming but very hard to wear, a precarious balancing act even if she lay down. And she stood up dropping berries.

Making
Believe

July's parsimonious grip on moisture (revised version; originally "parsimonious nature") may be loosening, bringing relief for our drought-stricken farmers. An advancing cold

front over the Great Lakes Region offers the threat of thundershowers late this afternoon.

At 10:00 AM, the temperature at Portland International Air-
port is 82, that's 27 celsius. Winds from the south at one knot.
Barometric pressure 29.75 and steady. Skies are hazy.

(For what other life was he keeping his opinions of
things?)

Handy Man

The Merry Maid was gleaming, gloriously gleaming when
the ten o'clock went out. She picked up her glint from the
general luminescence of the hazy day and the sparkle in her
captain's eye. He had swabbed her with her own dew hours
before and no salt spot marred her new varnish. He was fussy.
How had he gotten so fussy? It came with his gallantry and his
love of sharp knives and polished copper. Birthright or toilet-
training? Not passed on to his own children's nature anyhow;
whereas he would be pertinacious about certain details, certain
perfections of technique, they would be gently, obdurately
sloppy, like Martha. Anyhow, he loved them and they were
living their mysterious lives in faraway places, sending letters
which seemed to please Martha more or less, like everything
else.

At the moment, he was deeply pleased with his varnish. He
ran his hand over it, and if he still bent easily, would have lain
his cheek on it or even considered a slow childish lick. Such
smoothness. A fishing expedition was not what he would have
chosen to initiate the finish. But it couldn't be helped; everything coincided, the good drying days of the beginning of the
week, the perfect picnic time and tides, Ednah's imminent de-
parture. What a fool for a fish she was. He could not actively
hope against her pleasure but switched on the updated
weather, thinking, perhaps, the thunderstorms were upon
them.

There was no change; the storms were still for much later,

when they would be safely back here on their mooring, cleaning their mackerel if they caught any fish, after all. People were getting them at the mouth of the river. He pulled his old duffer's hat on tighter and leant over to untie the dinghy from the stern of the launch. He would take it ashore and organize the new lures in the tackle box. Then he could load the rods and lifejackets and be ready for Martha and Ednah's arrival; though they would be late. Each was reasonably efficient on her own, but together they managed to lose track of time, added errands, or forgot things which necessitated retracing their steps.

He floated idly in the dinghy, drifting along his boat to examine the varnish. Not a speck of dust broke the smooth golden mirror of her gunwales. He felt fear begin to mount from under his heart and did not try to escape its flood. How much longer will it be that I can keep this boat (or she me)? My powers slip away. Is this the last time I can take her down to the wood? In a few years, will the strength be gone from my hands, or will I even see the dust invading the brightness I can now lay on with smooth, long strokes? He knew that without the strength to leave his little bay, puttering around it would suffice him, but never in the Merry Maid gone shoddy. Without the gleam and polish of all his summers, she would be dying as fast as he. While with meticulous care constantly given she was immortal; bungs, planks, caulking over the years had been replaced by his own hands, working with the boat yard keeper who was his ally (but not his mercenary, he could never afford not to do the work himself).

When finally everything had been replaced once (it must have happened), was she still the same boat? He noticed his fear had dissipated for a moment. Was the river the same river, the sea the sea? Of course, only he might drown, let his boat turn to kindling on a shore. There was no holding it off, the tide of regret for what had not yet happened, his heart beat audibly (he the only hearer) and he shut his eyes to fix the hazy color to this summer morning with the golden boat awaiting passengers.

Looking for
Blue Eyes

The terrible stink came from the young gull that sat there blinking in the berry bushes. It seemed to list to one side but compensated with its head in her direction. It made no sound and seemed to be waiting for Karen to do something. She thought she would vomit. Controlling herself with either curiosity or mercy, she picked up a stick and poked it to see if it could move. It fell farther over, still looking at her, and she saw its legs were crushed and rotten. There were bugs on them. How could she nurse it? There was no hope, really, even if its affliction were not disgusting, how could she set its legs, teach it to fly, regurgitate chewed fish for it? She liked the way it looked at her, expectancy excited her. What might she do? If it had a chance to live, why not with her? Maybe she was making a pickup on this island after all. What if she came home with a bird in a box. —Well, Mother, I couldn't leave it there. She went toward the water to look for some little snails to feed it. When she had crushed them on the rocks and extracted the soft meat which she took back to the bird, it was dead.

She kicked sand on it to kill the fetid odor that seemed now to hang around her head, in her hair. She swept her hair with her hands and decided on the long-awaited shampoo. How long had she managed to put it off? Certainly, that was another of her mother's admonitions. Save something. You have to be careful. She would save plenty of shampoo, at least, for tomorrow; though she understood that that was the least symptom of her carrying-on. —If you carry on like I don't know what, what do you think will be left for you to do after you get married? —Isn't there always something left to do? —That is exactly where perversity comes from. That is exactly why you have to be careful. Karen had carefully saved some island, some berries (she had not saved the bird); now she would save some shampoo. No pervert she.

On the top of the little hill, shampoo, rinse, vinegar, towel in hand, brush stuffed in a deep pocket, she looked around and saw two boats converging slowly toward the island, or the buoyed passage along it, or the cove, or the other island, or the other island protecting the cove.

The one spot they could not be approaching was the southern tip, away from the cove and the ocean. The water was held there in long tubs between the parallel broken ledges. There was no passage because of outlying rocks, no entrance to shelter, only inviting clear pools.

They drew her down from her king spot on the rock, where she could see Jones's Garden jumbled at her feet, roses and berries and bay. She walked the narrow path that lay along the spine of the island leading to the ledges. Other people must come here, she thought, but not doubting the powers of her flag, motionless scarf on a pole, she stripped when she reached the end of the island. That is, she took off her bush pants, with all the pockets; she had not worn a shirt for hours. Where had she left it, she wondered. With the pack most likely. She supposed she might get a haze burn and had better wear it when she was done shampooing.

The water was warmer where it had been sliding in and out of the rocks, and she was able to slip into it and lie on her back while her hair spread out in the water, like some fine seaweed, or the gills of goose barnacles. She lathered it, not very successfully, because the salt water would not make voluptuous mounds of bubbles, but she could feel that it was working. She performed the whole ritual, two sudsings, a cream rinse, and then a dash of vinegar to remove the film left by the inefficient combination of salt water and shampoo. Then she lay there in her pool, blinking up at the pale blue traces of sky in the haze. It was really beautiful. What would she do with it?

Now I Would Not
Give You False Hope

—Dad, said Roy. Why do people talk about mermaids if
there aren't any?

—I don't know.

—Do you think it is a secret code?

—A secret code for what?

—Well, they didn't sound like nice people. They sounded
tough, like smugglers.

—Smuggling what?

—I don't know, Dad. I just am wondering.

—Like always. How about if you pay attention and don't
make such a mess with the fish line this time.

—I didn't do that. It just happened.

—That's what I mean. Pay attention and you can keep it
from just happening.

—The only other person I ever heard say mermaid was the
library lady. They were in the kind of story she used to like.
Girl stuff.

—Imagination isn't girls' exclusive property.

—You know what I mean. Not talking straight. Not about
real things.

—Like fish line?

—Like fish line.

Hank handed the rod minus tangles to Roy, who left the
tiller for a seat on the transom, where he could troll behind the
slow Auk.

—She's making about a knot and a half, don't you think,
Dad?

—If we're lucky.

—That's a good speed for catching fish. Isn't it, Dad?

—A lot better for that than for getting anywhere.

—What made people make up mermaids, Dad?

—I don't know. Most likely somebody saw one once and didn't know he couldn't have seen one.

—Weird.

—Of course, he could have asked his Daddy and then there wouldn't have been any mixup.

—Why didn't he?

—Maybe they didn't have Dads in the good old days. Just Moms.

—Aw come on. Why didn't he ask somebody? You know what I mean.

—How the hell do I know? Maybe the other person saw her too.

—How many people would have to see one before there'd be one?

—Jesus, Roy, you wear me out.

—There's got to be an answer to that one.

—There probably is. We'll get a book when we get home.

—What if it's not in a book.

—Then you're going to have to make it up. I'm tired of knowing everything.

Like why the sea is boiling hot and whether pigs have wings.

And what in the name of God was he doing with a little boy in the middle of this heavy calm, where every question the boy asked fell only on his ears, or, when he turned off, as he had now, would pass through him spreading pulsing circular waves out through the haze as far as voice would carry. The damage Roy would do with a CB! Everybody within ten miles would go crazy with anxiety over his questions. Except that wasn't really the question. It was the responsibility for answering that frustrated, almost physically. No more touching, I can't respond! Something would have to be thrown off, away, to lighten the air he breathed. And there sat his boy, looking down the line to his lure, jerking it up and right, up and left, up and right, expecting the fish any instant now, gathered to strike when it touched his hook.

Let a Working
Girl Lay Down

Jane emerged from the cabin expecting her milk to subside if she could change the subject.

—No way anything is going to come unstowed down there.

—The time you spent I should hope not.

—It's the only way to do it. Right. The first time. Otherwise it's a waste of time.

—We've got plenty of that on our hands. We'll never get anywhere today.

—I'm eager to see Hank and his baby.

—Well, no real problem. We can always get there under motor, and we're not due before four.

—That old boat of his is probably not so fast either.

—You'd be surprised. Some of the old ones go. If she's balanced, that's what counts, and he'll be reaching. He'll do a lot better than we.

—Are we going to put the sails up?

—Thought we'd nose out around the point and hope the tide is still going. We could pick up a little that way.

—I don't think it will be. Look at the ledges. Dead low.

—Well, slack anyway. We can still make that passage sailing if it is slack. How come we're always late? A real sailor would never miss a tide.

—Who do you know that's a real sailor?

—Well, you see them going by at the crack of dawn, or coming in out of the fog on a perfect course for the buoy. You know the ones. No crud. No diapers and soda pop, for instance.

—Just whisky neat, right?

—Right.

—And at least ten feet more on their boats, right?

—They're the ones.

—Well, it's not us, honey, and you might as well admit it. Even before the diapers there was some kind of little slack in our timing.

—You think we're hopeless?

—Hopeless? To whom? Who cares? We're going to get around this point somehow or other.

—Style is what you lack. You've no sense of style. The way to do things is terrifically important. Especially in boats.

—Go look at my stowing. Except you can't. Everything is completely put away.

—Well, that's it, and I'll never find it. You've got to master some style that communicates with somebody besides yourself.

—You're getting nasty. You're just hopeless at finding things and you won't admit there might be some system there.

—Method in your madness.

—If you will.

Beginning to seethe, she climbed on top the cabin and lay down between the hand rail and the hatch. Her face was forward, so she would catch the breath of air they generated moving out into the bay.

—Thanks for the dirty feet, said Dick. They were bare, dangling over the compass.

—You're mighty welcome, she said and shut her eyes. Had Ellen, in fact, left in anger; that was what she really doubted. Ellen could take shit as well as she, and make it for return. Ellen did not have the faults that subjected Jane to this particular maddening exchange. Look how she had pulled herself together and gotten out to medical school. Jane started contracting her belly muscles rhythmically, isometrically; she really had no desire to be tubby. Hold to ten, relax, lift it up off the deck again, hold to ten. What a bore. She decided to try it without counting. That was the supposed merit of this kind of exercise, it could be done anywhere without thinking, with no one suspecting that you, too, might have to do exercises to get rid of an ex-pregnant belly; that you didn't arrive just perfect on the half-shell, Venus Anadyomene without a sag or a wrinkle, half-wit on a scallop shell.

—What's going on up there? How come you're clenching your butt?

—I'm not.

—Yes you are. That's all I can see from here. Dirty feet and a clenching butt.

—I'm doing my exercises.

So much for the privacy theory: at your desk, in a phone booth, behind the wheel of your car, no one need know.

Need anyone know that her breasts were incompetent, her milk had been spilling? No one but Sal because there would not be enough for her if Jane could not stiffen her boundaries, set herself up some way. Which she could. And did. So exhausting.

But There Never Seems to Be Enough Time

The two sisters arrived on the float a few minutes late. They had had to put the hamburger away, and were very tempted to have a piece of blueberry pie. They dawdled. They daydreamed.

How many many berries it takes to make one blueberry pie. Enough for muffins was more possible. Little sister, berrying, do you remember dropping them into tin cups where they rang like soft bells when there were few; it seemed there always were few. Well, we ate every other one and the ones that made it to the cup were named like children until we ran out of names. But when we dumped the cups in Mother's sieve to wash the berries we would say —There's Henry. There's Barbara. —You can't tell, someone always said. —Of course we can. We love them, you said. Or I said.

Hen did not seem impatient from where they stood. Oars

cocked, he had drifted far along the near shore where he was examining the bottom for eel grass, which he hoped was returning. If eel grass returned so would flounder. At least there was very little kelp. Very little eel grass also. Rockweed, full of little clinging sculpins and crabs waiting for the tide to set them afloat again. No, the eel grass could not be said to be gaining.

—Yoohoo, yoohoo, called Martha.

Hen glanced at his watch and started rowing stern first towards them. They stood almost knee deep in a mound of foul weather gear stacked on the wicker picnic basket. It should not be possible to have such a quantity of equipment to bring; yet, as he approached, he began to see Martha's little pillow balanced dryly on top and Ednah's quilted bag in which she carried her glasses and needlepoint and whatever she was reading. He began to scowl.

—Have you girls brought everything in the house?

—Is that why you look so cross? I thought we were pretty smart to bring slickers, if it might storm.

—Now, would I take you out if I thought it was going to storm before we got back?

—Well, we got them this far. We'll bring them just in case.

—I'll put the dinghy on the mooring and bring the Merry Maid in to the float. I don't want to make three trips.

—The tide's not too low to bring the Merry Maid in?

—It's very low. But I know my way around. He rowed off energetically while they began gathering things to take on the boat.

—I'm looking forward to this, said Ednah.

—I know. I am too. Hen and I don't get out so much as we used to. He works a lot on the varnish.

—I never saw her look so pretty, Hen, said Ednah, as he slipped the launch smoothly along the float.

—I took her down to the wood this year. Come on aboard and you'll see your pretty face smile right back at you. He reached out his hand to her and she hiked her skirts and climbed over the gunwales. —Come on now, sister, hop on and give her a little shove, he said to his wife who was struggling to hoist and hike and hop simultaneously and arthritically.

—Give her a hand, Hen.

—You hold the boat.

—What's forgotten?

—Did you remember the lures?

—Daredevils. Got new ones.

—Lunch? That's in the basket.

—Rods? Well we don't need them all anyway.

—We're off. What a treat. What a pleasure.

Blinded by the Light

Karen, opening her eyes, sat up to go look for her shirt and saw two figures on her rock, by her flag, looking her way. She grabbed the towel and bush pants and clasped them to her front. Turning her back, she ran away looking for a jutting ledge to dress behind. As she slid over a sharp stone to shelter, she became aware that she might have covered the wrong side for flight. So much for instinct. And, of course, her shirt was up where they were, so she decided to drape her top with a towel and smoke a cigarette while looking out to sea and hoping they would go away.

Her Cricket performed quickly, and the little blue cloud that she made around herself was soothing. Her injured dignity responded rapidly to the rhythm of smoking, but still she was annoyed at the trespassers, who clearly had been practically standing in her belongings, right next to her flag.

The island had ceased to be completely her own, and it would be some struggle to get it back, if that were possible at all. What did they want? Had they looked like locals or boat people? She realized that she had only half-seen them, her eyes normally being a little slow on the uptake and affected by the bright haze even when shut. She was focusing nicely now, but forced herself to keep staring out to sea, rather than exhibit her curiosity. The sea was terribly boring, and she lit another cigarette. They were certainly men. Was it surprising that they seemed to be standing there with no intention of moving? Did they ever move? They might still be there. Had they laughed at her bare ass? What an ass. She laughed at her bare ass. That was maybe the dumbest thing she had ever done. They sure had an eyeful coming and going. She certainly would not have moved if she had discovered herself, naked like that. Were they still there? She could risk a glance if her hair were across her eyes and she only half-turned as if to stare more comfortably out to sea. They were gone.

Where now? There was a lot of mud on the other side of the island. It would make sense that they be clammers. She had only once tried digging clams and was astounded that they could move faster than she could dig. Never had she actually caught one. The ones that held still were dead or pebbles. Next low tide when the men were gone, she would go out in the mud herself and try again. The impracticality of clamming in the middle of the night struck her. Tomorrow then. That was a long time to eat nothing but berries. The tide would be completely wrong for meals. If she were going to have anything to cook for dinner, now was the time to catch it. She began scanning the rocks around her, not seeing much. This tip of the island was probably too exposed to heavy weather to make a good mussel bed; though the little snails traipsed around everywhere, and the Chinese hats, reputed to taste like erasers, were plentiful. She couldn't sit here all day after all. So she brushed her hair.

Right Before My
Very Eyes

—By Jesus. There she is. All of her.

—What do we do now?

—Clam. We don't have much tide left.

—We could hide. Jesus. Look at her.

—Yeah. That's a good one.

—What's going to happen?

—We're going to see.

—I mean she's going to wake up. We ought to be hiding.

—Clam. We've got to clam, or else we can't be here.

—Right.

—Well, let's get crackin.

—I'd just as leave stand here a piece longer.

—Shit. She's going to feel us looking at her pretty soon.

—There she goes.

—Whooee.

—What an ass.

—What an ass.

—Fuckin right.

—Now what?

—Clams?

—I guess she's not going much further.

—Not likely.

Nobody could see them except themselves. What they saw were rugged, handsome, Robert Redfords or Kris Kristoffersons with the New England gift for sparse but well-placed words. They were the tough progeny of those self-sufficient lobstermen, who were so tough themselves that, if the doctor saw one come into his office, he would forget all the cut fingers and bellyaches and get his adrenalin up for a life and death crisis. They didn't put up with shit, but went straight to the point.

—I don't know about these clams. They're gettin scarce as lobsters.

—Not scarce. Smart.

The water which lay there for a while at the oozing outer reaches of the island, neither retreating nor encroaching, began to inch in thin surges over Zak's black boots. Knucks looked at his slack-jawed friend, who was pursuing not clams with his fork but a half-thought with his eyes across the island.

—Get crackin, he said. —The clams are bout to go for a swim.

—Yup, said Zak and slopped off toward his skiff, which was nuzzling the mud at the edge of the water.

—Where you goin? That's not enough clams. We can dig another hour yet.

—Get my music goin here.

—Oh Jesus that crap.

—Been on low. You didn't even notice. Just make it a little louder.

—Call that a little louder?

—Hey. You don't have to listen. She's goin to like it. You just wait.

Looking for
Blue Eyes

—Dad. They're not biting.

—I see.

—What do you think about my lure?

—Nothing better.

—Can I fish from the dinghy?

—No.

—It's in the way. When I catch a fish, it's going to get all hung up.

—When that happens we'll do something about it.

—It's too hot for my scallop out there. I ought to give it some fresh water.

—Look. Suppose the dinghy came unfastened and you just drifted away.

—You'd come and get me.

—No.

—Poor scallop.

—You didn't change the water this morning?

—I forgot.

—It's going to die. You should have left it where you found it.

—I know it's going to die. Let me go give it some more water. Dad. Come on.

Hank, with long, full arm strokes was pulling in the dinghy.

—Hey Dad. you're fouling my fish line.

—Get that thing in.

—Oh hey no. Maybe it's a fish.

—Get it in then.

—Seaweed.

—O.K . . . . Into the dinghy. Take your rod.

—There aren't any fish out here.

—They're here. You're just not getting them.

—You got this thing tied up tight?

Hank had uncleated the line and swung the free end around his head.

—Come on, Dad. Tie her up.

—I'm just giving you some more line, said his father, who cleated it down again securely and tied a bowline on the back stay with the bitter end.

More line. How had the umbilical cord hooked in his gut? Through a glass window and a plastic box with controls, a red creature a little bigger than a broiler, eyes always closed behind flickering lids, legs lost in a diaper of such a harsh white might it not tear the transparent skin, revealed the pulse in its temple beating nearly double Hank's, an intense determination with no subcutaneous fat, a soul which had thrown itself into the world too fast, too soon, to risk what it was unprepared for, raising Hank's pulse by its helpless sleep until Hank thought his protoplasm could flow out like a medium's and envelop this being whose will outdid his and they could live together. —Get fat, baby. Get fat, he murmured. He was lost in his gaze and did not notice that people were polite about his mumblings and pressed into their own groups to point out little whosy, what a doll and just like her mother. The babies came and went. He stood there for long times. He never got a callous from leaning on the glass. His forehead continued to ache until the day he came back and brought Ellen, and they put the baby, now the size of a roaster, in her arms to take home, not knowing he had become the mother.

Shadow Captain

So boring, the flat calm, for some people, but the duffers were gleefully motoring out the inlet and turning into George's River. The ladies' white crew hats were startling as an advertisement for bleach. They settled themselves, Martha softly on her little pillow and Ednah with her emergency specs around her still long neck and her book, as if someone were about to serve them tea or some other treat in a parlor. One wore a pink cashmere cardigan, the other yellow, colors from a tussie-mussie garden buttoned snugly over full bosoms. Their captain, brother, lover, was discreetly costumed as a native in khaki pants and shirt from the dry-goods store in town. His visor hat was the hat of any captain. It was the way he wore it that set him apart. He stood straight and alert at the controls of his Merry Maid with the cap pulled tight, so the white hair at his temples bristled out over his ears. A beautiful picture, but they had not brought a camera. It was full of shots of the little white house in its garden, and besides, no one of them could leave the scene to capture the composure framed and mirrored in golden varnish. They were in deep water.

—I'm just going to sit here and keep my eyes peeled for naked hippies, said Martha.

—Now that's an odd thing to do.

—Oh no, Hen, said Ednah. It's all over town. We're going out among mermaids and whales today.

—You sisters are touched in the head.

—Never mind.

That was the fierce old librarian who sued the police for libel over remarks made on TV Instant Cam, the batty old bag and crusty old crab of their nightmares. Her fallen geraniums had been eyewitnessed by millions in the tri-state area, who also heard the degrading epithets of the police. It was a wonderful sort of news, as slippery as the weather, the outcome just as uncertain and compelling. This one more exposure of police oppression of the downtrodden had drawn a large group to her defense, many of them she judged hoodlums like the geranium kickers, but hoodlums for justice who were joined in their protests by the lawnorder segment. It was a powerful alliance, but she probably could have won alone.

—You really don't believe us, I suppose.

—I'll believe anything you tell me, Ednah.

—Then I will tell you that the butcher interprets the reports as the inevitable result of our welfare system.

—Where else do you suppose mermaids would be coming from in this day and age?

—I don't know. I am quite taken with the idea.

They were passing near an island which was the last protection of their anchorage. A warm breeze came from it. Martha leaned toward it, breathing deeply.

—Oh my.

—What dear?

—Can't you smell it?

—Ah, now I can. The roses and the bay.

Ednah, who could not smell a thing, looked hard at the shore to try and see the roses, at least. —Do you suppose it is too late to have a garden if you've lost your sense of smell?

Do you forget the other joys of gardening? Setting out berry plants one spring, your surprising warm hand in the dirt was a joy; the dirt was loosening but cool as the end of winter.

You washing my hands like a child's with Ivory soap.

You biting out the dirt.

I remember the smell of the sun when you were in it. Your hair like corn silk brushed my hand.

How did we achieve this balance? What have we achieved?

The golden boat with three passengers turned into George's River to catch mackerel on the rising tide.

Sometimes It's Heaven

When they put up the sails, the shackles along the genny's luff worked smoothly for Jane; the movement of the Gypsy was straightforward and pure, there was a little breeze on the beam. Dick cut the motor and the last clink of the winch was like a tiny bell in the sudden quiet as Jane cleated the halyard.

—I always wonder why I get so bad-tempered. It's the motor. That noise.

Dick had the main up and sheeted the two sails in. —This is nice. If this will only hold we can reach through the passage. I'll have a beer, too.

Jane dug in the locker. —I thought I put them right here on top. No. There we go. She pulled out two beers and handed them to Dick, so she could take off her shirt and shorts and spread out in the sunny haze.

—Better put some cream on. You can burn bad in this stuff.

—You do it.

So they had some nice moments with the breeze just abaft the bow, cool beer, slippery skin.

—We need a steering vane, said Jane. Then we could go below for a little bit.

—You can't set a steering vane in a place like this. We'd be on the rocks. Or run into somebody.

—Then we need to anchor.

—It's seventy-five feet deep.

—Well, you know what I mean. You know what we need.

—We'll just have to make do.

—So many sacrifices.

At the headland which was bold and wooded, they kept their course for the nearby islands marking the other side of the passage; it was such a pleasant point of sail.

—Can this hold, do you think?

—Light and variable is tricky. It's too early to be our afternoon breeze.

—I wish we could just go straight out past the island like this, just forever. This is perfect.

—You can't get there from here.

—We *are* there.

—But we can't stop.

Little squeaks and grunts began to come from below. — There goes Sal.

—Is it time?

—She'll be good, don't you think?

—She always is. She's so good.

Come on, Give
a Little Bit

Karen, her sweet-smelling hair a golden aura, did not climb back along the spine of the island to reach her shirt. Instead, she went slowly through the thick berry bushes on the exposed and rocky side, eating as she went. She did not relish encountering the dead gull again but thought she knew where it was, at the edge of which bushes. The berries were less delicious and not at all filling. She was starved. Whatever had possessed her mother to put her through this? Self-reliance. Wasn't she self-reliant? Could her mother imagine her starving for three days and having diarrhea for the next three? A true mother could never desire such a thing. Hers was weird and full of principles that messed up Karen's life. Before she could enumerate them, she came to her shirt tossed on a bush, not where she had left it. Karen put it on with a shiver, hoping they had not messed up her other things. She could see her flag intact, but she had better check whether or not her pack had been ripped off. Following rabbit runs, she climbed the island; as she approached, she could see it had not been moved. There was a song playing somewhere. She reached her flag and looked down on the small mud flat, where two men were digging as the tide rushed into their holes, and the music came out of a large, beached skiff. Good music. She lay down to listen and look. They could not help having found her strip stark naked. They had come to clam and had just checked her flag and there she was. She would have looked too. She really didn't care. She wasn't all that modest. For sure, she would have done the same. It did not take her long to decide that, if they were not too embarrassed when she came down to them, she would ask for some clams. It would seem less obvious if she came along the rocks gathering snails and limpets than if she came straight down the hill. They would meet by mistake again.

She took a couple of bandannas from her pack and knotted them into little bags. Then she descended to the shoreline just behind the curve of weedy rocks embracing the mud flat. Periwinkles swept easily by handfuls into the kerchief, but she only succeeded in prying loose two Chinese hats with her fingernails. The Swiss Army knife in one of her pockets must have a special blade for limpets, but there was no reason to waste a great deal of energy on collecting and preparing erasers if she had a chance to get some clams. She must not lose this chance. With a respectable harvest she rounded the tip of the island and looked greedily at two almost full clam-hods and two young men out near the limit of their boots rinsing the mud off their arms.

—Hey, look who's here, muttered Knucks.

—See? That's my music for you.

—Had nothing to do with that. She's looking for clams.

—Oh, hi, said Karen casually, as if they were about to pass on a crowded throughfare and she did not want to miss the opportunity to speak.

Hadn't they seen her someplace before? —Hi.

—Hey, you don't have a couple few extra clams or so, do you?

—Half of em's mudders . . . Take what you want.

—No kidding. Hey, I could really dig some clams! She went down to the full wooden baskets and began to pick out some of the fat, clean shells. They were not all like that. —Do you want me to help you sort them and get rid of these rocks and mudders?

—What's the use? We get paid for em. Just tuck em under.

—I can't pay you for these. I haven't got any money. I'll have to owe you.

—That's O.K. . . . Is that O.K., Zak?

—You know it.

They came slopping up out of the water and stood around.

—Is that too many?

—No. You better eat hearty.

—That's what I thought. Boy, I can't see eating berries all my life.

—You eat them wildberries?

—Sure, but they're too much of a good thing.

—Him, he never ate none of them things if his mother didn't put em in a pie. Me I eat em.

—Come off it, you never ate any plain berries? Here, I'll go get you some. That's how I'll pay for the clams.

—No, never mind. We're giving away the clams.

—What do you like, then? She asked Zak.

—Him, he only likes cupcakes and beer, said Knucks.

—Cupcakes and beer. Oh god that sounds good!

—Don't it though. Jesus, I wish I had some.

—Jesus, me too. I'd trade you back these clams for some cupcakes and beer.

—We'd give you the cupcakes and beer like we give you the clams if we had em.

—Why don't you go get us some, Knucks said to him. — With that fast skiff of yours you'd be to Friendship and back in no time. We got no lunch, you know.

—Yup, well you guys wouldn't be going anyplace while I'm gone, would you?

—Not hardly, said Karen. —Would you really do that? That would make my day.

—And you know I can't swim. How'm I going to get to my boat without your skiff?

—So, stranded huh? For cupcakes and beer. Zak was feeling his power again. Karen looked at him. It was becoming; some of his dullness went away when he talked about cupcakes and beer.

—Well, get crackin, said Knucks.

—Yup, said Zak. —But you better be here when I get back. He went to his skiff and lurched onto her to get her moving out. He started the motor to keep her headed away from the shore. —What do you want to hear? he said, fooling with his knobs.

—Anything. Anything at all. You've got good music, said Karen.

Zak smiled masterfully and Knucks went up and sat on a rock. Zak took his chances with what was on the air and lucked out, Supertramp. Wo wo wo...He blared out the cove. They could hear him for a long time.

Precious Mammaries
(Unseen Angels)

The little grunts and squeaks went on peacefully for a while. Then the snuffles and snorts were added and soon enough there came a full-scale shout for lunch. Jane pulled herself out of comfort to go below.

—Hey, how about a sandwich.

—We'll have to wait now. I've got to feed her. You should have mentioned it before.

—I wasn't hungry before.

—Jane rolled her eyes at him. —You're something else, she said.

—How about a glass of milk, at least.

—There's lots of fruit out there in the locker, and beer and soda. She was fast disappearing down the hatch.

—I'll never find it.

—Of course you will, if you look. If you're hungry.

Baby baby what a smelly kid you are. —Poor baby Sal all poopy. Oh what a poor red bottom. Her milk began to surge again, over the mess now. When the baby had just begun to call out, to cry, she had been in complete control; but here it came again, over this crap. She rapidly, too rapidly perhaps, for the tender bottom, wiped and washed and diapered Sally and grabbed her up. The baby breathed in one last hiccuping sob that filled with milk, and Jane sank down relieved to be working right.

When he leaned over to look for something to eat in the locker, Dick saw them staring at each other there on the bunk.

—You just go all catatonic with that baby, he said.

Jane only confirmed his judgment by not replying.

—Really, two more squawks weren't going to hurt her.

—That isn't it. This is really silly. You come nurse her.

—I don't have that choice.

—Do I have the choice?

—Sure. You could put her off another minute. He sat back at the tiller with an apple he did not expect to like.

—Poor pretty baby. Tell me, should I put you off? I think he thinks you are a piggy. Don't let him fool you, he loves you. I think you're a piggy too.

Before the birth they were lying uncomfortably together and he was stroking her big belly and wondering what would come of it.

Let's say there's this disaster and who are you going to save, me or it?

You, I think, you. Which would you?

You, for sure. A just begun life isn't anything yet.

I don't know, there isn't any line between us now. Will I forget that?

You see, it's not formed. It won't be anything for so long. I know who you are. You're worth saving.

But shouldn't it have a chance to go this far, at least?

We can make another baby. Never mind. I can see you're going to choose it. I would choose you.

The nearest and weep forever after. Die deciding.

The wind had shifted and the boat wallowed now before the wind. Jane could almost feel her inner ear slopping. She was queasy. She thought she should not take dramamine while she was nursing. But what are the other remedies?

Crackers, fresh air, distraction, Coca-Cola, but the one that really worked was out of the question. Get off the boat. Put your feet on the dock and wait for it to stop heaving.

For distraction, could she float to a conversation she liked, one that seemed to tell her something she wanted to hear, something she did not quite know.

How Ellen, in her white coat, had sat there on the edge of the hospital bed, without her baby and without Hank, too, and could smile and make Jane smile. Where was she coming from when they watched the nurse draw the curtain between the beds and she said, I told you about Althea?

And what about Althea: this is a regular soap, my head.

When Roy was born, she was my roommate, my perfect complement. She was all baby, just lying there trying to hold onto the fetus for another two weeks, and I was no baby. I couldn't touch Roy, you know, until they let me take him home a month later. She seemed to be just lying there waiting for me when they brought me down. She had already been there a week or so, and she had another two weeks to go. She felt like she could do it, which I guess was a help. Anyhow, I don't forget her. When she heard the doctor tell me "He has a fifty-fifty chance of living," it was good news, and when he was gone, she would say, "Honey, Althea's holding on, you can too." Of course, it was too late. I hadn't held on. I did a lot of crying those days, when they said my breasts would dry up and they wouldn't need me any more, or I could go home early what did they need me for. Althea said "Don't cry, honey. Wish I could go home." And she told me all about herself to take my mind off my troubles. She was married to a mortician.

Remembering. He dressed babies. Yuck.

I thought it was funny at first. I remember it as a crisis now, he had quit. She told me how he had always been called to embalm the little children for open caskets, he had such a touch, and he liked to make them pretty and cry. But then he couldn't go on. He used to like to cry... But then he couldn't stand it anymore "Like it didn't flush," she said. But what else could he do? She said, "He'd be a good preacher but he hasn't got no church. He says he's a no-good mechanic but reckons on finding a job doing that and maybe take an insurance course, sell insurance. He gets missionary about insurance, because most black people don't know what they're worth and have a fire or something and then have to start all over again from scratch. No wonder they don't never get ahead. Just a little bit of insurance."

Jane looked at Sally, who was just fooling around now, her belly full of insurance. She set the baby upright on her knee and Sally burped a high decibel burp.

—Jesus, I wish I could do that, said Dick looking in. But I haven't had enough to eat. Are you two almost done?

—Almost.

And back wherever. Ellen. Roy the baby. He might live. You can go home early. We don't need you here. When you can get around you can come back and look at him. You can phone for news. They'll tell you how many ounces he gained. Or lost. He will lose at first. He will not be blind. We think he will live. Your milk will go away. Isolette. Hank brought everything to wear home but underpants. You freeze your tail off. Look out there, it's a blizzard girl. You take a pair of mine. If you want. I'm suppose to lie here another two weeks yet so you can bring them back when you come visit the baby. I'm not coming back to see the baby. You not? That sweet little bitty baby. He doesn't know I'm here. I can't touch him. I'm lying here holding this baby in tight as I can and you going on home leaving you baby in a box. That's right. And you not coming back? When I can touch him. Well you take them pants anyhow. You can put them in the mail if I don't never see you again. You don't want to get your stitches frozen. I'll do that. What's your last name? Clay. Well, goodbye Althea. Hold tight. Hold on.

—What did you say?

—Nothing. Hold on. I'm coming.

Coming From
Behind You

Hen headed the Merry Maid into the clear river passage, no more obstructions along this shore for perhaps a mile; until they would come to the group of lobster pots he could see in the distance, hot-pink on the fair breast of the sea. He looked into his varnish seeing himself and moved about to reflect Martha, Ednah —no, only himself. He looked back at them.

They were there, smiling and responsive.

—Should we eat now?

But their images would not coalesce. The varnish had no interest in any other face than his.

—I don't know. What do you think?

—I suppose we can't fish at the same time?

—Absolutely not, said Martha. What a mess if you caught a fish right in the middle. I'd never be able to eat after.

—Personally, fish make me hungry.

—Well, not I. Let's do the sandwiches.

So everything that had been wrapped was unwrapped and the sandwiches they made were almost perfection, full of tomato yet not soggy, and crisp bacon with no grease.

—Pass the salt, please, said Hen.

Ednah rummaged in the basket.

—Hen always likes a little salt on everything, said Martha.

—It's possible we didn't put it in. Did you?

—Not I. You were putting in things like that.

—But there isn't anything else like that.

—Napkins.

—Not at all the same.

—Well, so it's not there?

—Doesn't seem to be.

—No salt, Hen.

—So I see.

Martha poured the coffee which was too hot to drink immediately from the enamel cups, another reason to be grateful for a calm day.

—I like picnics when we would have a bottle of wine.

—That's very nice on dry land, said Martha. But in the boat we would fall asleep and drown.

—I'd be quite willing to put on my life jacket to have a little glass of wine.

—Ednah, you goose. I believe you would.

They went slowly, not spilling their coffee and eating lemon chess pies. They did not save anything for later, because they intended to be home with mackerel by the time they were hungry again.

—Now I can fish, said Ednah, shaking her crumbs overboard.

—I don't know that it's worth the trouble right now.

—The more fishing I do the more fish I'll catch. Are you going to fish, Martha?

—You don't want to fish two lines at once, said Hen. You always tangle.

—Well, and anyhow, I'm just going to doze a little. Can I use the earphones, Hen?

—Sure. You can tune in the weather and give a listen.

—I just want to shut out the motor. I'm getting a terrific headache. The weather's fine.

Ednah rigged up a rod and dropped the daredevil overboard. —Take an aspirin, she said.

—I think silence and a little snooze will do it.

—Then don't fall overboard.

The red and white lure ran out into the boat's wake and Ednah stopped it just out of sight. She could feel it spinning back and forth in small arcs behind them, as they slowly dreamed along the deep shore.

—What if I catch the whale?

What if you had not married the voluptuous sister?

I didn't marry the voluptuous sister. I married the one who talked.

We have changed places now. Before I was the listener. Now look.

She was the one who said isn't this ham wonderful, isn't this wine just splendid, what a glorious day; so that one could tell what a wonderful time one was having, and she would say I think this and I think that. You were just your quiet self. It took a long time to hear you or to see you.

—What did you say?

—What if I catch the whale?

—You don't really think there's a whale out here.

—Yes, I do, but I don't think I'll catch it.

Hang in There

—Dad, I'm hungry.

—You're the cook.

—Well, pull me in.

Hank stood up and pulled the little dinghy in. —Got me a big fish, feels like a whale, he said. What you got?

—Nothing.

—How's your scallop?

—He's getting better.

—Well, I'll eat my big fish and you eat your scallop, said Hank, tenderly nibbling the salty bare belly of his kid, who was climbing past, using him for a boarding ladder and a ramp and finally a cushion.

—Nope, you're just teasing. Slippery Roy, slippery little Roy got away without a kiss.

—Hey, come back here.

—Nope. Roy did some acrobatics in the companionway. —You'll tickle me.

—Damn right. Mind out you don't fall on your head.

—What do you want for lunch. Peanut butter?

—No, give me baloney. Don't crack your skull, your brains will spill out.

—There isn't any more baloney. It got slippery and I used it for bait.

—No wonder you don't catch any fish.

—You have to eat peanut butter.

—Peanut butter's great.

—When we buy our CB, we could get some more baloney.

—What CB?

—You said we'd buy a CB in Camden.

—Boy, you get hold of something, you never let go, do you?

—Nope.

—Well hang in there. We'll get us a CB someday.

Hang in there honey/ It's gotta be worth the trouble/ Even if we find out/ What's true's a bustin bubble/ Just honey you mind out/ And Hang in there.

Hank could hear Linda Ronstadt or Emmylou singing the song. Since he had moved to D.C. to work for the Library of Congress, his style had evolved. It was now very Baltimore and Western, would fit well with other songs the biggies were singing. For a long time, through high school and college, he had tried to write nonsense verse in the styles of Lewis Carroll or Edward Lear, but discovering nonsense didn't exist anymore, he turned to song lyrics. At first he wrote them for friends with banjos and friends with guitars. When he went to graduate school and was always broke, he learned to sell them. Once he had written a hit, "When and If;" the Auk was bought with royalties from it, and he still earned spending money for her, which she always seemed to require. Almost ashamed now that he was a serious and professional person, he kept on doing it, because he was hooked, and because his thoughts often found themselves in a sort of blue jingle.

Life goes on/ Don't waste no time on us./ We just get in/ Stir up our own fuss;/ Bubble up truth/ Hang on it nail and tooth.

He could have made more money perhaps, if he had an ear for music. His songs were composed to a most vague kind of blue tune, very repetitive, but he could never quite repeat it. He only sold lyrics.

Roy passed him two peanut butter on stale bread sandwiches and a beer. —Thanks, you coming up?

—No, it's too hot to eat out there.

They ate in silence and then there was a funny rhythmic bumping noise from below, as if something had come loose and was swinging. Hank leaned to look through the hatchway. There was Roy, dangling between the bunks, his toes hooked in the stowing space along them, his arms rocking his torso peering up at the open hatch and grinning. —I think I'm get-

ting in the habit of this! It feels so great! He began to sing, —
Rockaby baby/ On the treetop/ When the wind blows/ The
baby shall rock/ No, the cradle shall rock.

—You goon. Quit that bumping. Hank sat back.

Giggling wildly, the song went on. —The cradle shall rock/
And when the bow breaks/ The cradle will fall/ And down will
come baby. Roy collapsed across the bunk and laughed up at
the little empty square of sky, —Baby/ Bough cradle and all.

—Hey, Dad. You missed it.

—No I didn't. I saw it all.

—No, you missed the best part. I'll do it again.

—I'm going to throw you overboard.

—I just ate. I'll get cramps and drown.

—Go catch us a fish. Do something. You're going to drive
me nuts.

What I tell you honey/ I tell you now is true/ You don't
believe me/ But I believe you/ You gotta grab what you see/
And hang in there.

What's Your Name?
(Little girl, What's
Your Name?)

So Karen went up and sat on the rock next to Knucks to wait
for her cupcakes and beer.

—So, what's your name, she said.

—Henry Nuckols and him he's Richy Zachary. They call
me Knucks and him Muzak.

—I thought you two were brothers.

—Nope, but everybody thinks so. Me and him been going
around tellin everybody we're twin brothers and about half the
guys believe it. And all the girls. We tell em we got separated
when we was little and haven't seen each other since and
didn't know where each other was until we met here. And
about half of em believes it.

She looked at him to see how badly she would have been fooled. He had blue eyes that hid a little, not dishonestly, she thought, but shyly. . .

—Look at this. I'll show you. He pulled out a bulging wallet and a string of clear plastic full of snapshots slipped out of it, unfolding.

—Who are all those people?

—Women, he said, folding it back. Do you have your wallet? I'll show you mine if you show me yours.

—I guess.

—Look, this is the one I wanted to show you. Bloodbrothers.

—There was a picture of two boys with beers, arms around each other's shoulders, grinning at a jostled camera. They looked more alike than she had thought and younger. She looked at Knucks again. He really was as young as she was, probably, just big.

—Him he's got an uncle here he lives with and pulls traps for and he's gettin a string of traps of his own now. Them nice hot pink buoys out there's his.

—You catch lobsters, too?

—Me? Yup. I been here just a while, from way up by Rumford where you already known every girl a hundred miles in every direction. Gets dead up there. But I've been around. See.

He dangled the photographs from his wallet, and yo-yoed them casually. —Show me yours.

Karen fished hers out of one of her pockets. It was more cigarette case than wallet. She opened it to her technicolor driver's license.

—You from Ohio? That's where they don't eat nothin but baitfish?

—Huh?

—That's right. These big buyers, you know, push up the price of bait every year selling it to you people. And that other stuff you eat is sharks.

—How do you know? What a shit!

—That's your name? What a weird name, Karen Jones-Jones.

—Would have been weirder if my mom had had her way, Karen Joan Jones-Jones.

—Three Joneses! What would she do that for?

—She's insane. She has this thing about family. Actually it's my grandmother's problem and it's a long story.

—You going to tell it?

—No. It has to do with one side being fancier than the other and keeping her maiden name. It's not important. She has these real fantasies, my mother. And I come out Jones Square.

—Jones Square. What's that?

—What they call me at school.

—You needn't worry about that. You're not square sweetie. You're weird, but you're sure not square.

—Cut the compliment crap. You don't know if I'm square or weird or what.

—That's just my cool line.

—I know. I hate lines.

Be My Breath
When I Grow Old

—Are you watching the tip of your rod, Ednah? It seems to me that it's bending. Do you have a fish?

—I know as well as you that it's bending. What kind of fisherman do you think I am. It's just seaweed.

—Well, pull it in. You'll never catch a fish that way.

—Just now we're in a terrible mess of seaweed. No sense pulling it in until we're through.

—Less sense in dragging that dead weight behind us.
—Come, hand it to me. I'll reel it in. He took the rod and her hand around it in his, encircling it as gently as ever and then

let hers slip away as he took the bending rod.

—Ednah, you have the bottom of the sea again.

—Not this time. I can see it floating out there. Unless I'm pulling the ocean inside out.

—Unless you're what?

—Never mind. Joking's hardly possible with the motor noise.

—You know, I'm afraid my ears are going a little, too, Ednah.

—You should see a doctor then. Sometimes it's easy to fix.

—I don't go to the doctor's in the summer. That is one of my firm principles.

—You have others?

—What is another? To take you for mackerel when you ask. To untangle your seaweed. He took the lure out of the mass of rockweed that came aboard with it and handed her the rod.

—That sounds like one of those lines we doubt ever got spoken, Hen.

She took it as he had, an easy exchange, leaving the warm cork handle for her. —But I have always admired your principles. If there's one thing I can't stand, it's an unprincipled man.

He grinned and turned back to the wheel. The launch which had gone perfectly straight without him, while he subdued the seaweed, continued as directly down the river and Ednah's daredevil slipped away to flash back and forth again just beneath their wake.

What can happen? A very difficult combination of very little and everything, small arcs reaching points just off somewhere, retreating reciprocal curves, tacks advancing as the wind shifts along some longed for plot.

Some would say everything was left out of her life.

—I've got one, I do!

—I believe you have. Pull him in.

—Martha, look!

Martha had left the scene, had taken her headache off dreaming in a blissful doze.

—She'd be overboard in a minute if her weight were in her brain.

—Which, thank God, it isn't. Here let me help.

—Oh, it's only a pogy.

—Foul-hooked at that. I'll throw him back.

—Oh, don't.

—You know they say everybody has eaten one pogy.

Could I ever throw a fish back? Would I be the only one to try it again, a mouthful of bones?

—I read you can split and fry them.

—You do believe everything you read.

—Well, sometimes I like crisp fried fish.

Of course she fried them with their heads on and left precious little for the cat. Once on a dare, Martha's idea to shock their mother, she had eaten all the eyeballs from the dishes. Like marrow, they weren't bad, heart of bones, fillet of soul. No, God, she did prefer flesh.

The fish could not breathe in the air, and she had to decide immediately to kill and keep him or toss him back.

—He'll just die with that tear from the hook. He'll just get eaten up. Keep him.

Darlin, If You
Want Me to Be

Dick and Jane and Baby Sally were all together in the cockpit of the Gypsy. Sally was reclining in her infant bucketseat on the cockpit sole, where she was rubbing mashed banana into the brim of her hat and into her ears. Her father and mother were having bananas for dessert, as well, but they also had Oreos.

—I'm going to give her an Oreo, said Dick. —Do you think she'd like that?

—I know she'd like it but don't give it to her.

—Why not? She eats everything in sight.

—It's a cholesterol sandwich, that white stuff, and chocolate's lousy for you.

—You think she's going to get acne already?

—If she doesn't get bad habits now, she won't have to change them later.

—How come we get Oreos?

—That's the whole point. It's already too late for us.

—You mean she's never going to get to take them apart and eat out the middles.

—Not if I can help it.

—Shouldn't we throw them overboard then?

—Not at a dollar nine a bag we shouldn't.

—Well she's going to get these bad ideas. Babies aren't dumb, you know.

—That's true. These will be our last Oreos. Better enjoy them.

Did they eat them all or save some for later to eat under the cover of darkness when Sally couldn't see them? She couldn't see from under the brim of her hat, anyhow.

—That hat of hers is really getting to me. Couldn't we wash her up a little bit?

—Jane looked at her and was disgusted too. —I'll get seasick if I go below right after eating.

—Well, you hang that thing overboard to rinse it, and I'll look for a damp towel or something. The boat isn't going anywhere anyhow, he said.

—I know. I hate it. Jane removed the baby's hat and dangled overboard with it to slop in the trough of the next swell. —Oh God! Oh Dick! she yelled.

Dick leapt through the hatch, ready for action.

—There goes mine! I was holding onto hers so tight I lost mine.

—Jesus. You scared me to death. It's just a hat.

—I'll get sunstroke.

—We have to turn the boat around for a damned hat.

Jane had the tiller hard over and was sheeting the main.

—No, he took the sheet. —Get out of the way. I'll do it. Look at that tide take it away! We're going to lose all the ground we just made. No wonder we weren't going anywhere. When am I going to learn never to sail through here? Get that kid out of here. Where am I supposed to put my feet? No, don't pick her up, you'll drop her overboard too.

Jane was starting little actions in all directions, but they were all wrong; so she sat down with her feet resting on Sally who was yowling because she had sun and banana in her eyes.

Sally thought the toes were a consolation prize, a gift to pull on and eat. —Silly Sally, I love you, said Jane, bending down between her knees.

—I've got it! I've got it! said Dick who might have fallen overboard.

—Our hero, said Jane.

His Blue Eyes Saw
Better Than Mine

—I don't know if I can wait for the cupcakes and beer, said Karen, leaning back on the flat rock. —My stomach's growling.

—Don't you have anything better in that wallet than a license?

—Cigarettes, she said, offering him one.

—I mean pictures. Your boyfriend.

—I don't have a particular boyfriend.

—Stacked like that and you don't have a boyfriend. Come off it. You just don't want to show me.

—Here, said Karen. —See for yourself. She handed him the wallet, and he pulled the things out that were behind the license: a library card and a snapshot.

—What's that? A cat!

—See. I knew you'd think it was weird.

—That your cat?

—My professor's.

—Your professor's! Professor of what? Cats?

—Communications.

—You look pretty normal, he said admiringly, but you sure have got a weird wallet.

—You want to hear about it?

—About a professor's cat. Sounds great.

—First off, it was a picnic at his house and I took a picture of him and his wife and baby, but they didn't turn out. Just the cat. But it's a nice cat. I'll tell you the whole thing if you want.

He was looking at her and seemed to be listening.

—This professor's not old. He's not good looking like a jock, but he really turns me on. I heard there was this one professor in Communications who fooled around and I thought about it being him all the time. I didn't do very well on his quiz because I was doodling a lot. He was friendly, too. So I decided I ought to ask people if he was the one before I did something dumb. When I asked around, nobody but me seemed to think he could be the one, but I made an appointment to see him about my quiz anyhow.

—I told him I didn't think I remembered what he wanted me to remember when it came to his quiz; that when I looked at a film I couldn't remember it all and that he always asked questions about the parts I forgot.

—Well, what do you remember, he said. Let's start with that. Tell me about the one I gave the quiz on, the Renoir.

—So you should have seen this great film. It was a fairy tale.

—A fairy tale? And you go to college?

—It was a fairy tale. You know the one about the little match girl?

—Don't know too many fairy tales. He was pretty sure she didn't have on a bra.

But she was just looking out at the ocean now. —In the movie there was this poor little girl named Karen.

—That's why you liked it.

—Well, anyhow that's a part I remembered pretty easy. And the subtitles said she lived in the distant north in a humble shack.

—What's a subtitle?

—They hadn't invented sound. They had to write everything they couldn't act out. So this poor little girl, Karen, is trying to sell matches, on Christmas Eve naturally, and it's snowing. Nobody will buy them but she can't go home until she sells some. There's this window full of toys and she looks through the reflections and begins like daydreaming. She gets in with them and they come alive.

—She bust in?

—Don't be dumb. She just like dreams in. Well now, I really don't remember if she gets in while she's looking through the window, or I think she has this dream while she's lighting her matches to keep warm.

—What happens when she runs out?

—She dies. But the good part is the middle. There's this toy soldier you can tell is supposed to be handsome. She's sort of pretty, but he is just blah. I mean he didn't turn me on but he did her. So they're having this kind of fairy tale thing in the toy shop and some big bugger jumps out of a box. The subtitle says "Suddenly a Killjoy," and the next one says "I Have an Appointment With Karen Tonight. I am Death."

—I think you remember good.

—Yeah, but it's the wrong things. So, of course the toy soldier, does he put her on his horse or do they both get horses? Anyhow, they dash off into the clouds and that's where it really gets fantastic. There's this wild music.

—You said they hadn't invented noise.

—Well, they put it in later and it's a little much. When they first showed the picture some lady used to play the organ. But it's this wild horse music, and they are galloping away from Death with this skull on his cap. It's downhill — steep — like falling out of heaven and then Karen is dead, draped over the soldier's saddle with her pretty curls tangled and one of the curls gets loose and drifts away on the breeze.

—She get cut up?

—No, it doesn't show how the curl gets loose. And it lands on this marker like a flag where they're going to bury her. Then there are these roses opening up. And that's the end. Unless the end is where these old ladies find her all dead in the snow and the subtitles say "Imagine Trying to Keep Warm With Matches."

—That's what I think.

—Well, for a fairy tale it was really great. Sad.

—I thought this was about your professor.

—It still is.

—So, what did he say?

—He said seems like to me you remember pretty well.

—That's what I think.

—But, he said. What about the camera? What was the camera doing?

—How are you supposed to know that?

—Well, that's what I wondered. I mean, I was really digging this little match girl, right. But he said, and I guess I should have known from the stuff we'd been supposed to be reading, that I ought to be able to tell from the pictures what the camera was doing. Well, I just drew a blank. I mean, I would have flunked that quiz all over again. So he said O.K., maybe you've just got a real literal mind. We're going to be making a film in my advanced class this Saturday. Why don't you just come over to my house at 2:30 and we'll be talking about the effects we're trying to make and how to make them and then we're going to do it.

—So, of course, I said yeah, that'll be really great and he said, hey I really like the way you tell that movie. You just need to get some of the technical points and you'll do fine. So I felt really good, like maybe he was the one who fooled around.

She turned over on the rock, and he studied her backside to see if she was wearing underpants at least. It did not seem that way. He slid back on his elbow to look closer. No, for sure.

He's Bad
Production

The Merry Maid was in the mouth of George's River, fishing seriously. The pogy had been treated with some scorn by Hen and lay dead but uncleaned in the bottom of a bucket. Ednah had set her complete attention on the lure which was out of sight; and Hen let the boat have her way, knowing balance and pure lines would always keep her straight, barring the unexpected encounter, less than likely this still afternoon. He stood by the wheel but watched Ednah. He thought she was about to turn and smile at him. She did, brushing her hair under the brim of her hat, but too quickly returned her expectations to the sea.

Foolish woman with the beautiful, almost transparent skin, the forehead of a new-hatched bird with blue at the temples, the merest sunlicked freckles of age, I saw you and thought your head would fall over, your neck was so long, almost laughable, almost Alice when she bit the right side of the mushroom. Might I have played Leda to your swan, your sway, your first ridiculous and beautiful surprise? And your hands that could lay quietly in your lap so long, then suddenly no longer, and they flew around your face—hands like wild things; so that I forgot what I was saying that roused such flight. Do you remember? Martha was pregnant, and you nursed her indolence and gave her some cakes and tea, and you wanted to take the crib upstairs. I went to look for the neighbor so he could help me, but you were in a hurry, want-

ing to see the room ready for the baby before you left, and,
before I was back, you had dragged the crib more than halfway up, and even when I was there I think you carried more
than half in those hands—whose skin doesn't really fit as it did
then. And still is so fine, and when you turn your head the thin
folds are like the most amazing cloth. The names of cloths?
My literary knowledge: cambric, tulle, *peau de soie*—admitting there is no difference. And there you are still wearing
Liberty lawn (no one wears that any more, because it lasts
forever and who can stand it, something so delicate and eternal). In the old cashmere that buttons more tightly there are
thin places and vague spots that will never go away. A drop of
mackerel blood. A smudge of humus. As much nostalgia for
the things that didn't happen as for those that did.

—For all the good this does, she said over her shoulder, I
might as well be reading my book.

—Oh, now, don't give up. What are you reading? I need a
good book.

—Emily Dickinson.

—Poetry, oh. That won't do. I need a good story.

—Well, so do I. wouldn't have started this if I hadn't had to
look up the same reference three times this past spring. You
know those lines "It might be lonelier Without the
loneliness"?

—Not really. Not at all.

—I didn't either. But people were quoting it left and right in
April. And so irresponsible about sources.

—They come in and ask you where things like that come
from?

—Or call up. Could we be in the wrong place? There aren't
any fish here.

He knew how much he needed her myth of a peculiar loyalty, an embellished devotion to fact, not unlike the varnished
Merry Maid slipping through the flat calm of his reality. What
would he have done if she had ripped into him, thrust into his

consciousness with more than the receptive touch, the acquiescence of smiling eyes?

—Hen! Look out! The sound which had slowly begun to
intrude on their personal peace, became huge and charged
across their bow.

—Where in Hell did he come from?

—He wasn't looking.

—Nor I. We could be dead.

—What happened? said Martha, almost thrown overboard
by the wake but tenacious even in sleep.

—Nothing. He didn't hit us.

—Near miss is as much as a mile.

—Wasn't he looking?

Zak was looking now, waving his arms over the pile of
lobster pots, as his skiff careened toward Friendship.

—As if we could hear what he said with that hideous music
blaring. Now that's what I call a clam tough.

—You should report him to the Coast Guard.

—You know, they're really just not interested in matters of
this sort. If you don't say Mayday you needn't bother.

—I'll never be the same, said Martha readjusting the earphones for comfort and settling down again.

C'est La Vie
Said the Old Folks

The Doppler effects, passes.

Follow the lonely fisherman in his quest, learn how he
avoids catastrophe in his dangerous calling, get between his
ears, commune with the sea. He is going to Friendship. We
know he does not see where he is going; what does he hear?

You're supposed to be feeling good now (cause everybody
said you would). Momma don't take my Kodachrome
(Momma don't take my Kodachrome). I'm looking for blue
eyes (Has anyone seen him?) Blinded by the light.

What's your name (Little girl what's your name)?

It goes to show you never can tell.

Out on Thunder Island.

Coming down. Coming down.

Beset with restlessness, he fiddles with his dials seeking the random right song. There's a change in the ocean (change in the deep blue sea). Diddy wa diddy (mean)? If I had a box just for wishes.

—Holy shit, he said, standing up and looking behind him. Nearly run down them golden oldies.

—Goddam Summer Pukes, he hollered. You're in the channel!

It Goes to Show
You Never Can Tell

He was about to put his hand on the unbroken curve when she leaned back on her own elbow and said —That was sort of interesting that afternoon, and he found himself rudely facing her zipper. She didn't seem to mind. —We used his camera to make a movie about a farmer's daughter, heroes and stuff. We took a lot of stills to use for montage. That's when I got the cat picture. It got really pretty cold by the end of the afternoon and I got all goosepimply on my arms and even under my shirt. We were standing pretty close and he was patting his cat and talking about I forget what, but in a minute he looked at me and said hey you look really cold. Here, I'll lend you my cat! And he draped his cat around my neck like a furpiece and petted it to make it stay, and I warmed right up I can tell you.

—You're weird. With a cat? Did you get screwed?

—Not yet.

—He did later on?

—No, I mean still not yet.

—You think he's going to?

—I don't know. How do I know?

—He might?

—Yeah sure he might. You want to go swimming?

—In that cold stuff, you're kidding. You got seal blood?

—Come on.

—I can't hardly swim anyhow.

—Bet you can swim good enough for me.

—You think so? A little faraway lightning flashed like a dim idea in the sky. —You got your suit?

—What a turkey.

—Well, I wasn't sure. I thought you might be hung up on your professor, or his cat.

—Turkey turkey. She kicked him gently in the gut, because he was still looking at her zipper. —Watch.

She started to unzip and then stood and walked to the big rock at the top of the tide.

I Know,
It's Been Coming
for Some Time

—It's thickening up. We're going to set some courses and use the motor.

—You think that's fog?

—Something is going to happen. Something is going to come of it. If the wind shifts one way it might be fog, the other way God only knows what.

—We're not getting anywhere anyhow.

—That's the thing.

—Fisherman's Passage just gets longer every year.

—Or shorter. Remember reaching through it when we came home last August. It was blowing a gale.

—Like flying through mountains. What a chop it can get in here.

—I don't like it. Let's really get out. Put Sally down below.

—She's O.K. . . . .

—I can't take care of the sails and the courses and the motor and the rocks and the baby all at once.

—I'll take the sails down, you start the motor.

—She'll fall overboard. Put her below.

—From down there on the cockpit sole? You think she can fly?

—I'll step on her. Get her out of here.

—What is the matter with you? You're flipping.

—Look. I wouldn't be surprised if I just heard thunder.

—I wouldn't either. You're so paranoid.

Sally went below. The sails came down. The motor fired quickly. With paranoia the worst imagined evil of the moment, no one listened for thunder. They went to set a course from the bell, which would mark their leaving the passage. From there they could go straight for sound buoys or calculate more frequent marks closer to shore.

—Which will it be?

There was a certain imminence in the weather that even Jane, still playing games, could feel. Heavy heavy hangs over your head. Forfeit.

—I would rather the inside way.

The land looked gentle and mild in the haze, the sea blind and warning beyond that particular bell.

—In either a blow or fog I don't want to be off this point.

—I don't see much choice.

—There isn't any. That's where we're going to be. A little farther out or a little closer in.

—This could go on forever.

Yesterday's Wine

I'll always be the same, the silent retort. Forever. Ready ready ready. Ednah stood up and impatiently scanned the horizon for the riffles of schooling fish. The mouth of the river was fuller and fuller but not with mackerel. She sat down again discouraged. —Why can't I catch a fish?

—Perhaps, the tide isn't good between these islands.

—We've always caught them here before.

Here she was ready to tangle again in the blood and guts, the incredible iodine, slippery gore. But no fish.

—Hen, are you sure this is the right spot?

—It used to be.

—No one else is here today.

—There's no telling what makes fish come and go. They do seem to be gone.

—Why am I fishing then?

—I thought that was what you liked to do.

—I do. I do.

I hardly dare think of cleaning the fish. How the organs lie in their smooth sacs, colors rich and delicate, and the odor of the sea, ozone, iodine. The slippery fish escaping our hands on the decks. Our hands together, freckled with silver, rich with the blood of the sea. Your old black knife lays them open and I lift out the guts and feed the gulls.

We were tumbling with the baby (which? I forget. It was George. He was naked.) I was too rough and suddenly you cried like a child. I thought you liked it. I do. I do. Martha was dozing with her head on the picnic hamper and we finished the wine together, the dark wine filling our sort of silence with the saturated calm.

—Martha, have you been listening to the weather? Martha! Hen had to touch her shoulder to make her hear. She had been enjoying the sweet lull after her fright, resting her eyes on the nearby rocks where either half-dressed hippies or naked myths might be. She took off the earphones.

—Yes?

—Have you been listening to the weather? I really don't like the way it feels.

—No. I was listening to the Lobster channel for mermaid sightings. There's no such thing.

—Such a skeptic, said her sister. And you, Hen. What's the matter with the weather?

—Hen's sinuses are the best barometer on the east coast.

—I do feel this pressure.

—I just feel discouraged. It's true. You're right. I always feel depressed just before a thunderstorm.

—Turn it on Martha. And listen.

—I can't stand going back without mackerel. Take us over there, Hen. Is that what those ripples are?

—Tide and ledges.

—We can't go there.

—No.

—I don't want to go back.

She

Because Roy had installed himself comfortably in the little puddle at the bottom of the dinghy, a wet hat (which had been a hatful of water) pulled over his eyes, his handline held between his overboard right toes, secured elsewhere Hank hoped, Hank half-slept also. Otherwise, how could the Auk produce such a silence? What he had partially in mind was the extinction of the species, the need for translation, the birth of the blues. Heavy. His tapes excused the Auk's presence, and his, passively wresting a living from the airways over the sea. But this year the restless locals had gone to CB . . . New regulations made the former channels too expensive for fishermen; so, if Roy were right and his tapes half-empty, his material would be too scanty come Fall. He had to have more. He had to get the CB. It was difficult enough to justify grants to ethnographic semanticists without nothing coming of it. Hank no longer believed in conversation with the anthropologist as a tool. Trying to keep an informant from translating, when personally you were grateful for any little inclusion, demanded more rigor, more deadly seriousness than he could command facing another. So he put it, even when the insider was six foot two, gap-toothed, with skin made of fish leather and steady, pale eyes that looked at you until you went away. That was a possibility: that his discovery of the logorrhea of these men on the air had been so completely the opposite of his projection into their self-sufficiency, their savage and intelligent solitude, that he had to record it to prove he could face it, on the outside chance that some day he might understand how this talk replaced the taciturn sincerity he sought.

In this business asking questions was no way to understand. If the insider took to translating, followed his tendency to speak as he expected Hank to understand, to explain rather than continue, all was lost; the repetitions with their differences were covered with an imagined view of his own view. Could this hope for comprehension be like the lovers' dream of silent intimacy, crossing boundaries between senses to a surprise? The only way he could come to what a word meant was to know all the ways it, another body, naturally met its surroundings. The only way he could know that was to hear it over and over again.

The only thing he required was everything. Plenitude. This might be his death by drowning except he had accepted his lazy Auk's trajectory as a limit. What she could not handle, he could not. And if the words beat like rain, she did not leak. If the silence were thick and oppressive, her tough bow cut it and kept to the steady ellipse. A forgiving boat made everything possible, even the dire mistakes of a captain, freed him to risk a dream.

His eyes were closed. Now the sorrow was that, the silent race of fishermen already gone, he felt his own presence slipping away, as if it had never existed, as if he had never been an adolescent or a child.

He was passing on, progenitor of a desire for truth and nonsense that could never be.

So he was slipping into a dark gloom, in the cockpit of the Auk, which keened a low melody of rigging, planks and waves. When he tried the harmony, he came up with only percussion, a beating heart, or was it thunder?

Making
Believe

Mariners should be on the alert for signs of approaching heavy weather.

A small craft advisory is in effect for the coastal waters from Rockland to the Merrimack River. A line of thunder-squalls causing severe wind and hail damage extends from eastern Vermont and New Hampshire into western Maine where it is moving across the lake region at thirty-five miles an hour. These squalls should be considered dangerous and all mariners are advised to seek safe shelter immediately.

Listen What I'm
Putting Down

Old and gay, old and gay, Ednah refused to consider the possibility of return.

—Listen to that, Hen. Ednah, reel in.

—It's a small craft advisory.

—We should go straight home.

—We're two hours out. Safe shelter immediately means sooner than that.

—Aren't you glad we brought the foul weather gear?

—I will be, I expect.

—Why do you two take them so seriously? They're most unreliable. I don't believe them for a minute.

—This isn't vague. Someone is seeing those squalls now and reporting them. This is not what might happen; this is happening.

—So what are we going to do?

—Get out the chart. We're not going to find a snug harbor out here, but we can find some shelter.

—Those are nice islands.

—They may be the ones. We can duck in behind Jones's Garden. The entrance is on this side, I think. Fold the chart, Martha, and show me.

—You've got your geography skewed. You've got Jones's Garden in the wrong place.

—No. I know where it is. Turn the chart the right way.

—It's that one over there.

—No. It will appear just behind this point.

—They all look about the same.

—You see those sticks? Those are ranges to keep us off the rocks here. I know exactly where we are.

—Hen, aren't you going too fast? Look at my poor lure out there bouncing up and down.

—Don't you have that thing reeled in yet? We can't be trolling along any more.

—You're such an alarmist. Nothing has changed in the weather. If something really does happen, we can get in quickly enough. It's not like you, you're no coward.

—I have no prejudice against cowardice.

—Ednah, you are perfectly gratuitous. Hen has to be responsible.

—I think it's the new varnish. It's gone to his head. He doesn't want it hailed on.

—Oh, Hen. I never thought of that; what a tragedy if that should happen. What are you going to do?

—Get you old girls to lie down and spread out and cover as much surface as possible.

—I believe he's serious.

—Don't be ridiculous.

—It's not certain that it will hail here.

—If there's hail damage in New Hampshire won't there be here?

—Not necessarily.

—He's only believing what suits him. A minute ago, we had to take the weatherman's word as gospel.

—Ednah. Stop it. This is serious. What has gotten into you?

—The mackerel. My heart was set on fish.

—Listen for thunder.

—We can't hear. We're all more deaf than not.

Out on Thunder Island

Karen had already tucked her clothes, neatly rolled, behind a rock just out of reach of the tide by the time Knucks stood up. There was something in the scenario that he could not quite get his finger on, something askew. He was not about to drop his britches so fast. Karen was wading out into the briny deep as if it were not ice water.

—Come on, she said over her shoulder.

Under her shining brown skin with the indelible white imprint of a bikini, she was covered with an enchanting layer of fat, which smoothed every angle that might be harsh, making every corner seem compliant, and most effectively insulating her against the cold water. Knucks knew something about the appearance of his own body, muscles with gullies where they joined the bones, tendons like ridges, prickly undergrowth. He was more a man of the darkness. He could have waited until night.

—Come on, she said again.

—I can't swim.

She sank into the cold water, shuddering.

—It's fantastic! Aren't you roasting?

If he only had known it, Knucks was on the horns of a dilemma, between the devil and the deep blue sea.

—What if I just sit here and watch?

—That's not good enough.

—It's thundering.

—At least take off your boots.

—One place worse than being in a boat in a thunderstorm is standing in water.

—It can't come that fast.

—Honest, I can't swim. Aren't you freezing your tits off?

—Look. She stood up. They looked dangerously brittle. —
I'll teach you to swim. That'll be fun.

It began to seem pleasantly inevitable. So Knucks went
ahead and pulled off his boots and his pants, wishing the girl
had some scrap of decency and would turn her back as he
thrashed out into the water.

—O.K.! O.K.! she exclaimed. —You see, it's not bad.

It was, as far as he was concerned, awful; the farther he
went in the more he shriveled until finally his apprehensive
genitals disappeared in the enormous icy gulp of the deep blue
sea.

—Ah, that's better now, isn't it, said Karen. —You'll get
used to it. Come on over here and I'll give you a swimming
lesson.

—Mmmm. Safely under cover, though he was freezing his
tail off, Knucks was getting into the spirit of things again.

—You have to lie down in the water.

—Lie down! I'll drownd!

—You can't do it standing up.

—Sure you can.

—Float?

—Well, float. Who cares?

—That'd be funny. You and me bobbing around together
like two bottles with messages inside.

—You got these weird ideas.

—Just lean back in the water and let your feet come up to
the top.

—I'm not lettin my fucking head go under.

—Oh, go ahead. Just don't breathe.

—Whadya going to do when I'm lyin on the bottom?

—You wait and see.

—Why not just skip this part?

I Wanna Know
Have You Ever
Seen the Rain?

The next thing he knew, the rain was pouring with an intensity he had never felt before, its sound almost covered the thunder, it left no room to breathe. It dropped like a curtain between the Auk and the dinghy. It held back the wind like a thick wall.

—Dad! Dad! Pull me in!

Hank was pulling. —Get in the boat baby. We've got to get these sails off.

—Let me do the jib for once.

—You know how. Go ahead. Just don't let it fall overboard. And don't you.

Hank dropped the main and furled it rapidly, snapping the new elastic sail stops he and Roy had made out of shock cord. They were much faster than conventional ties. The bow of his boat was almost out of sight, less than thirty feet away behind the sheets of rain. —Are you still there, Roy?

—Yes.

—Hurry. Before the wind gets here. He could barely see the small figure trying to stuff the jib in its sack, too slowly. How long the rain would hold back the wind was the question. He went forward to help.

—It's so heavy, Dad, with rain in it.

—It's almost done. Thanks. I want you below. Let's go.

The rain hurt. Looking at the opaque green surface of the sea, they could see the force of each drop in the splash of displacement. If they looked at it one way they would see it as the surface erupting, the crater walls liquid, the circumference bursting upward, the center empty.

—Wow, said Roy. Let me get out of here.

Hank started the motor, but kept it in neutral. There was nowhere to go and he had to hope he was no closer to any ledges than when he had shut his eyes. He had lost his bearings.

—Go below, Roy. Secure everything. Close that hatch behind you and check the other.

Inside the boat, the roar of the rain reverberated like the sound of his own head when Roy listened in a conch shell. (Blood, he was told.) He stood in the hatchway and peeked out between the slides at his father, who was putting his raingear over his wet clothes.

—Why are you doing that?

—What?

—Why are you doing that?

—I don't know.

—You sure can't get any wetter.

—Well, too late now. It's on. I won't get cold.

The lightning and thunder began to seem as constant as the rain; it was almost impossible to remember which flash went with which crack, boom or roll, estimating distance. There was no distance, and then the wind began.

I Wanna Know

—It's opting for wind, Janey. Look how black it is northwest of us.

—God, somebody's getting wet. I'm going to put on my suit. I'll get yours.

—My boots. I'll need my boots.

—Do you want me to listen for the weather?

—We can see the weather.

—Aren't we too close to this point?

—I'm just going to take it straight out to sea from here. At least, there aren't any unmarked rocks in the mouth of this bay.

—It gets so rough out there.

—Still it's safest.

Because of the outboard's steady firing, they were always

shouting. It was a sound which created discontent (opposite to the continent and soothing white noise in buildings they weren't in). Dark and cruel, it was guaranteed to lay bare their nerves.

—I can't stand this suit. It's too hot. I'm going to take it off again.

—God, Janey. You can't do anything for more than two minutes without changing your mind.

—That's not what you said when I was stowing. Or nursing.

—You get all excited about doing something, then you just go out like a match first draft that comes along.

—Thanks. I'd give anything for a draft right now. It's rolly and hot and I'm sick.

He thought if she would get up off her butt and actually do something, she wouldn't be sick. He saw her, forlorn and separate, watching his actions and longing to be part of what he was doing, he who could sail, he who could swim, could ski, climb mountains. Whose body did what he told it.

—I wonder if we ran into trouble if you could handle the boat.

—Some time to wonder about that.

—Well, really. I fall overboard. The wind is blowing. You're barfing. The ledges uncovering. The baby screaming. What do you do?

—Jesus, how am I supposed to know. What's this, an etiquette quiz?

—You quit barfing. You bring the boat up into the wind and then you go through the wind and you fall off and come down below me and come up with sails drawing enough to get you going and you coast right up to me. Got that?

Snatched from the jaws of death.

—The sails aren't even up.

Now I am dreaming about the land someplace and making a little garden and pulling the dirt over my head and waiting for the rain. Now I am dreaming that I don't need an excuse. I am arranged in an orderly row waiting for the drought to be over; then the earth begins to heave like water and tosses me back to lie like a parable on the side of the road.

—You look green. Think of something else and you won't get sick.

Give Me the Beat Boys

Zak was elated. By his feet was a sack with a couple of cool six packs, and he had bought a pair of each variety of Hostess cupcakes found in the bait store. He aimed to please and share his pleasure. Never in his wildest dreams would he have considered the friendly welcome a possibility. His wildest dreams stopped at the stills of his Now Showing case: of him fucking a real doll they had to hold down at first, then of Knucks' white butt doing it, and her tired eyes still smiling over his shoulder at him, Zak. Then, there had to be four pictures to fill the case, him doing it again and again but his hands over her eyes so she couldn't look behind him at Knucks the way she looked at him. She would have to close her eyes for him, or he would close them for her.

He sang along —And free my soul I wanna get lost in your Rock and Roll and Drift Away.

When the rain came down in torrents, he upped his amps and outsang it. Luckily, he knew where he was and the water was pretty good there, because he was about as prepared for disaster as a rock band taking a shower.

There's a Calm Before the Storm

Martha, Hen and Ednah, however, were completely suited up in yellow slickers and anchored in the cove behind Jones's Garden. They had time to watch the haze condense into a thunderous black sky, and they looked at a bandanna hanging motionless from a piece of driftwood on the top of the island.

—That's one of the children from that place, said Martha to Ednah.

—What children? What place?

—You know, that camp. They row around together in all kinds of weather and then they each spend three days in solitude on an island.

—The bay is full of them. Everywhere you look there is a bandanna on a stick.

—It's not as bad as all that, Hen.

—Well, the woods are full of them, if you ask me. It used to be we could go ashore and pick berries and dig clams and not worry about bumping into people.

—We never bring the dinghy nowadays anyhow.

—Maybe that's part of the reason, dear. The islands don't belong to us anymore.

—I wonder who he is. I wonder what he is doing.

—Who?

—The camper.

—Moping around, I suppose. It's just as likely that it's a girl, you know.

—Oh my, said Ednah. How lonely. Well, I should like that.

—It must be a little scary.

—I think it is vastly overrated.

—Now, with this storm coming, I think not.

The dark sky crossed the invisible peninsula and gestured toward it with a series of brilliant strokes of lightning. It was coming soon enough.

If we had not prudently hurried for shelter, were still there. In the mouth of the bay we cannot see in the rain. We are in sight of land, but it has hidden. I will die if I lose my boat. That is likely. Put on your life vest. We won't live long in this water. The rest is a long hibernation. No one will be looking for us. Hope intrudes. We are all here balanced around. Does any one of us know exactly what we are hoping for?

We're hardly going to run from one end of the boat to the other to this elusive embrace. Don't rock the boat.

Every flash is a pleasure of edges, of nerve ends, of boundaries.

We refuse to be reductive.

It is not all, it can't be all rain and wind and fish and blood. If it is (or were) we are crazy. Fiercely apart because we want to be together. What thoughtless fish ever knew its child, its father, its mother (its sister, its brother)? What beautiful free absent fish?

Coming Down
Coming Down

So the rain obscured the surface upon which Knucks was trying to float. He had required a great deal of help. He had inadequate adipose and sunk every chance he got, but Karen was very supportive. When the sky and the sea were indistinguishable, they agreed that prone was the safest posture with lightning all around and found a smooth spot where the morning glories came out over the sand into the rocks. They were there for the whole long storm. When the pouring and blowing stopped, they would almost separate and then it would start again, modulating not moderating.

No one had much time for words. Zak was trying to sing along with the handy man: Comma comma comma comma come come, but the traps were creating too much windage, and the boat was hard to handle. They were coming unstowed and had to be lashed down. Then his antenna broke and water got in his equipment and it all blew. Thank god for the cellophane on the cupcakes.

Hen put out a second anchor and started the motor again, while Ednah and Martha hoped against hope it would not hail. They all kept low because the lightning was banging around on the islands.

The sea was building and Jane was sick. She went below with the baby who seemed perfectly happy to bounce around and watch her mother vomit. Dick was prepared with enough space to maneuver. He steered each wave separately. His muscles ached, but he didn't wish to be anywhere else.

Hank didn't know where he was. The wind snapped his elastic sail stops and the escaping sail was drawing; it was impossible to keep headed into the wind. She was heeling and sailing desperately, and probably being put down into the islands. Roy's head was sticking out of the hatch and he was cheering.

—Dad! Wow! This is out of sight!

Suddenly, the break in the clouds was final. There was air to breathe where there had been water, no wind.

—Let's just lie here, said Knucks.

—What about Richie?

—Who, Zak? All them amps. We'll hear him coming.

As it cleared, Hank thought he knew where he was again; the new brilliant light transformed a distant dot, a buoy he thought, yes, a red nun. Studying the contour lines on his chart would sort out the islands before he had to go too close. Sighting along the main which he had lashed down with a sheet when it began unstopping itself in the wind, he saw what seemed to be a tear. There were some large hailstones around his feet. —Come on out, he said to Roy. Look at those.

—It's ice. Where'd they come from?

—That's hail.

—In the summertime?

—That's when it hails.

—Come on, Dad.

—You're thinking of sleet and snow.

—It was so hot.

—Up there it was cold and these are just raindrops that bounced around adding layers of ice. If you cut them open, it's like tree rings inside. Or, I think, pearls.

—Can I use your knife?

—You probably need a special little saw.

—Can I keep them in the ice box until we get one?

—I think you need a freezer, but you can try.

—They're already not as big. I better hurry. I'm going to get the bailer to scoop them up.

—Just save a couple of big ones.

—If I get a lot they'll keep each other cold.

—O.K., get the bailer.

—Dad.

—What?

—The dinghy's gone.

—Oh fuck.

—I can't get the bailer.

—Fuck the bailer. Who needs a bailer without a dinghy. How did it come loose?

—My scallop was in it.

—Fuck the scallop. Were you screwing with the knot out there?

—My whole collection of drift iron was in it.

—Your damn drift iron. So were the oars and the oarlocks and the seats and the bow and the stern. The whole fucking dinghy's gone because you can't keep your hands off things.

—We're not dragging the painter. The line's gone too.

—Yeah. I see. I wonder how that happened. My fault.

—We've got the life raft Dad.

—That's for emergencies.

—I bet this is an emergency.

—Yup.

—I bet my scallop thinks it's an emergency.

—More than likely.

—With all that rainwater in the bucket, it's going to die.

—Yup.

—Aw. I wish I hadn't kept it.

—You better get your hailstones if you want them.

—They'll just melt.

—We'll never find it.

—Are we going to look for it?

—What's the use? Maybe some kind soul will find it and call the Coast Guard.

—The fishermen are pretty nice.

Jane lay still and shamed, knowing her insides had only half an hour of grace ahead unless she could get her feet under her and go out in the bright light and air. She would force the clarity into her lungs, pump it through her blood, communicate peace and atonement to her resistant gut. Who? Who was going to stiffen the weak knees, balance the head; who the gyroscope, who the gimbals? She felt immensely disloyal sitting up. Puking in a bucket while Dick steered the Gypsy through squalls. He was not speaking but he had not blown overboard because the boat was moving straight. To whom was she disloyal? Why was she ungrateful? She did not even want to be alive when she was seasick. If she had been captain she would have taken them veering from Scylla's teeth straight down Charybdis's gullet. And then who could tell her she would not have been spewed out again, rejected, belched. Go breathe. She stood up in another wave of guilt. Why can't you do it? Whatever it is.

I am dying of abstraction. Without a point to make. Splashing off milkily or rearranging hidden objects and still things happen without me. The boat is heading for the rendezvous with someone I used to know and my other friend who is more present because she chooses to be absent. If the storm is over where is my state of grace?

So together we had been laughing blithely in the face of adversity, because after all, the hairs on our heads are numbered like the days of our lives and new little gray hairs poke out to replace the falling dark ones, and the fluff of the newborn with light behind it is sufficient halo. So if this is the end it is and if it isn't it isn't.

Until suddenly Ednah realized that perhaps her hope had been that she was something put away for a rainy day. Which had come and gone. That indeed the balancing act was arranged as she had tried not to perceive it, a matter of magnification and shifts of attention, and not an overwhelming drive to some final passion, which, in a way, had she hoped, lay just beyond her consciousness.

Or was that really just what kept her balance and she liked it very much?

—My heavens, Ednah. You look like you could use some Geritol.

—God. Don't give her any Geritol. We can't stand her as it is.

—Hen, she looks pale. Don't joke. Are you all right?

Ednah's funny retorts were somewhere else and they were worried. She was just absorbing another dose of disappointment and in a second she said, —I read somewhere that in a thunderstorm the ozone level changes, especially with a lot of lightning. I think I'm having an ozone reaction. Does the air smell sweet?

—You'll be all right?

—You couldn't have read that anywhere. You're making that up.

—I did indeed. I think so.

The fishermen *are* nice. Zak has found a dinghy that he might let Karen use for the next two days on the island. It is a perfectly good little boat, broke loose in the storm. She might like it. He might like her. She might like him. What a fucker that his set blew. But he was a lucky shit not to be on the rocks. Even with his powerful motor he was blown down, sailing sideways with the windage of his traps. Later he would go ahead and set them. The lightening of the weather made it more worthwhile. Nothing like a boat when it's fine. Tomorrow was Sunday and he couldn't set them then. The lobsters were going to be in church. Or something. His wits were sharpening with the breeze. Shooting the breeze. He needed someone to joke with, you know, to describe his close call to, to drink beer with and jesus was he hungry even horny now he had time to remember the knockers floating in a tide pool and the purpose of his cupcakes. They were dry but he didn't even eat one so she could have first choice. You never think of how nice the fishermen are and how really gallant.

That stupid Hen had his anchor fouled on something so they couldn't leave. The girls were in a snit. The one anchor was hauled and the rope coiled neatly.

—Why did you ever put out two?

—You were here when it was blowing. You saw what it was like.

—I don't think we really needed two anchors. Look how that's holding.

—How could we ever be blown off that?

Hen rested his aching back and cramping hands and looked at his mates. —This is the second anchor. The first one is the one that came up so nicely.

—Are we going to have to cut it off?

—I hope not. I don't want to do that, they're expensive.

—Maybe the Coast Guard is nearby.

—You think they're your private valets.

—Well, they certainly do help people with engine trouble, or even out of gas.

—But all I have to do is decide that I've thrown $75 overboard, and we can go home.

—Well, is that what is going to happen?

—Or I could dive down and unfoul it.

—What an idea! You'll have a stroke.

—I think it would be worth $75 for you not to have a stroke.

—That's how I always have unfouled them.

—But you haven't had one hung up in centuries.

—There's another trick I read about but I can't believe it works.

—Oh?

—We take the boat around and around in circles and the anchor comes up.

—Let's do that.

—But I don't think it works with this kind of anchor.

—We'll never know unless we try.

So Martha took the helm and the Merry Maid slowly circled the anchor, around and around, while Hen pulled and Ednah leaned overboard to see what the problem could be. Nothing happened.

—Got trouble? hollered Zak.

—We sure do, said Ednah.

—The anchor's fouled.

—Hold on. I'll give her a yank.

He came alongside and jumped aboard with his own bowline which he cleated down. He held his skiff off and pushed her astern so Hen's varnish wouldn't suffer.

Hen gave Zak the line which he jerked vigorously in several directions. —She's some hung up, he said. And he took off his boots and jumped overboard. —You got her in neutral? he said. —I don't want to get run over. Martha made sure she was in neutral. Zak dove down the length of the anchor line, and the whole boat felt it come free. He exhaled explosively as he hit the surface and explained. —Some awful mess you had down there. They were very grateful. Also grateful that he climbed back on his own boat. —Oh Jesus. Don't let me forget them boots, he said.

—No siree, said Ednah colloquially. She handed them to him.

—What can we do for you? asked Hen.

—Not a thing. Turned off some fine ain't it?

—Thanks to you all is not lost.

Zak began to feel like a character in a book he would not have looked twice at and backed his skiff away.

—Thank you so much.

—We're certainly glad some fisherman can swim.

—That's a myth I believed, said Ednah, questioning him.

—Some can. Some can't, he said. We'll see ya.

They headed out of the cove towards home waving cheer-
fully and admiring the light on the water, wondering which
part was light and which part thought.

While Karen and Knucks lay not thinking nor even dreaming in the technicolor wash of light that bathed their tangled
legs and the morning glories where their sleeping heads lay,
they never worried about lines that bothered them. The sleep
of reason engenders monsters, for instance, never entered
their heads.

And Dick was very reasonable when poor Jane came up, no
longer green, but ashen. —Honey, do you want to put the sails
up? The wind has shifted.

—In a minute. Let me get my legs working again.

—Do you want a soda?

—Yes.

—Is Sally O.K.?

—She got bored and fell asleep in the middle.

—The least she could have done is appreciate the climax.

—And the denouement.

—When was that?

—This is it.

—How much longer before we get there?

—Oh, an hour or so at most.

—Well, she'll probably miss that too. She's out like a light.

—That's how you go out, not how you stay out.

—How would you say it then?

—I don't know. Better. She's out cold?

—She's not cold. Look at her. Of all the cozy warm
creatures.

She was lying on a towel on the cabin sole with her little

butt, heavily disguised in diapers, in the air and her tiny toes showing like beach pebbles at the edge of a disappearing wave.

—Look at that, Janey. We did well, honey.

—We did.

—Do you feel better?

—Do you guess it's always like that for everybody? Putting it all into one little package like that. All your eggs in one basket, so to speak.

—What are you talking about?

—I mean there are moments when it works, when she just holds everything together, things almost make sense for a second.

—You're so abstruse.

—You know what I mean, Dick. You know perfectly well. Just then. We were looking at her together. It was a nice moment.

—Yeah, it was. She's cute. Not as cute as you though.

—Oh shit, that's not it.

—Well, you're not so cute when you're green.

—Oh damn. That's it. It's gone.

It may always not have taken place.

But they didn't even wake up they were so happy and exhausted. They were expecting and were tuned for Zak's musical alarm, hollering into the cove on the wings of song. The commonplace drone of motors did not penetrate, spawning a sound that was absolutely unparticular and powerless to attract their sleeping attention. So they were knotted together as naked as on the days they were born when Zak, who suspected something when he was not even greeted on the beach, came over the rise and almost stepped in them.

—You fuckers, he said and they sat up.

—And I brung the cupcakes, which he threw at them with his right hand. Then with his left he hurled the sixpack, which

Karen, dodging the rain of twinkies and hohos, met full force with her temple and that was that.

—Oh Jesus shit, look what you done, he said.

—Me! Knucks could no more believe his ears than his eyes.

—You her, everybody.

—And she so friendly.

—Oh God in heaven.

—What's that shit?

—Maybe she ain't dead.

—Just conked out.

—Don't know my own strength.

—She sure is dead O.K.

—Them sixpacks weigh a ton.

—This one's a bloody mess. What the fuck are you going to do? They're going to catch you.

—First thing the police gonna do is fish around inside and see whose little buggers are swimmin around in there and they ain't mine, that's for sure.

—But what'll we do? She's so pretty.

—We'll just float her out to sea and they'll think she drownded.

—Big hole like that in her head?

—She maybe bumped into a rock. These dumbshit kids swim anywhere.

—Anyhow how can we get rid of her? She was so sweet.

—She didn't never say no?

—She didn't never.

—Fuck.

—It was her idea.

—A nice little thing like that. Shit I wisht I was cuttin you up and puttin you in bait boxes.

—Look it just happened.

—I oughta just take off and leave you right here. With them buggers of yours inside like fingerprints, ain't nobody gonna care about me.

—Except me, and I'm tellin.

Roy said —Hey, Dad, don't feel bad about the dinghy. That was a great storm. I'd like to do that again. Remember when the sail started flapping. You were great, Dad. Just because your knot didn't hold. It mighta been me. But I didn't touch that end. Hey, Dad. Just really don't look like that. I mean that's just how terrible that storm was. Our dinghy got sunk. Do you guess it got sunk? That was really great. Wait till I tell everybody about it. I could leave out the part about the painter coming untied. It could just swamp and we could cut it free. And we'd be saved. Hey, Dad. You're really a great sailor. I'd like to do that again. Wouldn't you? If it got sunk nobody'd find it though. But my scallop wouldn't be dead. It's hard to decide. Don't you think, Dad? Guess we'd rather find our dinghy with a dead scallop. Right?

Dick and Jane set the sails again. The freshening breeze would take them as fast as the motor, and they could almost see the island now. Because the tide was not quite high and Ednah still had not caught a mackerel, the Merry Maid was taking the long way home and stopping to cross and recross certain passages. Hank gave Roy the tiller and charge of the motor, while he got out his kit to mend the torn sail. Zak and Knucks, however, did not know how to proceed. They did decide to cover her up with their shirts so she wouldn't get sunburned. They debated whether sinking her in one piece was so dangerous that they had to divide her up among several lobster traps. She might pop right back up if they didn't. Neither one wanted to say that he could or couldn't cut her up into bait. Whatever they did had to be done when the tide was out again, at night, so that no one, even they, could see, and so that whatever traces of mayhem they left would be in the mud flats and covered up and washed away by day. Zak pointed out that they had to set the traps by midnight because the next day was Sunday and setting traps was illegal Sunday. What they had was time on their hands, the whole time and space between tides. They decided to set themselves up on the cove side in case any summer people showed and had to be discouraged from going ashore. Knucks could work on a couple of traps so they would hold more. Zak could work on his audio equipment so they would have some music again. And they would eat the cupcakes and drink the evidence because they had never had any lunch. Nor had poor Karen but she did eat a lot of berries beforehand.

The only one who was still hungry was Jane, because she had lost her lunch and was feeling fine now. She had to think twice about what she ate, because her post-maternity metabolism was not up to her appetite. Her body just kept adding to itself. Taking an apple, she hoped to con herself into feeling full. The breeze was wonderful and they sailed on, almost directly, toward the anchorage off Jones's Garden to meet Hank and his baby. Jane had picked the spot where they would meet and was beginning to feel responsible and apprehensive, thinking it was like undressing to show someone a favorite place. At first, when she had seen it, she was sure it was a joke, that Jones was a very bad gardener immortalized on the chart with a mess of rock and weeds, but when they landed she thought she would choose such a stone for her memory, because the tangle and profusion was so completely beautiful, incomprehensible, ungardenable. Unpossessible, it became the island of herself, whether it was her own island or not, no matter who was the true Jones, or if there was one. Dick was on the kitchen telephone deciding where to meet, and she was right there making supper and said Hank would love that island. Dick agreed because it was also a terrific anchorage with good clam flats if they hit the tides right.

But now she wondered who in the world could love that mess but herself, and it was clear that the mudflats would be under water for the rest of the afternoon. In the morning, if she knew Dick and Hank together, they would have become very competitive about their duties as cruising sailors and be sailing into the sunrise before she was out of her sleeping bag. We will never get to Isle au Haut if we don't start . . . Sailing this way, there was always a destination, hard to perceive occasionally if you were slatting around in the swells, but there; though you might not make it.

—Hey, Dad. How much farther?

—Almost. Almost. It's behind that big island there.

—Are we going to get to sail anymore?

—About the time I get the sail mended we'll be there.

—You need some of that neat tape stuff.

—Wouldn't work.

—Sure it does. It's great.

—You have to sew afterward. That's just for quick mends.

—It says it lasts forever.

—I like to sew. It makes me feel like I'm taking care of the boat.

—You know what we really need?

—What?

—A new sail.

—That makes a lot of things we really need.

—Just a CB, a dinghy and a sail.

—That's all?

—Well, baloney too. Maybe we can get all that stuff in Camden.

—What you need is a mother.

—What for, Dad? I just like it you and me.

—You need somebody to tell you sufficient unto the day is the evil thereof.

—What? Mom wouldn't tell me that. What's that mean?

—My mom did. Almost every day.

—What's it mean?

—Make do. You have to make do.

—How could it mean that?

—Enough bad things happen in one day without wanting anything else.

—Then it doesn't mean make do.

—Sure it does.

—Make do means you're not going to spend any money.

—Same stuff.

—Dad, you're wacky. You're not going to spend all that money they gave you, huh?

—Well, sure. But I want to think about it for a while.

—We do need Mom. You know what she'd say: sure honey you want it do it.

—Yeah. Well. That's too easy.

—What's too easy about that?

—You have to choose.

—Mom doesn't. She just does what she wants.

—That's great. Why do you think she's not here with us right now.

—She doesn't like the ocean. If she had a vacation she'd rather go to the mountains.

—That's not choosing?

—Not for her, it's not. She just knows.

—Suppose I chose to go to the mountains.

—You'd never get around to it.

—I'd just say fuck the ocean and forget the fishermen and we'd go live with your mom again.

—I wouldn't come.

—Who's going to take care of you?

—I can sail.

The trouble with fishing when you don't catch anything is that it is very boring and most people don't want to do it much less hear about it. One solution is to pay a great deal of attention to negligible details, the light on the water, the waver of the lure, the feel of the rod, the eyes that are steady then look away, what they see or think they see on the horizon. Another solution is to pick up a detail and take it as far as she dares; possibilities unfold, but one word, one touch limits another. Before she knows it, even the ellipses touch down. The trick she hopes is not to go under when they do, to live a long life by changing lures, to refuse until the end to know yourself, which is to fix and kill if it can happen. The tragic end. It happens too soon.

Ednah reeled in and replaced the daredevil with a Mepps while Hen sighted what seemed to be a tiny boat in the mouth of the bay. He was not sure he could see that far and asked Martha to look at it too.

—I don't see anyone in it. What do you think it means?

—It's a tender. If anyone was in it he would not have survived.

—Oh no, Hen, the boat's still floating. He would be alive.

—Unless it was a child.

—And he couldn't swim.

—Suppose a child went out in the afternoon.

—His mother shouldn't have let him.

—We'd better pick up the dinghy and turn it in to the Coast Guard.

—Someone will need it.

—Someone might be in it. Just napping.

—He floated too far out.

—We should tow him back to shore.

—When I was a little boy I dreamed of rescuing someone and being richly rewarded.

—We all did.

You Can't
Always Get

The music was just beginning to start up again; it flicked in and out of the static at first and then came in steadily.

—Can't get no volume out of this thing, said Zak.

—Good.

—It just won't come in.

—How come do you guess?

—Shit. I don't know. Blew something I don't know about.

—Hey I thought you knew about all of that.
—Yeah me too.
—I don't mind it low.
—It's O.K. but it's not the same.

What You Want

—You want to sail, Janey?
—Sure.
—See that can up there. You have to stay below it.

She concentrated on the feel of the boat, the balance, the way the wind drew it along and the little swells were cut by the bow. At first she did very well maintaining the relationships, but then it became a little less clear how to do it. Had the wind changed, was the current among the islands putting her down so she would miss her mark? She tried to put the boat up a little higher into the wind.

—Fall off. You're pinching her.

So she let it wander down a little, looking for the same feel to the helm as she had at first.

—Now come up. You're sailing bare.

Didn't she wish. Naked as a jaybird and alone, flashing over the water and showing them, just showing them she could do it, alone. If she had learned. Herself. A natural genius. Untaught.

Just Try and Try
Try and Try

Didn't they all. But they never talked about their dreams. She knew that Hen had always wanted to rescue someone and obligingly dreamed it was herself. But why were they still at it. It was too late, time to give up and go home rather than run out to sea another little mile to see why there was such a tiny boat alone where no one should have taken it.

—We must go and help them. We have plenty of time.

—Or at least go see.

—Reel in Ednah. It's full speed ahead.

—What a nuisance. And me with no supper.

—You've got your pogy.

—Marvelous. I'm not going to clean it yet. That would be giving up.

—You're never going to catch a fish.

—Waited this long, I can wait a little bit longer.

—Reel it in or it will get tangled in seaweed.

—You rescue your dinghy. I'll attend to the fishing.

—No one ever caught a fish going ten knots with the lure bouncing on the surface.

—Maybe I'll be the first.

No, Don't
You Tell Me . . .

—Dick, could that be the Auk out there putting up her sail?

—Give me the tiller and let me sail. You're hopeless, anyhow. Get the glasses and see.

—I believe it is.

—Have you ever seen it?

—No.

—Then how can you tell?

—I don't know. It just is. An old boat.

—Let me see the glasses. I think you're right. She looks pretty from here but I bet those sails are lousy.

—You're too far away to tell that.

—You can tell by the color.

. . . He Gave Up
on Me

—Dad, there's a sailboat. Is that your friends?

—It's hard to tell. Those new ones all look alike.

—Clorox bottles.

—That's it.

—Why would anybody want one of those?

—To get where they're going. They're efficient, fast. They're nice. It's just different.

—I love this boat. Will you give it to me when you die?

—Not planning on dying just yet.

—Maybe when you just get too old.

—Thanks.

For what. His least mediocre moments were spent in the Auk with Roy. Nothing irrelevant. No intrusions. Clinging together on an old boat that seemed to understand on her own what the ocean was up to, so that he could even say his most perfect moments, except for the lingering superstition that when he could claim the most perfect moment it would be taken away. He could not remember if Auks were extinct because of an excess of perfection (like dinosaurs, intent on one moment and not the next) or if they had been killed off by man, seeking auk feathers in Auckland to augment his income. Awkward. He had just begun to feel what must be admitted to be a reasonable fear, of doddering into extinction, more and more this awkward self and no one could say to him anymore don't be silly, a promising young man like yourself. After a certain age can you be promising? He would be 'set in his ways,' a lousy punster who could not remember the difference between a dodo and an auk.

He was not answering Roy. It was not as simple as being hurt that his kid could ask him to die—essence of kids. It was that even dying was not a big enough gift for Roy. Even if now he gave him everything he could think of, everything he had, everything he didn't have, there would still be a gap that no magic three wishes could fill. He had to make do, he had to dodder on, he had to stow it, he had to stuff it.

Just Lookin for
Blue Eyes

—Shall I grab it, Hen?

—I will.

—It would be a nice little boat.

—I'm always surprised that people don't keep things neater.

—He must have been using it like a trailer.

—If his dinghy looks like that, think of his boat.

—What does that bucket have in it?

—A chip to keep the water from splashing out.

—She took on water.

—Some of it came from that bucket, too. Why would you carry a bucket of water around in the ocean?

—Pick up the painter there, it's dragging.

—Did it break? Did it come untied?

—You can't tell.

If We Never
Meet Again

—They're waving at us, Dad. It's them. Your friends. No look. They're not coming towards us anymore. They're changing course. What are they doing?

—Picking something up?

—They're scrambling around. Look, Dad. What are they doing?

—It looks like they found a dinghy.

—Oh boy. That's our dinghy.

—Not possible.

—It beat us here.

—Roy. That damn dinghy wouldn't even have come in this direction.

—Well, everybody couldn't have lost one.

There's No One Else in the World

—The person isn't in it.
—Lord, I hope he hasn't drowned.
—The oars are tied down, Martha. No one was rowing it.
—What a lot of junk there is in it.
—It is a yacht tender.
—What is all that rusty stuff in the bottom of the boat?
—It looks like old pieces of things, a ratchet, a block.
—There's something jumping around in that bucket.
—A scallop! Look at all those eyes.
—A scallop! Well, I like scallops almost as well as mackerel.
—There's only one.
—I guess that will have to be enough.

Your Eyes . . .

Some not quite extinguished hope had Jane looking very hard at Hank. She had the binoculars to her eyes and he turned and she felt him focus on her gaze. Is that possible, magnified? The glasses reverse and he must have imagined the vanishing points of pupils to have seen anything at all. Still she was sure of it, some little juncture of still points; could they ask for more?

—I really don't want to drag this extra dinghy around.
—We shouldn't leave it to be banged up on the rocks.
—I don't know what we want with it.
—If it goes on the rocks it will be kindling by tomorrow.
—I don't want to take the time to go by the Coast Guard.
—We could give it to somebody at the anchorage. Somebody will turn up.

. . . Got Me Reeling

Hank was surprised by the binocular's focus. They were not looking at his mended sail or his waving son. They were looking down his eyes. He was too far away to be embarrassed but close enough to be touched.

—Hey, Dad. Who's got right of way?

—We would.

—We're going to bump right off that point.

—They would have to fall off and let us pass. But I'm going to come up and give them room to come in beside us. We can sail into the cove together.

Hello Stranger

—Perfect timing, shouted Dick.

They were all waving and then tending their sails and then coasting slowly together into the cove.

—This is Roy. Remember Roy?

—Not like that we don't. Hi, Roy.

—We're Dick and Jane.

—Where's Baby Sally?

—She's down below. She's asleep.

—Where's Spot and Puff?

—We left them at home.

—Really?

—No. Silly.

—You've got two dinghies. Was that what we saw you doing just now?

—Just found it ten minutes ago.

—Well, we lost ours.

—Roy.

—Yeah. It sank.

—That was an awful storm. You were in it?

—Where else?

—As soon as we get ourselves anchored, we'll give you the dinghy.

—Oh boy. You hear that, Dad? But it's not as good as ours. Is that why you look that that?

—Hadn't you better give it to the Coast Guard? Somebody may be hoping as hard as I that that is how he will see his dinghy again.

—Well, if somebody turned yours in and you got it back, you could turn this one in.

—I guess I'm still trying to work on the honor system.

—You haven't heard of the salvage system. The law of the sea. If it's come loose and you find it, it's yours.

—I'm not sure when you switch systems.

—When you need a dinghy, Dad. That's when. You really need one so I can row around the cove and get out of your hair.

—We can just borrow it for that, Roy.

—Look. I want to get rid of the thing. I don't want to go to the Coast Guard. I don't want to leave it tied to a pot buoy. Borrow it from the loser.

—Right, Dad, right.

—I just think maybe we should be reporting it. You don't know what awful thing happened in that dinghy. If the big boat sank. Or what.

—Well then, Christ. Borrow it from me. You don't know where it came from. I came out with two dinghies, O.K.?

—Take your dinghy where you can get it. I knew you guys would start fussing. We haven't even anchored.

—Right, Mrs. Dick.

—Jane's O.K. Call me Jane.

Roy blushed, had goofed.

—That's O.K. Was that your sea etiquette?

—Are we anchoring?

—That looks like a mooring. If we picked up a mooring we could raft up.

—Better be sure it's a mooring not a pot buoy. Pop right up in a blow.

—Sure hope it's done blowing.

—That's a mooring. You get it, Dick. I'll loop around and throw you some lines when we come back around.

This Side of Heaven

—Well. We're going home.

—I suppose I almost caught a fish.

—A pogy, a scallop, a dinghy. What do you want?

—Everything.

I don't know why we didn't all die. Going back to my little house in the grassy garden, why could we not all have died? It isn't paid for. It isn't bought. We could have died as well here. Or, am I, with the night coming now simply to be fuscous as a mushroom under the black pines, in the forest floor, or in the carpet of a rained-in car where the leaves have mulched down dragging the machinery into rust and me with it no longer rusting out cyclically, monthly, but only hypothetically. Dreaming of elusive fish, mingling in the blood of fish. Could I ever throw one back? Even if everyone has eaten one pogy, would I be the only one to try it again, a mouthful of bones, but believing everything I read.

—Still?

Put Your Loving
Hand in Mine

As soon as they were tied up, they shook hands and kissed all around, realizing it was quite a storm they had survived to arrive in this peaceful cove nowhere together. Roy wanted to go ashore but was not allowed to go alone because he tended to forget details like tying the tender to something on the beach. More than one of his vagrant boats had been rescued by a swim. So he just went rowing all along the shore in the extra dinghy. Before the sun disappeared, the tidepool at the bottom of the boat was full of scallop shells, moon snails, starfish. The grownups sat together and drank quantities of beer; until Sally reminded them that she was getting very hungry and was lying in a puddle.

They tickled her hand while she nursed, and she would hold on to any finger the way all primates do.

—What are you doing with this child out in the middle of the ocean, said Hank. She needs to be on the land where she can swing in the trees.

—She doesn't care where she is. She thinks you're a tree right now.

—I am. Mine is a long and sad tale.

—Enchanted dormouse eh?

—You remember that?

—It *is* a long tail certainly.

—What's that from? said Dick.

—Pool of Tears.

—Janey reads stuff like that to Sally. She's out of her head.

—I am not!

—A knot! Oh, do let me help you to undo it.

Jane and Hank broke up in the wild beery giggles and Sally was bubbling and cooing and perfectly happy with breasts and fingers.

Diddy Wa Diddy

Roy rowed up to the tough looking fellow who was working on something in his big skiff and listening to his radio.

—What are you doing? he said.

—Walkin the horse, said Zak.

Roy looked around for a horse and decided the man meant shut up and go away. So he did. He saw another man on the shore mending traps and, not wanting to be crowded with the whole ocean around him, he went on over to another one of the islands and poked along the shore. It got dark and he was hungry too and went back to the sailboats.

—Hey, Dad. You know your theory about fishermen telling the real truth.

—Yup.

—It's full of baloney.

—Oh yeah?

—There's a guy over there told me he was walkin a horse.

—He did?

—He didn't have any horse.

—He didn't?

—Quit that, Dad.

—O.K. Sorry. I meant what did he mean?

—I think he was a suspicious character.

—Roy. You always think everyone is a suspicious character. Too much TV.

—Suspicious characters aren't on TV. They're in books, Dad.

—Then you don't have to worry about them, said Dick. They're almost extinct. The only people going to believe in them are your Dad and this lady here.

—What do you mean extinct?

—Nobody reads anymore. It's all going to be visual. All the characters on film or video.

Diddy Mean.

I don't know if it means anything or not and why do I still expect I will know before I am erased, all my little lines and smudges, wrists written on in blue vein characters and the blotches of time showing on the papery backs of my hands, and nearly erased all my hope. I have to think that even if I caught the fish it would not be enough. I still would want to see the hearts that will beat for days in a cup of saltwater and still want the sweet flesh and my hands washed and my face kissed. I suppose I could have died sooner.

Someday

—That's the whole big thing in communications these days. It's all going to be more direct with pictures.

—You can see how things are changing. How maybe what we used to call subtlety is muddle.

—I've seen some mighty muddled pictures in my day.

—Well, it's different. With pictures someday it could improve. The stimulus is more direct.

—When are we going to eat? Roy said.

—Are you fixing supper Jane?

—Sort of.

—Sort of? What do you mean sort of?

—I mean I'm just going to open some cans since nobody caught any fish. I'm just waiting for the signal.

—I'm starved.

—That's the signal.

Sally was ready to sleep again, obliging baby, and her mother washed her up and kissed her face and put her down on her blanket. Then she opened two big cans of spaghetti.

—Worms, said Roy. —We're going to eat that stuff? I don't want it.

—Be polite, said his father. —You better want what you get. So Roy politely quit the scene and, inside the Auk, comforted himself with a few peanut butter sandwiches and his two dollar transistor radio.

Someday Never Comes

They tied up in the last gleams of light, and while Martha and Hen unloaded the boat, Ednah cleaned the dead pogy which she intended to fry the daylights out of. The scallop was large and she took it to cook in a little butter. Hamburger at the end of a day of fishing was still against her principles; better to eat almost nothing (which wasn't necessary because of Mrs.

Thibault's pie). Blueberry pie, arranged long in advance, simplified her need for principles. Though, it must be said, she was fully prepared to choke to death on a bone before she got to dessert.

Zak and Knucks had eaten all the dessert for lunch. Zak's receiver was not working very well. Sometimes it was off. Sometimes it was on. They were waiting for the sounds of activity on the rafted sailboats to die down.

—There goes that kid. He's getting in the boat with all the rest of em.

They were crammed together inside the Gypsy, full of beer and wine and half asleep. The children were soon completely asleep and the adults debated in a halfhearted way whether *Murmur of the Heart* did social damage in its depiction of the pleasures of incest.

—What I really wanted to know about, said Jane, —was if boys actually do that.

—Do what?

—Measure their pricks.

—Some boys.

—French boys.

—Boys of a certain age.

She went outside to do the dishes overboard. The night was not too cold and she was astounded at the fluorescence caused by the swishing dirty pan and the particles of food sinking down to the fish. She wanted to show it. She looked below to ask if anybody knew about fluorescence, feeling sure Hank would, but they were all asleep, leaning against each other, the children and the men. Breaking the circuit before it was made. She missed Ellen. Ellen, who never had a fantasy to speak of, who *did* her ideas, if Ellen were there they would be below together in the warm heap by now, instead of Jane alone with her empty curiosity. She got into a dinghy and cast herself off, adrift under the stars. She arranged herself on the boat cushions and life jackets Roy had left in the bottom of the boat and floated aimlessly, feeling something which was not a metaphor. At first she attempted to interfere and define it. It was physical but also dangerous abstraction, which she connected with her maternity. It was not a question, looking down at the heaped people, of King of the Mountain and one experience displacing another, one love, one life, one explanation sufficing, it was more like the fluorescence of garbage, contagious from cell to cell, sweeping through, insatiably curious, her unusable blooming.

On the emptying mud flat they were trying to stuff her into a lobster trap. Finally, they admitted they could not possibly cut her up. Even so much as a finger, an arm or a leg, much less the tits and boxes of their dreams. A little bit of her hair blew in the breeze as they lifted her and hauled her around.

—No way this is going to work.

—You gotta get a big rock in there too. Else she won't stay down.

The idea that she had to be sunk in a lobster pot would not go away. The thought to dump her with a rock in the middle of the bay would not come, unable to edge its way past their original scheme. Part way in and hanging out both ends of the trap was not sufficient burial. So they lashed three traps together with a heavy, flat rock in each, and stuffed her in feet first. The music which they had thought was long gone came back with "Goodby Thunder Island," and as they embarked, as if leaving were the energy required to get the set going again, it came in with "It Goes to Show You Never Can Tell." Zak threw himself at it to cut the volume.

—Don't want to wake up the summer pukes, he said.

Miles away, Martha and Hen were already snoring together, but that was not what kept Ednah awake. She had anticipation again and indigestion. Fried food no longer set very well with her, and she would have to call the realtor in the morning to fix the spot for her declining years, her dark descent.

Zak and Knucks moved slowly, giving the sailboats wide berth so as not to awaken the people inside. Once past, they sped up and nearly ran down a dinghy with a sleeping woman in it. A pot buoy was draped over the bow to hold the little boat in the cove. The wake did not disturb Jane but dislodged the pot buoy.

Zak and Knucks went out into the bay and found a spot where setting traps was risky because the currents often enough took them out to sea and never washed them ashore to be retrieved by fishermen or little boys. They set their unwieldy trap, letting the pot warp run out, as usual, to be marked by a hot pink buoy. Then they went back to town without forgetting their other boat or needing to open another wound and mingle their blood, swearing a swear to be secret.

I Get By With Some Help
From My Friends

She was rowing responsibly back to the boat when Dick awoke at dawn to the sounds of Roy's little portable. His father told him to turn it off because they didn't want to hear any news this trip.

—Just this one song, Dad.

—That was pretty goddam irresponsible, hollered Dick into the brilliant cove.

Jane just rowed along not looking back over her shoulder at him. She was perspiring even in the morning cool and her hands were blistered.

—What the fuck did you do that for? You could have washed out to sea.

—I did, she said approaching the boats.

—What? said Dick.

—I did.

—Thank god you didn't really.

—What was it like? Where were you?

—Great.

—You weren't scared?

—No. Yes.

—If we want to get to Isle au Haut we'd better get going. Sally says she's hungry.

—Did you miss me?

—When we woke up.

—You must have slept well.

—Sleep of the dead.

They unrafted the boats and left the cove off Jones's Garden. The breeze was already lively.

—I bet it's going to blow, Hank called over.

—Can't be like yesterday anyhow.

—Nothing again will ever be like that.

They were sailing out through a brilliant patch of pot buoys, the boats still very close.

—Look, Dad. It's like sailing through a sea of M&Ms. Already licked.

They all heard and laughed at Roy and sailed out to sea.

Coming toward them from another island was a launch. They passed at some distance. Another ellipse.

Dave landed the launch and found no Karen. He found her camp unslept in, unmarauded. He found her clothes neatly rolled and tucked behind a rock. The dangers of solitude were all too apparent to him. He had been waiting for this to happen. Drowned drowned drowned. Back at the launch he grasped his little microphone tightly. Was he ruined? He called the Coast Guard. Mayday.